Michele Richard

MOCKED BY FAITH

PRAISE FOR MOCKED BY FAITH

Alexia Cross is like most girls her age, worried she'll never find someone who would want her, or accept her. The only difference comes with the fact that at eighteen, she's considered to be an old maid simply because her parents haven't contracted her to marry anyone yet. Alexia and her family live in a small community where they practice arranged marriages. To an outsider's eye, this practice would seem odd, or even outrageous, but for the families who live inside The Gates, it's just their way of life. When she finds she's finally been contracted to marry a man she's never met, or won't meet until their wedding day, she struggles to deal with the fear of who this man is, and why he's settling for her.

Across the globe, Justin McNear has been searching for the woman with the emerald green eyes, the very one who's been haunting his dreams. In his haste to find her, Justin turns from his faith, venturing into the outside world in hopes that she'll be waiting for him. Realizing his mistake, he returns home, only to face the shame from his community. In an effort to purify himself, he goes to drastic measures to become the type of man that a father would want for his daughter. When he learns of his contract to Alexia, he struggles to come to terms with the fact that he won't meet his wife until they are standing at the altar.

Through the emotional battles of being newly married, they try to get to know the person they've bonded their lives to, while fighting the plagues of doubt that threaten their faith in each other, and the church they love so dearly. Justin and Alexia's journey of self-discovery leads them down a path of hope and love, only to have the rug pulled out from under them time and again. Together, Justin and Alexia find their faith tested one final time, by something so harrowing; neither may be able to recover from.

Lisa Bilbrey – *The Review Lounge*

Second Edition Published by
Renaissance Romance Publishing

Renaissance Romance Publishing
PO Box 22 Clarendon, TX 79226

ISBN-13: 978-0615673332
ISBN-10: 0615673333

Cover art: © Jahn|Dreamstime.com © Dan Collier|Dreamstime.com
© Teodor|Dreamstime.com © Yana Gulyanovska|Dreamstime.com
Cover design by: Melissa Condor

www.michele-richard.net

About the Author

Michele Richard is the proud mother of two daughters. She has been married since 1997 to a wonderful husband, who for twenty-five years has been her best friend and supporter. Being an overly creative and caring person, she has been a volunteer co-leader for the Girl Scout Troop for five years. She takes great pride in teaching and guiding our future generations.

Her desire to continue her education drove her to attend night classes at Waltham High School. She refuses to just let life be. There is too much to learn than to stand about and watch it go by. Though she is not fluent yet in either, she has learned to speak French and Spanish in school. One day her dream is to be fluent in both.

"I suppose that makes me a lover of languages. Never stop learning is my motto."

Travel is one of her great passions. Having seen the beaches of the Bahamas, Aruba, and Mexico and the deserts of Utah and Arizona, her personal favourite was bicycling down Mount Vail and standing on top of the Intercontinental Divide, followed closely by the Grand Canyon.

"America is truly a beautiful place to see. I recommend seeing as much of it as you can."

THANK YOU

Thank you to Lisa Bilbrey and Laura Braley for helping me stay sane through this adventure and for helping me when I spiraled and lost my way.

As always, I owe my family a huge thanks for supporting me through the process. I love you, Maurice, Danielle, Virginia, and my mom, Pat.

I owe a huge debt of thanks to Gloria Keenan for all she does for me, including helping me in the earlier chapters.

From TWCS Publishing House, thank you, Lauren, Amanda, Jenn, and Donna. And how could I not thank M.A. Stacie for her wonderful British additions? She gave Justin his colorful accent.

To the staff at Renaissance Romance Publishing I thank Lisa, Laura, Elizabeth, Melissa, and Serenity for all their unwavering faith and endless hours.

For more information on TTTS please go to http://www.tttsfoundation.org The site is a wonderful resource for those affected by the loss of a child due to Twin to Twin Transfer Syndrome.

CHAPTER 1

ALEXIA CROSS'S CROSSROADS

How can a girl who is about to graduate from high school and embark on the next stage of her life be so unhappy? It probably had something to do with the fact that I'm a complete and utter failure to my parents. How so? Well, in our church, things worked a little differently than in most.

At the ripe old age of sixteen, the members of our church started to match us with our future husbands and wives; not matchmaking, but arranged marriages. If you think that's why I was so unhappy, you'd be wrong. My displeasure came from the fact that I would be eighteen in a week – just one week before I graduated – and my parents, along with the Council, had been unsuccessful in procuring me a husband. I was set to be the only one in our graduating class – actually, the whole community – to be unmatched.

I guess I hadn't been of much assistance in that area. Since I wasn't the most stunning creature out there and a little too quiet for most, I pretty much stayed by the sides of my two best friends Ginger Mula and Madison Johnson. We'd grown up together, attending the same church and school since we were five years old. They were lucky; as soon as they'd turned sixteen, their parents had no problem finding them husbands. Don't get me wrong; I really am happy for them, and they love the young men their parents picked. So what would happen to me? I had no idea.

"Lexie, we're having dinner at the church tonight, so stay dressed in your uniform," Mom spoke from the stairway. "Oh, and put on a little makeup, will you?"

I sighed and stomped to my bedroom door. "But, Mom, the dinner tonight is for the introductions of new couples. Why do I have to go?" I whined, crossing my arms.

"Alexia Ann Cross," my mother raised her voice, "you will be ready when your father gets home, and that's all there is to it!"

Thankfully, she didn't hear me grumbling under my breath. I looked at Ginger and Madison, who sat on my bed snickering at me. They didn't know how lucky they were; they had already been introduced to their future husbands.

"Come on, Lexie; let's get you ready." I huffed, giving in to Ginger's demand. "You know, you really have beautiful hair. I love the golden highlights." Ginger twirled my red curls between her fingers. "We should do an up-do for tonight. What do you think, Madison?"

"Without a doubt. I think an inverted french braid wrapped into a tight bun would do the trick. Oh, and I have got to do your makeup. Trust me – your mom will love it." If Madison bounced any more, she would shake me off the bed.

"Whatever; it's not like Prince Charming is going to be there to sweep me off my feet," I sulked.

When the torture began, I couldn't help but shut my eyes and daydream about what it would be like to be the only member of my church to be unwed. It was more of a nightmare than a dream.

"Wow, this eye shadow really brings out your green eyes." Madison said that every time she fussed over me.

Granted, I had unusual emerald-colored eyes, but I didn't see the big deal about it. Most people found emerald-colored eyes distracting. The first time I'd meet someone, all they'd do was stare at my eyes. It was a little unnerving.

Once the girls had decided I'd reached perfection, it was time for them to go home and get ready, too. The whole community would be in attendance, much to my dismay.

"See you tonight, ladies," I called, watching them run down the stairs.

Looking in the mirror one last time, I couldn't help wishing I looked more like my friends. Madison had the perfect oval face with dark, chocolate-brown eyes and matching wavy, long locks. Ginger had a round face with straight, sandy blond hair and hazel eyes that changed colors depending on what she wore. Joey and Johnny were lucky to be getting them as wives.

Joey and Johnny McNear were twins, so the girls would be having a double wedding next month. Both boys had the messy, curly blond hair of their father and their mother's icy-blue eyes. It was in their personalities that they differed from one another. Joey had received the nickname "Crazy Eight" at a very early age. The name in itself explained his behavior. Johnny, though, was quieter and more laid back, like myself.

"Lexie, let's go; we're going to be late," my father grumbled.

He wouldn't admit it, but I could see it on his face every time we attended an event like tonight's. He was not proud of my status. He tried to smile when I came down the stairs, but it ended up looking more like a wince. My mother, on the other hand, smiled approvingly at my appearance. That at least made one of us happy.

Following behind them, I couldn't help thinking that I would be spending my life living in my parents' home and doing whatever they asked. After my father opened my door, I slipped into the backseat before fastening my seatbelt.

I tuned them out, gazing out the window while they chatted on the ride to the church. I really didn't want to hear about my father's new law cases or my mother rattling off about the new drapes for the living room.

Heaving a heavy breath, I stepped out when my father opened my door. He didn't have to say a word; I knew what he was thinking: I would be the burden that wouldn't leave.

Wrapping her arm around my waist, my mother guided us in through the basement door. It was no surprise that, when we walked into the meeting room, everyone turned to see the future spinster enter.

As soon as Ginger and Madison came running up, everyone turned back to their own conversations. "Hey, you! We thought you'd convinced your parents to let you stay home." They giggled in unison.

"Not a prayer of that happening." I waved good-bye to my parents and went to hide in the furthest corner.

Joey and Johnny joined us to tell us all about their honeymoon news. Their eyes lit up when they described the pristine beaches and clear waters. Aruba sounded like a really nice place to visit. I sighed, watching the two couples holding hands.

When the Council took the stage, I cringed. I really didn't want to see all the happy couples being announced. That was when I saw another couple I'd never seen before talking to my parents. Suspiciously, the four of them left the room. What was that all about?

"Hey, who's that with my parents?" I asked.

"Oh, no; that's not good. That's my dad's brother James and his wife Jane. They're visiting from the English community, but why are they here?" Johnny looked shocked to see them. Before he could say more, the ceremony started.

"Good evening, families of Les Portes de l'Ange. Tonight, I have the pleasure of announcing three new couples who have been promised to each other." Minister Jeff waved the newly-signed contracts in the air. For an older man, he was still handsome, with curly, short, dark brown hair and light brown eyes. Compared to his wife, he was quite tall, standing almost six feet.

"If I could ask for Tori Leone, Danielle Atwood, Sydney O'Neil, and their parents to please join me up here so we can announce them to their future husbands." The smiling ladies made their way onto the stage at his left.

"Now, if Andrew Reynolds, Ryan Michaels, Matthew Mills, and their parents would please join us." We waited while they settled in on his right side.

Each sets of parents held the traditional long, white, silk ribbon. When instructed, Tori and her parents stepped forward and waited. Soon Ryan and his parents joined them. Tori and Ryan stepped toward each other and held hands while their parents took turns wrapping the ribbons around their wrists.

"With these ribbons, we bind more than just your hands; we bind your souls, your life spirits, and your futures as one," exclaimed Tori's parents in unison.

"From this day forth, you will be a single entity, one united pair, you will remain forever faithful to one another and to our church," finished Ryan's parents.

Of course, the mothers cried, the fathers shook hands, and everyone clapped. The two other couples repeated the same process. As much as I didn't want to admit it, I was somewhat jealous that they were getting something I would never have. My heart ached every time I thought about it. Just when Minister Jeff started wrapping up the evening so we could eat, he was interrupted by none other than my father. Whatever my father whispered to him, it made Minister Jeff smile wide.

"Okay, folks, if you would be so kind as to allow a change in tonight's program. We have a very special announcement to make. Alexia Cross, would you please come up here?"

My heart beat frantically in my chest. I balled my shaking hands into fists and pinned them to my sides.

With everyone's eyes locked upon me, I weaved through the room to join my parents on stage. Before I could even ask what was going on, the other McNear couple joined us. Looking at my friends, I could see the ladies were beaming, not so much for Crazy Eight; he was in hysterics. Johnny just dropped his face into his hands and shook his head.

"Tonight Alexia Cross has been contracted to marry Justin McNear, son of James and Jane McNear from our sister church in England! Since he was unable to make the trek himself tonight, we'll be holding their tying ceremony next month, on Saturday, June twenty-sixth, the day of their wedding. So, please join me in congratulating the future bride." The announcement left me flabbergasted and gaping.

Did he seriously just say I'd be marrying a man I wouldn't meet until the day of my actual wedding? My thoughts swirled around the realization. It was really going to happen? As soon as the clapping died down, the whispers started about my impending nuptials. Some thought the arrangement was just so people wouldn't feel badly for me; others thought about the condition of the man I'd be marrying. I had a feeling I needed to find out what Crazy Eight knew.

"Alexia, it's a pleasure to meet you. I think you will be just what our son needs," gushed Jane as she gave me a tight hug.

Stepping back, she made room for James. "Your father is right; you'll make the perfect wife for my son." James hugged me, too.

Grabbing me away from James, my mother took her turn, "Oh, Alexia, we finally found someone who will love and take care of you." She sobbed into my shoulder.

Once she passed me off, it was time to look my father in the eye. "This will be good for you, also." My father sighed, relieved.

Thankfully, Ginger and Madison spared me from the rest of the people wanting to congratulate me. "C'mon, the guys want to tell you something."

Ginger rattled, grabbing my hand and dragging me behind her.

"Lexie, I'm so sorry they did this to you." Johnny grabbed me, pulling me into a bear hug.

I huffed into his chest and let the realization wash over me. Rubbing soothing circles on my back, he held me until I released him. Looking up into Joey's stormy eyes, I nodded for it to begin.

"Crazy Eight, how bad is it?" His face fell, preparing to tell me about his cousin.

"Justin's not here tonight because . . ." he nearly choked on his own words, "he's at the revirgining retreat."

He's not pure!

I saw everyone flinch at this news, and my chest started to heave. The air refused to enter my lungs. Panic rushed over me in waves. I finally got it. They hadn't been able to find anyone pure for me, so they'd settled for someone who already had a track record. Could it get any worse?

"Apparently, he rebelled against our practices for a while, and now everyone is making him recommit to our lifestyle." Johnny shrugged, avoiding looking me in the eyes.

"The fact that they couldn't find him a wife didn't help either, but I guess that's all taken care of now." Joey hip-checked me, chuckling.

Staggering back, I leaned against the wall and slid down until my backside landed on the ground. I tucked my head between my knees. No one knew what to say while the seconds ticked away.

"You're awfully quiet, Lexie. What's going on in that brain of yours?" Madison spoke softly.

"I'm just trying to figure out who I harmed in another life to have this happen to me," I whined.

"Come on, guys, there have to be some good qualities to your cousin, right?"

"Yeah, Ginger. He's good-looking, and his parents are beyond rich, which is really cool. I guess Lexie won't have to worry about fumbling through the sex. He's had enough practice to know what to do," Joey belly laughed, causing me to groan.

"Great, so while he's out sleeping with anything with a heartbeat, I can go shopping." I hissed.

I saw my parents making their approach, so I jumped up and smoothed out my skirt. "Lexie, it's time for dinner. Let's go have a seat and get to know your future in-laws."

I just waved good-bye to my friends and followed my parents to our table.

It was all I could do not to break down in tears after learning the only man whose parents wanted me had *experience*. The McNears spoke very highly of their son while they chatted through dinner. I remained my usual quiet self. I already knew enough to know that he would be the best I could get. Nibbling on my dinner, I tried not to vomit. It wasn't the penne and broccoli that had me on the verge; it came from thinking about the man who couldn't keep his manhood in his pants until after his wedding.

They did tell us they were moving here next month with Justin and his sister Krista; she was only fourteen. They were hoping to find her someone here as well. From their conversations with my father, they did indeed have a lot of money from several high-end car dealerships they owned. No amount of money could make up for the fact that their son had used women strictly for his own pleasure.

In our world, you did not have sex with someone before you were married; hence the revirgining retreat. Having sexual relations before marriage, if left undisclosed, would breach the contract. Even disclosed, most fathers wouldn't accept the preexisting condition. I couldn't wrap my mind around why God would do this to me.

It was be my guess that it was why they had thrown in the car; perhaps they wanted to sweeten the deal. The contract demanded that I be well cared for, so plans were made for us to go to the new dealership they had just bought in town, where I would have my pick of a new car.

I giggled when I received a text from Crazy Eight asking me if he'd mentioned that my future in-laws were loaded. Luckily, all the parents thought I was laughing about the car. I looked over at Joey and caught him making faces at me, no doubt trying to cheer me up. One scowl sent his way from my father was all it took for him to snap his head forward.

When the evening came to a close, we made our way home. My parents were in unusually high spirits; I, on the other hand, only felt more miserable, if that were even possible.

My father sat on the couch to unwind with a slight smile gracing his lips.

"Lexie, come sit with us, please?" He patted the open seat next to him.

"Yeah, Dad?" I sighed, joining him.

"Are you pleased that we found someone for you?" His was voice now lighter than it had been in two years.

"Of course, Dad. I'm sure you did the best you could," I reassured him with a fake smile.

"His family meets all the requirements, and I have spoken with Minister Jeff about him. He's equally convinced this young man will be a good husband for you."

"I'm sure he will be, and I'll do everything to make him happy, also." I knew I had no other choice, and I would have to make the best of a difficult situation.

"I know you will. You've accepted everything we've taught you." He grasped my hand, squeezing it.

I needed to know more about Justin. "What can you tell me about him?" I uttered without looking my father in the eye.

"I won't lie to you; he's currently at the revirgining retreat. He'd been dating outside the community, and Minister Peter suggested he attend. As for his personality, he's a gentle young man who spends his time working for his father's business and volunteering for the church." I tried to hide my cringe at the thought of his previous interactions with women.

"How old is he?"

"Eighteen."

"Eighteen? Was he still available because of his indiscretions?" I knew the answer, but I wanted to hear it, hoping my information was incorrect.

"Yes." He glanced back and forth between me and my mother.

"Do you have a picture of him?"

"No, but his parents showed us one along with his medical history at this evening's dinner." From the way his smile gleamed, I couldn't help but think they liked what they had seen in his portfolio.

"Well, if that's it, I'm really tired. May I go to bed now?" I really needed to slip away and reflect on tonight's turn of events.

"Yeah, good night, Lexie. Sleep tight." With one last pat on my hand, he released me.

I couldn't walk up the stairs quick enough. I wanted a little peace and quiet to come to terms with my parents' sudden decision.

Grabbing my sleep pants and T-shirt, I changed in the quiet darkness of my room, using the moonlight to add a slight glow to my bedroom. Slipping into bed, I thought about why they'd had to make such a quick decision tonight.

Our community had very few demands; however, the main one was marriage. Our scriptures dictated that a blessed union was required to make every person complete.

As parents, it was their job to remove the emotional factor and find a spouse that would complete our lives. The Council searched out proper pairings first, and then it was up to the parents to accept or decline their choices.

Most husbands worked outside of the community in high-paying jobs or owned businesses in the local town of Small River, Minnesota. Very few of the wives worked, but those who did usually were the teachers at our school, although most volunteered at our private clinic or school.

Our ancestors had learned early on that the general public didn't understand our beliefs, so they'd found it better to close themselves off from the influences that would corrupt them.

Long before my time, the people in Small River had heard about our practices, and a young couple had received a tongue lashing from a mob on how wrong it was to marry without love. We do love our husbands and wives; it develops after we say "I do."

CHAPTER 2

ALEXIA CROSS'S COMING OF AGE

The night of the dinner, I ended up falling asleep crying over the man I'd soon be marrying: Justin McNear. I'd always thought that when I married, we'd both be inexperienced and learning the mechanics together. Instead, the only parents who would take me had a son who was promiscuous.

That night, I dreamt about a faceless man surrounded by gorgeous women who pawed at him. There he lay on a bed of white, moaning and urging them to continue. His hands searched out their curvy figures, stroking them with sensuous adoration. Just when the women had started peeling off his shirt, I was jarred awake.

I woke up panting, my chest heaving in a futile attempt to breathe. My body thrashed in protest of the horrific dreams. Every time I closed my eyes, the same vision would haunt me.

I sat back quietly while we drove to the courthouse. I tried my best to not look like I had spent the night crying, but with my eyes red and puffy, I wasn't certain if I could pull it off. Being the only lawyer in the area gave my father all the knowledge he needed to assure us that we would have no problems getting a marriage license. Fifteen minutes after we'd arrived, we departed, successful in our venture to get the only document we needed for the ceremony.

Our next stop was the dealership. I wasn't sure what I was supposed to select. All I knew was that they sold very expensive cars, and they'd told me that I could have my pick of anything.

"Ready, Lexie?"

Glancing over the rows of cars, I tittered. "Sure, Dad. Any suggestions before I start test driving?"

"Might I make a suggestion?"

"Of course, please do." I quickly nodded to James.

"I think something child-friendly would be a good idea, since I'm sure you and Justin will want to add to your family right off." I bit my lip, thinking about it.

I knew I wanted children, but I had no idea how Justin felt about them. His father thought we would, so maybe he did want them. A thought occurred to me: the contract we generally used specified for children. Maybe that's why he thought we would be adding to our new family so quickly.

I took my time scoping out the lot, narrowing my choices down to three possibilities. I agreed to test drive the child-friendly cars, and eventually I selected a white Mercedes R350 Crossover. My hopes were that Justin might want children or maybe he would just do it because it was in the contract. Either way, I picked the Mercedes because it would be perfect for children.

While Mr. McNear handled the paperwork, my father went down the street to add it to his insurance policy. When everything was said and done, I drove away in my new car. It felt strange and exhilarating to be driving my very own car. Up until today, I'd always shared my mother's. Now I wouldn't have to plead to use hers. I could come and go whenever I pleased.

Luc grinned when he waved me through the gates that led to our gated community. He seemed pleased with my choice in cars. Luc Pelletier and I were in the same graduating class. He did our security part-time on the weekends and full time during the summer. His dream of becoming our head of security came from his father, who now held the post.

Ginger and Madison were waiting outside Madison's house when I pulled up. "Oh my gosh, Lexie! It's beautiful!" gushed Ginger, running her fingers along the glossy front fender.

"This will be perfect for a family. I can't believe they gave you a new car on top of the house and dowry! You so have it made!" Madison laughed.

"Well, get in already. Let's take this baby for a proper ride." I blushed. I'd never thought about the money involved in a marriage contract. Not that it would make me any happier, but at least we wouldn't have to struggle, which was a good thing.

We spent the afternoon driving around until just before dinner, when my mother called and gave me the address of a potential home for Justin and me. When we pulled up, I gasped. My mother, with the help of Mrs. McNear, had found a cottage on the waterfront. I don't know what Justin would think, although his mom said he'd love it. I thought it was perfect. It sat nestled in the woods with a deck facing the beach, and there was even a dock for swimming or a small boat if we wanted. As I walked from room to room, I knew it needed work; however, I would be willing to do whatever it took to make it my new home. A professional makeover would be too expensive, but I knew where to get free help for that.

"Mom, this place is amazing!" I twittered.

"We just knew you'd love it!" She rushed up and hugged me.

"Thank you, Mrs. McNear. You and my mom really did find a perfect home. Do you think Justin will like it?"

Jane took her turn to hug me. "I think he'll love anywhere you are."

I didn't know what Justin would think, but if his mom said he would love it, then that would have to suffice.

"I'll go tell Patty the good news." Jane grabbed her bag, rushing out the door.

We milled around a bit before heading home ourselves. After dropping off everyone, I headed home to see if we'd heard from Patty, Minister Jeff's wife. Patty ran the realty part of Les Portes de l'Ange, or Gates of the Angels. She assured us that everything could be processed in time for the wedding day.

I didn't get the chance to see Justin's parents again before they left the following day to go back to England. The week crawled by with my mind filled with thoughts of Justin. The realization had settled in that it didn't matter now; the contract had been signed. Regardless of the facts, I would be marrying Justin in less than a month's time. I would do everything to make the best of the agreement.

~*~

I never thought I would wake up this morning with a case of the birthday blues, but I did. It had been a week since my contract was signed, and even though I knew I'd been promised to Justin McNear, he wouldn't be there to share my birthday with me. As of today, I'd yet to see a photograph of him. Celebrating my birthday with just my family and friends had always been our traditional way, but this year would be different.

Turning eighteen in our faith was the most important birthday. After today, I would no longer be a child, even though I'd still have to graduate from high school next week. My parents decided to throw a huge shindig at the church to celebrate my birthday. I think they were trying to make up for the late marriage contract, but they'd never admit to it.

When I approached the back of the church, I could already see the pink and white balloons, matching streamers, and twinkling lights covering the churchyard. Everyone had already arrived to help me celebrate — well, everyone except the one person I wanted to see there.

Not having any idea about the man I'd be marrying was starting to drive me insane. I wanted to know everything about him, yet my friends had no details about him to share with me, even though some of them they were related to Justin.

I understood he'd been enduring the retreat to better himself for our future together, but I was still impatient to meet him. I'd never been an insecure person, but I was quickly getting there. Even dressed in my best white sleeveless cotton sundress and golden goddess sandals, I couldn't help but be worried if Justin would approve. With all those wild thoughts running through my head it was no wonder. Maybe he wouldn't like me in it, if he were here. Would he think I was pretty enough to stay with me after he saw me? Stupid, I know, but he'd done things with women that I had no clue about. What if I disappointed him? What if he married me and then didn't want to touch me?

I forced myself to push all those thoughts away for tonight. This evening I refused to think about anything but the band playing our favorite gospel songs and dancing with my friends.

"Happy birthday, Lexie!" Ginger and Madison screeched when they approached.

"Hey, happy birthday, old lady!"

"Thanks, Crazy Eight. I hope you bought me some of that wrinkle cream you use." I giggled.

"Sorry, sweetheart, I don't share my anti-aging secrets." He winked, causing us all to laugh.

Everyone enjoyed the festive party mood while we laughed, danced, and ate. As usual, there was way too much food; I swore I'd be stuffed for a week. My mom left me speechless when she brought out the cake. It had to be absolutely the prettiest cake I'd ever seen her make, and she'd made too many to keep track of.

If someone needed a cake for an event, they went to my mother. People even paid for the honor of having one of her cakes. My dad said if it made her happy to sell her cakes she could, as long as it didn't interfere with the house, church, or family.

"Do you like it, Lexie?"

"Are you serious, Mom? It's without a doubt the prettiest cake I've ever seen," I gushed, hugging her.

"Thank you for saying that, but I think you're biased when it comes to my cakes." I chuckled because she was right; I would always be her biggest fan.

Thankfully, I was saved when the music slowed down, and my dad asked me for a moment alone. "Lexie, walk with me, please?" I wouldn't turn down the offer because I didn't want to see everyone slow dancing with their loved ones.

I took the arm he extended and followed him down the path that led to the lake. "Alexia, I need to know you're happy. You haven't said much to us since the dinner." He gestured for us to sit on the wall that lined the beach.

"Dad, I'm fine with getting married. It's actually a relief that someone wants me after two years of waiting." I looked away, hoping he wouldn't see the shame on my face.

He nudged my chin so I looked him in the eyes. "Alexia, there was a lot of interest in you. Didn't you know that?"

"What do you mean? I thought no one would take me, and you had to accept the McNears' offer." I gawked at him in disbelief.

"Heavens, no. We were rather picky. I didn't find anyone worthy of you, and I was unwilling to settle." He smiled, reminding me of the way he used to smile at me when I was a small child.

"Really? So, the McNears aren't the first to show interest in me?" I couldn't believe what I'd heard fly from his lips.

"Lexie, there were many offers, but we waited, hoping for someone better to come along. I'm sorry you thought you were undesirable, but I assure you that wasn't the case." He released my chin, looking over to the water.

"Dad, do you think he's a nice person?"

"Yes, I do. I asked his uncle all sorts of questions before I agreed to the contract. I needed to know you would be in the best hands."

I nodded. "How bad is it at the retreat?"

"Well, from what I have heard, it's not easy on them, but they always come out of it a better person and spouse." From the far off look in his eyes, I wondered how much he wasn't sharing.

When he held back elaborating on it further, I had to ask, "Have you seen a picture of him?"

When he grinned I knew. "Yes, he's a very good-looking young man. He looks a lot like his father."

"Did you send him one of me?" I held my breath, hoping they had sent him something better than a snapshot. My senior picture would have been the best choice.

"No, we didn't have one handy, and since we signed the contract so quickly, I never had a chance to get his parents one before they left." I released a shaky breath. Justin, too, would have no idea what I looked like.

"Dad, how many indiscretions did he have?" The curiosity was eating at me.

"I don't know. His dad said he went looking for love and discovered the hard way that it doesn't always happen that way. That's why our church believes in the parents handling the arrangements. Our way, we match you with a person you might not have given a second look at walking down the street. I don't think it would be a good idea to judge him for looking outside our faith; instead, you should judge him for the fact that he came back on his own accord after realizing our way was the better way."

I nodded. "Okay, Dad, I promise not to judge him." I smiled, genuinely relieved for the first time in months.

"Now, I don't want to keep you from your party any longer. Let's head back and cut your cake. It's your favorite: strawberries and cream." Walking back to the churchyard, I felt better about my situation.

If they had turned down numerous offers for me, then Justin must be worthy of my parents' expectations. If that was the case, then I would do my best to believe in Justin. I figured I would look at it as my mother did. She saw it as Justin's version of the Amish tradition of Rumspringa. I just hoped he was as understanding about my inexperience.

After a chorus of *Happy Birthday* rang in my ears, I blew out the eighteen candles and cut the pink-iced cake with eighteen perfect white and purple flowers decorating the trim. The guests began devouring the cake before my mother had even finished cutting it. Nothing beats a vanilla cake with pink whipped cream frosting and strawberry filling; nothing. Nausea set in, however, when we were forced to watch Joey and Madison practicing the correct procedure for shoving cake up your bride's nose. After that sight, I prayed I wouldn't have to endure it.

No birthday party would be complete without presents. When Crazy Eight and Johnny held off to the end after I opened all the other gifts, I couldn't imagine what they'd bought me. To my surprise, when I opened the pink opalescent wrapping, there sat cradled in white tissue paper a sterling silver five-by-seven inch picture frame with a picture of a young boy nestled inside.

Okay, I didn't get it, until Johnny whispered in my ear. "It's Justin, the last time he visited. Do you remember him now?" A sharp gasp escaped my chest.

I'd seen him once during the summer when were eight years old at a barbecue the church had held. We swam together in the lake.

That summer, I'd started dreaming of a man. There was no other way to describe him than that he appeared to be a young man of about eighteen with deep, sapphire-colored eyes. Even now, I'd see him hiding in the back of my dreams. In all the dreams I've had of him, he only said one thing: "You are mine to love."

Thinking more about the day I'd met Justin, it dawned on me; Justin had said those exact words to me that night while lying on a blanket under the fireworks. I was eight, so I'd giggled and told him, "I'll be waiting." And that had been it. His parents had taken him home, and I'd never seen him again.

I nearly knocked Crazy Eight and Johnny over in my rush to hug them at the same time. Of course, Madison and Ginger couldn't help but join in, so together we all toppled over laughing. It was officially my favorite birthday.

Granted, I still had no idea what Justin looked like now, but I at least knew that at one time he'd liked me; maybe he remembered me, too. Just maybe — the young boy in the picture frame grew up to fulfill his promise. In three short weeks, I would find out whether that was true or not.

That night while I slept with the picture frame next to my bed, I dreamt of the man again, only this time I wrapped myself around him, stroking his body with loving hands.

CHAPTER 3

ALEXIA CROSS'S PREPARATIONS

Two days after my birthday, Madison, Ginger, and I spent the day in Small River to register for our weddings. Ginger's father owned a chain of home goods stores scattered throughout the northern half of Minnesota. They were nowhere near the size of an actual Home Goods franchise, but they were very popular in the smaller towns, where the workers knew the customers by name.

When we arrived, Steven Mula, Ginger's father, greeted us, "Good morning, ladies. My wife told me you were coming to do your registries for the weddings; let's get started." He motioned with his hand for us to follow him to the back room.

When we entered the private room, there was only a black computer desk with a laptop, paper, pens, and a black leather couch in the corner of the room. We sat on the couch while he sat at the desk and started preparing everything. From the drawer in the desk, he pulled out three clipboards with checklist forms on them.

"So, this is what you need to do. Just check off the things you will need like towels, etcetera. I will help you pick the colors, makes, and models on the computer. Easy enough, right?" He grinned at the three of us.

After passing one to each of us, he left us to fill them out. The second the door shut, the giggling began. "Okay, replace these lists with the ones our moms sent." Secretly, our mothers had taken a copy of the lists and had filled in everything we'd need.

Ginger pulled hers from her bag first and attached it to the clipboard. Seriously, how did they expect eighteen-year-olds who lived at home to know what they needed to set up a house?

We had made a plan about cooking dinners. Together, we were going to make a week's worth of meals all at once and freeze them; all we'd have to do would be to defrost and reheat. Ginger was the cook in our group, so she'd be the one giving us instructions. Personally, I would be willing to pay her to just make the meals with heating instructions. I hadn't inherited my mother's love of cooking and baking. Baking wouldn't be an issue since my mother had already promised to just bake extra for me; that way, I wouldn't burn down the cottage.

For the next hour, we kicked back and just talked about all the things we didn't want to talk about inside Les Portes de l'Ange; things that would make us blush in the presence of our faith. Ginger shared the story of her first kiss with John. He had been so sweet about it and waited until her eighteenth birthday. Just hearing her tell the story had me wishing mine would be just as romantic, even though that was doubtful since our first kiss would be in front of our wedding guests. Madison's was less romantic. Joey's kiss was impulsive and passionate; it would seem the twins' kissing methods were as different as their personalities.

Soon Ginger's father joined us again and started inputting everything our mothers had thought we would need. My only request was for everything in the bathroom to be emerald green for my woodsy theme. Thankfully, he selected the best items for us off our lists. He even ordered us pizza for lunch. While he worked, we ate. With everything now in place for the weddings, we each hugged and kissed him goodbye.

On the way back through the gates, Madison received a text telling us the guys were at the beach. After spending the day indoors, a swim sounded wonderful. Since we had grown up in a community with a lake, we knew to always wear a swimsuit under our clothes, and today had been no exception.

"Hey, guys!" Madison called to them, waving like a lunatic.

"C'mon in; the water is awesome." They didn't need to be told twice. Ginger and Madison stripped off their clothes while they ran for the water.

I took my time in order to give them a moment to splash and play chicken in the water. Apparently, I took too long because Joey ran out to grab me and proceeded to drag me into the water kicking and screaming. He won!

The afternoon hours slipped by with us splashing, swimming, and soaking up the serene beauty of the lake. Once we were too exhausted to move anymore, we lay on the sandy beach to enjoy the sunset. "So, Lexie, are you excited about graduation this weekend?"

"I guess so, but I'm more worried about the wedding. No one will tell me anything about him. What if Justin doesn't think I'm good enough? They won't even let me call him." I pouted.

"It's not his parents that won't let you call him. The retreat forbids outside contact." Johnny squeezed my hand in support.

"As for us, we haven't seen him in years. We have no idea what he's like now. We've told you all we've heard." Johnny shrugged.

"They never call?" I asked astonished.

"Sure they do, but only my parents have talked to them. They don't tell us all the day-to-day crap." Joey chuckled.

I let it go, knowing I wasn't obtaining any more information from them tonight. At eleven forty-five, I started dropping everyone off for our midnight curfews. In a few days, we wouldn't have that anymore.

~*~

Two weeks after the announcement of my impending nuptials, graduation day arrived. I was decked out in a white satin robe as I slowly walked across the stage of our school's auditorium to receive my high school diploma; I was the first of my friends to receive my certificate. Looking across the sea of black and white robes, I smiled and waved my diploma in the air for my parents to see. Our graduating class consisted of only forty-three seniors, but our school had a dropout average of zero students, which unequivocally beat the state record.

"Lexie, we did it!" *Like there was ever any doubt.*

"Yes, Ginger, we sure did." I pulled her into a hug, only to be joined by a giggling Madison.

Half of the student body would be attending college in the fall, most of them males. The females in our community usually opted to be stay-at-home wives. It wasn't a requirement; it was just the way we preferred it. I'd already enrolled in online classes for the fall. I had chosen to study Fine

Arts.

"It's hard to believe that in three weeks we'll all be married," Madison swooned.

I was surprised they weren't the least bit upset that I would be getting married before them, even though, they'd had their date set long before me. One thing about my friends: there was no jealousy among us. We loved each other for who we were, not who had what.

"Just think, Lexie, two more weeks for you," Ginger cooed.

"Then it's both of your turns," I crooned.

"You'll be back in time for our weddings, right?" Madison wrinkled her brow.

"Yes, my mom arranged for us to have a surprise honeymoon a week later, so I won't have to shirk my maid of honor duties." I smirked.

"A surprise, huh? Did she give you any hints?"

"No, Ginger; hence the word 'surprise'." I laughed.

Arm in arm, the three of us walked to Madison's house just one block from the school. We hadn't walked like that in years. I missed the closeness we had shared as children.

Madison's parents threw a fabulous party after the ceremony. None of us went home until three in the morning. You'd think we'd never be seeing each other again, when in fact: we would all continue to live in the gated community where we had grown up.

Once again, Justin wasn't there to experience that with me like everyone else's promised ones. He hadn't been there for a lot of firsts, like helping me pick out my first car, my eighteenth birthday, the prom, and the selection of our wedding registry items, just to name a few. On a happier note, he was expected to be released in just one week.

Our mothers were planning the entire wedding; they talked daily on the phone or via e-mail. My only wedding responsibilities had been the marriage license and my dress, which Ginger's mother had agreed to make for me. Like my mother, she worked from home, and she loved being a seamstress. They were thrilled when I chose to update my mother's traditional wedding gown. It felt right to continue with a tradition that not many were following nowadays. Since all the invites and everything from the music to the honeymoon were set, all I had to do was start working on the house.

~*~

The little cottage and its breathtaking view still amazed me.

"Wow, Lexie, I hope we get open invites to swim," Joey joked.

"Of course; you're all welcome anytime you want," I muttered, walking around thinking about what I wanted to do first.

"Okay, I think the bathroom should be painted first, so I can paint it tomorrow." Everyone dispersed and took a different room.

Johnny did what I asked and started prepping the bathroom with tape and paper. I went and did the same for the bedroom. Madison and Ginger attacked the kitchen, leaving Joey the living room. At noon, my mother showed up to deliver lunch. I think she had an ulterior motive and wanted to check up on us.

"Lexie, I love the green in the bathroom. Johnny did a great job." She smiled in approval.

"It's the only room I'm painting with a color; the rest will be white, with the woodwork remaining natural."

"I like it, especially in the guest room. That way, when you have a baby, you can paint it blue or pink depending on what you have." I gasped, shocked.

"Mom! Please, I have to get married before I can even think about having a baby."

"Now, Lexie, there's no reason you can't start planning on a family. Your wedding is just over a week away." My friends just laughed at my embarrassment.

In the end, it took the five of us two days to have everything painted and ready for my mother to begin unpacking the few gifts that had been sent early and moving everything she wanted me to take from the house. I don't know how I would have accomplished it all without my mother and friends.

~*~

On the day Justin would be released, I found myself surrounded by every female I knew. Jane called in on Skype so she wouldn't miss a thing at my shower. She was so happy to be included; after all, it was her son's future, too. My mother even made her a keepsake photo album of everything about the wedding. She snapped pictures of me every chance she could, from writing invitations and thank you notes to painting the cottage.

The house was all decorated in a majestic blue, my favorite color now. It was the color of the eyes of the man in my dreams and the boy in the photo frame I now knew to be Justin. I really couldn't explain it, but I think in my mind I'd held out hope that one day he'd come back to me, and now it looked like he would be. As I opened each gift, my mother ooh'ed and aah'ed and laughed with Jane. Actually, everyone seemed in high spirits, laughing and joking about our future. They certainly had higher expectations than I did. When all was said and done, everyone clapped, pleased that I'd received everything I needed to make Justin happy.

The most embarrassing gift came from my two best friends. Yes, you guessed it: a skimpy piece of cream, satin lingerie. How could it have been that not a single female in the room wasn't appalled? I'll never know. I blushed ten shades of red just handling the pink box that contained the cream-colored chemise.

When the celebration quieted down, I took a moment to talk with Jane. "Hi, Jane. How's England?"

"Wonderful, sweetheart. Justin's due home in a few hours. Lexie, everything was beautiful. Thank you for allowing me to video in. I'm sorry I couldn't be there. You received so many wonderful gifts." She beamed through the computer monitor.

"Thank you for the wonderful china and crystal set. Where is Krista? I thought she would have watched, too."

"Out with friends; you know how fourteen-year-olds are. I'm giving her a little leeway since we fly out tomorrow."

"I can't wait to meet them both. I'm just scared I'll disappoint them." I wasn't sure she heard my whisper until she answered it.

"They will love you! Krista is already asking about you, and when James tells Justin today about the marriage, he'll be thrilled, too."

"He doesn't know yet?" I whimpered in disbelief.

"No, we weren't allowed any contact with him, so James will tell him on the ride home. That way, they can talk man to man." She sounded nonchalant as the panic rose in my chest.

I'd spent the last three weeks preparing to marry a man who didn't even know he was getting married. He'd had no time to acclimate to the idea of being married to someone he'd never met. How could Jane be so nonchalant about the fact that he didn't even know I existed? Great, my nightmare was now a living horror show.

"We understand, and we look forward to seeing you soon," I muttered, still thinking about the fact that he didn't know about the wedding.

"Our flight can't come soon enough. Justin is going to love you, I just know it in my heart." With that, the screen went black.

Mocked By Faith

CHAPTER 4

JUSTIN MCNEAR'S ATONEMENT

When I checked in a month ago to the revirgining retreat, I knew the reasons behind the need for it. I'd gone out with women outside our community that I wasn't promised to.

I closed my eyes and took a deep cleansing breath as I thought about how foolish I'd been to think I could find love on my own.

It had all started when I turned sixteen and my friends celebrated with a day trip to the beach. Sitting in the sand watching my friends messing about with their future wives, all I could think about was the green-eyed girl in my dreams. The dreams were nothing new; I'd had them for as long as I could remember. When the time came to leave, I couldn't do it. I knew my father had begun talks to find me a wife. I'd already searched our community for her; she wasn't there.

My friends were flabbergasted when I refused to return with them. In the end, they relented and left me on the beach. Dreading what I had to do, I made my way to the phone box down the road. My fingers trembled when I rang my home number.

"Hello?"

"Dad, it's Justin. I'm not coming home. Please understand. I need to find the woman of my dreams. I know it sounds silly, but it's just something I have to do. I know she's out there waiting for me, I just have to find her," I begged over the phone.

"Justin, don't be ridiculous! We will find the right one for you. Just come home. Your mum is worried sick about you," he demanded.

"Sorry, Dad, I can't do that. I have to find her. She haunts my dreams every night," I gritted out before hanging up the phone.

The next month was horrid. I moved from place to place, sleeping anywhere I could find. I made a few acquaintances; mostly I found women who only wanted me for my physical attributes. None of them had the eyes from my dreams. The harsh reality settled in; I would never find what I desired most. Feeling defeated and abused, I did the only thing I could and called my father.

"Dad, I want to come home," I cried.

"Son, where are you?"

"A small town on the coast named Plymouth. Please, Dad, come get me. I was wrong to ever leave!" I sobbed harder.

"I'm coming, son. Just don't move!" he growled.

I knew there would be hell to pay, and I didn't care. I just wanted to go home and forget I'd ever left. Dropping onto the sand, I waited the two hours it took for my father to reach me. I'll never forget the sight of him pulling in and jumping out, seeking me out with his eyes. Leaping to my feet, I rushed toward him.

"Dad!" I yelled, running right into his open arms.

"It's okay, son. We'll fix this," he vowed, hugging me tighter.

"I promise, Dad, I'll marry whomever you think will be right for me. I won't fight it!" I promised from my heart.

Even over a year since my indiscretion, no parents in our community were willing to accept me as a possible husband for their daughters. There had not been many encounters, but enough to automatically have everyone mark me off their lists with a big, red X. My reputation was now tarnished forever. It had only taken one short month to destroy any future I had with my church, my family, and my friends.

When a car entered on the dirt road that led to the compound, I knew who it was, since only one family was due to arrive today: mine. And only one man would drive a Lamborghini out there: my dad.

Minister Mark met him at the car and no doubt filled him in on my progress. Minister Mark and his wife ran the retreat for wayward souls like me. I could only hope my father thought my progress warranted my release.

Watching the man, I found I did share most of his facial features, from his caramel-brown hair to his crooked smile, except for my eyes; they were a few shades deeper blue than my mum's. I found it surprising that he had come alone. I'd have thought my mother and sister Krista would have been with him.

"Hello, Justin. How are you, son?" He clapped me on the shoulder.

"I'm good, Dad, but I'd like to come home now." When he nodded, I couldn't help but smile.

"Yes, Minister Mark agrees with you, and so do I. Why don't you go to the car, and we can talk more on the way home?"

I practically danced when I threw my duffle bag over my shoulder, heading to the passenger seat. It felt like forever before he finally joined me. When he smiled getting into the car, I knew something had changed. At first, he didn't say anything, though that didn't last long.

"Well, Justin, I have some good news for you. We have found you a wife while you were here." He paused to see my reaction.

My heart hammered in my chest. "Do I know her? Is she nice?" I tried to keep my voice unstrained.

"No, you've never had the pleasure. She's very nice, incredibly sweet-natured, and beautiful. There is one glitch though."

There always was when it came to me.

"And what might that be?" I muttered, looking out the window, trying not to let my anxiety show.

"We're moving to Les Portes de l'Ange in Small River, Minnesota, near your cousins, since that's where she lives."

I gasped, fisting my hands against my thighs. After hissing out a deep breath to calm myself, I said, "I see. So in order for you to acquire me a wife, we need to leave everyone who knows what I did?" I chided.

"No, your mum and I have been talking about this for quite some time. A new business opportunity opened up, and everything just happened to fall into place." His cool exterior never wavered.

"Do they know?"

He nodded. "I have told her parents about the situation, and they still willingly agreed to the marriage."

I could only imagine what they had to pay for that exception, or could it be no one wanted her either? The thought crossed my mind that maybe she'd had her own indiscretions.

Closing my eyes, I huffed. "How old is she?"

"She turned eighteen last week." I might not know her, but it would have been nice to have been with my future wife on her birthday. I always thought I'd see my future wife coming of age like my friends had.

"How is it that she's still available?"

"Her parents were rather *picky* when it came to finding her a husband. They turned down fifteen other offers before accepting ours."

There was only one thing I could think of that would have them easily forgiving my indiscretions. "How much, Dad?" I ground through my teeth.

"Twice the standard fees."

I winced at the thought that they really might have only been looking for the money. "Basically, they only wanted the money?" That simple thought appalled me.

"Actually, no. They didn't ask for anything above what is customary. I offered more in the hopes it would help."

"How soon until we leave?" I asked dryly, not wanting to share my fears with him.

"Everything's been packed and shipped. We fly out tomorrow." He grinned.

"And the wedding?" I choked.

"Saturday." For the first time, he grimaced.

"Less than a week?" I bellowed. "Are you serious? We haven't even met yet. What about the tying ceremony?"

"Justin, we've waited long enough. This girl is definitely better than anything we've seen here. She'll make you happy, and you will return the favor. As for the tying ceremony, Minister Jeff has agreed to do it for us on the wedding day." I hated when he used that smug tone of voice.

"That was very nice of him, and you're right, I'm sorry. I guess I just can't wrap my mind around the fact that someone accepted me," I admitted. That, after all, was the reason I'd agreed to the retreat. I had known that it would be my last chance at a contract to wed.

"Well, she is something special, and this union will be good for both of you."

Still stunned by the turn of events, I decided to submit to the entire idea. "So, what's she like?"

"Well, she's very easygoing and faithful beyond her years. She's best friends with your cousins' wives-to-be; they'll be able to tell you more when we arrive."

"Do I at least get to say good-bye to my friends here?" I implored.

"We're going to a have a farewell dinner tonight in the meeting hall, so you will see them there." Well, I would have that, at least.

I spent the rest of the ride trying to envision what my bride-to-be would look like. You can imagine the wild things that were running through my mind. There had to be something wrong with her if she'd made it to eighteen before finding someone willing to take her. There were too many things to count, from excessive facial hair to an ungodly amount of warts – and that didn't even cover the possible physical deformities, like several missing limbs.

I finally gave up thinking how bad this could be and tried to focus on the good things. They'd had fifteen offers; she had to have some redeeming factors. Once we were married, I could move out of my parents' house and be my own person; we could have sex if she agreed; and I wouldn't have to hide my secret passion for drawing. And if she was willing, we could have a child.

I knew it was a standard clause in the contract for us to try to have a child in the first year, but that didn't mean her family hadn't asked for it to be removed. For all I knew about the girl, maybe she couldn't have children; maybe that was why she was still available at eighteen. It was possible she couldn't or wouldn't want children.

My mother and Krista were standing on the porch when we arrived. It was nice to finally be back with my family again. My mum, of course, pulled me into a giant hug before I could even say, "Hello, Mum."

"Welcome back! You look too skinny; didn't they feed you there?"

"Yeah, Mum, they did." I stepped back to see Krista anxiously awaiting her turn.

"Hey, squirt, miss me?" I ruffled her hair.

With a gleam in her brown eyes, she teased, "Nah, too busy packing your room with Mum." She cackled, throwing her head back.

I stepped back to get a better look at her. I think she had grown while I'd been away. She wasn't going to be hard to marry off with her long, curly, mahogany hair, deep brown eyes, and long legs. We had both inherited our height from our parents.

It was shocking to see the house almost empty. As a precaution, I drifted off to my bedroom to make sure nothing had been left behind. When I cracked open my secret hiding spot, I noticed my drawing stuff was gone and immediately panicked.

"I packed everything up before Mum could find it." Krista smiled from the doorway.

"I owe you, squirt." I sighed as the relief washed over me.

"Who is she?" She quirked her eyebrow.

"Who's who?"

"The girl you keep drawing with the emerald green eyes?"

"I don't know; just someone I see sometimes when I dream. I can't figure out why I dream of her."

"Is that why you started seeing the outsiders?"

I nodded. "I just kept hoping I'd find her, but I didn't. It doesn't matter anymore. I am getting married, and that's all that counts. I found my way back to the church and my family," I vowed with total confidence.

"Mum keeps going on about how wonderful she is." She cocked her eyebrow, no doubt hoping for more information.

"So I hear from Dad. Haven't you met her yet?"

"Nope; they went solo this trip. I stayed with Katie's family while they were gone. They didn't even bring home a picture or anything." My mind ran right back to thinking about her possible ghoulish appearance.

I really had to stop freaking out about this, since it was a done deal and the contract had been signed. Thankfully, the time for the dinner arrived so I didn't have long to dwell on it. The meeting hall looked like it had every other night when we'd attended meetings. Of course, I got the usual distasteful glares from the attendees. As I usually did, I just shrugged them off and went to see my friends, who were huddled together in the corner.

"Welcome back. So, are you now a reborn virgin?" Paulie ribbed.

"Funny, Paulie. You're a regular comedian." I elbowed him playfully in the gut.

"No, seriously, how bad was it?" Jonathan winced. We'd all heard the stories.

"Fine; a little intense, but I'm good with it." I shrugged.

Before we could say any more, Minister Peter took the podium and addressed the group. "Good evening, everyone. Thank you for coming tonight to say good-bye to a family who've been with us since 1979. As some of you already know, the McNears will be moving to Les Portes de l'Ange, our sister community in Minnesota. I have also just learned that Justin's been contracted to marry Alexia Cross, who currently resides there.

Minister Jeff has contacted me, and I informed him of Justin's remarkable reconfirmation to our beliefs, so the young woman will be very lucky to have him. If you will raise your glasses, I believe a toast is in order." When everyone had done as he asked, he continued, "Your family will be missed, and we hope you will all visit us again soon. This is not goodbye, but until we meet again. So, let's celebrate!" He stepped away to speak with my parents, and I turned back to my friends.

"Did you know about this?"

"Yeah, Paulie, my dad told me on the way back today." He gasped, surprised by the sudden turn of events.

"And you didn't tell us – why?"

"Because there is not much to tell. I know nothing about the girl." *I wish I did.*

"Seriously? But you know what she looks like, right?"

"Nope, no idea."

We hung out and caught up on current events. They wanted to know if I would be back for their weddings in August, and I told them I would try my best. They were also surprised about the date of my wedding. The best I could hope would be that they *might* be able to attend mine. When the evening finally ended, we hugged everyone and bid them farewell.

We flew into Minnesota the next evening, and a crazy week ensued. We went directly to my family's new townhouse to start unpacking, but my things remained boxed since in a few days I'd be leaving.

"Do you like the new house?"

"Yeah, Mum, it's great. I'm sure everyone will be happy here." I didn't convince anyone.

"You're going to love the cottage her parents bought. We picked it out together before we flew back to get everything ready." She beamed with pride.

"Mum, you don't have to convince me. I'm sure everything will be perfect, and if it's not, that's okay, too. I *will* make it work." My father walked in with his arms full of bedding, so I helped my mother make the bed.

"I am so happy to hear you're willing to devote yourself to this, son. It proves the retreat was the best thing for you," he said with knowledge he didn't possess.

"I couldn't agree more." Truth be told, I hadn't needed the retreat to devote myself back to my faith, but if it had made everyone happy, it was worth it. "Will I see her before the wedding?"

"Right now, everyone is working overtime on getting everything ready for the ceremony and the house, so I can't say for sure. You don't have to worry; she's just as anxious to see you, too." I decided to try another approach.

"Why didn't you bring a picture home with you?"

"We never received one. Your cousins have one, but they didn't have a copy, and they wouldn't part with the one they have. We did see her in person the night we signed the contract, and she looked like an angel." Great description of my future wife: extremely vague.

"Has she seen a picture of me, then?"

"No, but her parents did, though." At this point, I gave up. It was apparent that they weren't going to share anything further.

"Do we need to do anything for the state's requirements?"

"No, we took care of everything. Her dad's a lawyer, so he knew all the laws. Minnesota doesn't require blood tests, and as long as all the required information for you was provided, only one of you needed to apply for the marriage license. We had all the proper identification and your Social Security number from when we lived in the States before." Well, there went that shot at seeing her.

The more they blocked my efforts to see her, the more curious I became.

The second day, we continued to unpack and help my mother set up the new house.

At lunchtime, I was thrilled when my cousins came by for a visit. Unfortunately, they didn't bring a picture of my future bride. When my mum went inside for some tea, I pounced.

"Come on, guys. You have to give me something about her, *anything*," I pleaded.

"Well, what do you want to know?" Johnny chuckled.

"Everything." I looked up to see they were smiling with mischief in their eyes.

"You still haven't pieced it together yet, have you?" Joey snickered.

"Pieced what together?"

"Who she is. You really don't remember, do you?" Johnny taunted.

"Are you saying I've seen her before?" They just nodded, grinning like the cat that ate the canary.

My mother interrupted us before I could ask more. I gasped when their words clicked in my mind. The only girl it could be was a young girl I'd met the year we'd visited from England. I couldn't exactly picture her face, but I remembered that I'd felt connected to her when we played on the beach. When I closed my eyes and tried to concentrate on her, all I could see in my mind was emerald green eyes – the same eyes that had haunted my dreams for years; the same ones that covered my sketch book.

Was it possible she was the one I'd been looking for all along? As much as I wanted to hope it could be true, I refused to believe it. It would hurt too much if it weren't.

We didn't get another chance to talk before my cousins had to go.

"Just remember, cousin, she means a lot to us and is one of our best friends. If you hurt her, we will hurt you." Joey gestured between them.

I sighed. "Not a chance. I'll never hurt her."

The third day, I spent at the dealership, helping my dad take over the business. While we were there, he gave me an early wedding present: a black 2010 Mercedes S600 sedan. "Dad, this is a fantastic gift." I laughed from behind the steering wheel.

He also told me about Alexia's car choice. "We gave Alexia a white Mercedes R350 Crossover. I hope you approve." Grinning, I nodded, hoping she picked it with the possibility of children in mind.

"Yes, it's a great car, and my future bride deserves only the best."

Since talking with my cousins, I hadn't decided whether or not she was the green-eyed girl of my dreams. I realized I was very fortunate to have someone as well liked as she was, which seemed to be the common theme in everyone's description.

On the fourth day, I started moving my belongings into the new house I would live in after the wedding. As I got out of the Mercedes, I found the view breathtaking. Her parents had bought us a lakefront white cottage-style home. I could already see that some improvements needed to be made, but that didn't worry me. I'd always been good with my hands. I'd hoped when I moved my boxes into the cottage I would share with Alexia that I might catch a glimpse of her, but instead I found her mother setting up the house.

"Oh, Justin, right? You scared me to death." She held her hand over her heart.

"Yeah, sorry about that. I just wanted to drop off my boxes." I quickly placed them on the floor, freeing me to shake her hand.

"Justin McNear," I knew she was aware of my name, but proper etiquette required that I introduced myself.

"Katrina Cross." She dropped what she was doing, making her way over to me.

"It's a pleasure to meet you, Mrs. Cross." She accepted my hand to shake with a smile.

"Please, call me Katrina. After tomorrow we'll be family."

"Mrs. – Katrina, can I ask you about Alexia?"

"Sure, what would you like to know?" Her eyes lit up at the thought of talking about her daughter.

I exhaled. "Everything."

"Justin, you don't have to worry. Alexia will be the best wife possible for you. She is a very caring, loyal, and a quiet person. She loves to read and garden. She also likes her solitude; that's why this place will be perfect for the two of you."

"Thank you, it's lovely. It really is," I said, gazing out the glass doors that led to a spacious deck with several lounge chairs and a small patio set.

I was so lost in the beauty of the view, I didn't hear my mother come in. "Justin, come on, I'll give you the grand tour." She grinned.

"Sure, Mum, lead the way."

"So, here's the living room. It has a wonderful fireplace for those cold winter nights. Lexie picked out the living room set. She said blue is her favorite color; it almost matches your eyes." She continued to rattle off all the little things that didn't really matter to me. "And in here is the dining room. You'll remember this set from our home in England. I think your grandmother would have wanted you to have it."

"Thank you; it's nice to have a piece of home here." I followed her when she moved on to the kitchen where Katrina had been putting away the gifts from the bridal shower.

I'd missed so much already; I could only hope she didn't resent me for it. If I'd known before I entered the retreat everything I would be missing, I'd have postponed it to be here with her. But then again, if I hadn't gone, would her parents have signed the contract? It was a catch-22. It was one thing to miss my own prom; however, including her birthday, prom, and graduation, I'd missed way too many important occasions. I did make a special trip the day we were in town to get her a belated gift for each.

"This is your new bedroom. Lexie moved her stuff in a few days ago. Do you like the bedding? It's a gift from Minister Peter and his wife. I watched the whole shower on a video chat your dad set up for me. That's why I didn't come with your dad to get you. I thought it was important to participate in the party." She looked so sad.

I almost wondered about the logic behind white sheets on a honeymoon bed. I couldn't help but wonder if my earlier thoughts about her virginity were correct. I prayed they weren't.

"Here is the bathroom. I just love the tree theme, don't you?"

"Yeah, it's definitely better than yellow with butterflies." I chuckled, wondering who could have done such a remarkable job on the leaves because they had clearly been painted freehand. I really liked the room being painted pastel green with emerald green leaf prints painted onto it. It reminded me of the eyes I'd seen in my dreams for years.

"I saved this room for last. Right now it's the spare bedroom, but hopefully soon it will be a nursery." She beamed at the thought of becoming a grandmother. If she thought that was a possibility, then maybe the clause remained intact.

"Oh, my gosh," my mother glanced at her watch. "We have to go. Your father will be home soon, and I haven't even started dinner yet." I followed her to the door with one last wave to Katrina.

Thankfully, the ride back to the townhouse was quick. She had just enough time to whip up a quick dinner before my dad walked in. One thing about my dad was that he demanded things be done a certain way. I'd seen him flip out if the house wasn't perfect or if dinner was late being served. I never wanted to be like that; it caused too much stress on the family.

After I finished my sausage and chips, I slipped away to take a walk alone. Even after ten years away, I found the beach easily. I couldn't help but marvel at the size of this community.

In England, our community property sat on only a quarter of the land of Les Portes de l'Ange and had half the population. Here, they had one private school that housed all the grades and a private clinic that handled all the day-to-day medical needs. I stopped and admired the small shopping center that they were constructing, and I recognized the future spot of Joey and Madison's beauty salon.

Joey thought progressively where his future wife was concerned.

When he told my mother she'd be attending cosmetology classes in the fall, she had nearly fallen off her chair.

However, his thinking was sound, because if Madison wanted to work, at least she'd be working inside the confines of our belief structure. He also explained that her older sister Alison would be working for them since she had already worked as a hairdresser after graduating cosmetology school. I had no idea what Alexia thought about furthering her education or working. I only hoped that if there was something that made her happy, she would want to pursue it. After all, many women in our community did, and I thought it made them more interesting.

When I finally reached the beach, I sat on the sand to relax before tomorrow's mayhem began. Closing my eyes, I could see the green eyes that had held me captive for so long. I thought more about what my cousins had said about meeting Alexia before, and I kept coming back to the barbeque where I'd met a young girl on the very beach on which I now sat. The harder I concentrated on the memory, the clearer it became. I had focused on her red hair blowing in the breeze while she watched the fireworks exploding overhead. I'd spent the entire day mesmerized by her shimmering green eyes. They were the same eyes from my dreams, and they belonged to the girl I always thought should be mine.

I was elated to discover that I had been promised to the girl I'd vowed years earlier to make mine; the same girl who had promised to wait. One thing that I did learn from the retreat was that I had to let go of the irrational fear that my parents wouldn't find me the right wife. It was my one deepest fear in the world. Now it seemed I had worried over nothing, because they had found me the perfect wife.

I nearly jumped out of my skin when I heard two voices approaching from behind me. "I told you we'd find him here." I turned to see my twin cousins smirking.

"You twits! You scared the piss out of me," I chided.

"Yeah well, serves you right. Your parents are about to call out the militia to look for you." Joey chuckled.

"Why would they do that?" I questioned.

"Well, when Alexia and her parents showed up for a formal introduction, you were gone. I don't like when one of my best friends cries. She thinks you ran off on her," Joey snarled.

"I didn't run off on her; I was relaxing before tomorrow. I should get back and tell her I'm sorry for making her worry." I sighed. This wasn't how I'd wanted to meet her.

"You should get back, but apologies will have to wait. She was so upset, they had to take her home." Johnny gestured for me to follow him back.

The walk back was torturous, not because of the company. I'd blown my one shot at seeing Alexia before the wedding. I'd had no idea they were coming over. If I had, no one could have pulled me away from the house. When I looked down my parents' driveway, disappointment washed over me again. There were no extra cars, so they had indeed gone home.

My cousins were right, of course. Everyone freaked out when I got back. "Where have you been?"

"I just went for a walk to the beach, Dad. I had no idea she was coming over tonight. If I had, wild dogs couldn't have dragged me out. Why do you still doubt me? I said I would marry anyone you chose, and I will!" I couldn't wait to move out from under his iron rule.

"I'm sorry for doubting you, but do you realize how devastated they were not to see you tonight? The poor girl ran out of here crying. She thought you ran away." I cringed at the thought of making her cry. She should never have to doubt her reliance on me.

"Well, we'll just call them and explain that I meant no disrespect to them. If I had known they were coming, I would have been here. I've been waiting and desperately wanting to meet her."

"James, please call them so she doesn't end up crying herself to sleep," my mum begged.

He did call, and thankfully, Mr. Cross answered the phone. Once everything was explained, I'd been forgiven, though I'd lost my only chance to meet her before the wedding. She claimed she was too tired to come back; however, I think she was embarrassed. I wanted to ask her to reconsider, but my dad wouldn't allow me to talk to her father.

I decided to write her a quick note and begged my cousins to deliver it. Fortunately, they agreed to take it to her. When I headed off to bed for a futile attempt at sleep, I just kept seeing green eyes and hearing, "I'll be waiting."

CHAPTER 5

ALEXIA CROSS'S WISHES AND A WEDDING

As the morning light crept through my window, I slowly opened my swollen eyes, the reality of last night's event still fresh in my mind. Even though his father had called and said everything was fine, I had no way of knowing if they'd dragged him back kicking and screaming or what. I wished I knew the truth.

I wished his mother had never said he didn't know about the wedding. Those words had started my downward spiral a week ago. Every moment of every day since then, I'd heard them over and over, replaying in my mind like a bad horror movie.

Looking at the shiny silver picture frame, I saw a note tucked inside that hadn't been there before. I didn't recognize the writing. I reached out, grasped it with a shaking hand, and read it.

Alexia,
You are mine to love.
Please, still be waiting for me.
Justin

With those words, a new floodgate opened, and I started crying again, although this time, my tears were of pure joy. He remembered me; he never forgot; he hadn't run. For the first time since the arrangement had been reached, I felt secure in knowing this was the right thing to do. I'd still been waiting; deep inside I'd always remembered my vow, and now I knew he did, too.

When Madison rushed in, she thought the worst. "Oh, Alexia, please don't cry. It'll be okay." I just shook my head, handing her the note.

"What does it mean?" She looked baffled.

"'You are mine to love' is what Justin said to me on the beach ten years ago before he left for England." I smiled through my tears.

"And?" she prompted me to continue.

"My reply was 'I'll be waiting'."

"So, he's telling you he never forgot you?"

"Yes," I giggled.

"Then, why are you crying?"

"Because I'm finally happy. He's the one."

"Well then, what are we waiting for? We have to get you ready." She grabbed my hand, dragging me from the bed.

"He hasn't seen me since I was eight. Do you think he'll be disappointed?"

"Not a snowball's chance in Hell. You get showered; Ginger's making your breakfast." She shoved me toward the bathroom.

"Madison, your gown looks lovely on you." She smiled at me, twirling to show it off.

"Why, thank you." She curtsied, letting her inner diva shine through.

When I padded off in search of a hot shower, I found I was very excited about today. Up until now, I'd been going through the motions, doing what everyone expected and just hoping for the best. Not anymore. I wanted this; I wanted to marry Justin, and I wanted it now.

Normally, I took my time in the hot stream, letting it pelt away at the tight muscles in my back, but not today. I wanted time to speed up. In my head, I started to count down the minutes until the wedding.

One hundred and sixty-seven minutes left.

Quickly, I washed my body with my favorite lavender body wash, shaved all the pertinent areas, and shampooed my hair with my matching lavender-scented shampoo. Feeling refreshed and ready for what the day would bring, I wrapped myself up in a fluffy pink towel and made my way back to my room to let Madison begin blow-drying my hair.

One hundred and forty-three minutes left.

While she worked her magic on my hair, I began eating my blueberry muffin and fruit salad that Ginger had delivered. Laughing, I explained about the note from Justin and what it meant in between bites of my breakfast. She thought it was romantic and couldn't help but hug me. Once my plate was empty, she took it back to the kitchen, and when she returned, my mother followed her in.

"Good morning, sweetie. You're practically glowing. Are you happy today?"

"Yes, someone left me a note from Justin. Who brought it?" I waved it at her.

"Joey and Johnny said he begged them to bring it to you last night, but when they arrived you were already asleep." She started to whisper. "Johnny snuck it into your room when your father wasn't looking."

"Oh, my Johnny is so sweet," Ginger cooed with that wistful gaze he invoked in her.

With my hair finally dry, Madison began banana curling it with her curling iron. No wonder she wanted to be a hairdresser; the things she could do with hair reminded me of an artist with a blank canvas. She pulled all the curls up with a white ribbon, tying it off in the front. The curls cascaded around my head, and she pinned them as she went around the ribbon until they bowed to her wishes.

One hundred and eleven minutes left.

Madison and Ginger tag-teamed my makeup. On a normal day, I wore just the basics like lip gloss and mascara, but today they applied the works. I was almost worried that one of them would poke out my eye when they ferociously applied the cosmetics Madison had made me buy for today. With one last coat of gloss, they declared themselves done.

Ninety-seven minutes left.

"Good morning, ladies. Here's the dress. What do you think?" Charlene swept into the room, carrying my mother's wedding dress.

All I managed was a gasp at the beauty of the gown she'd reinvented for me.

"Oh. My. Gosh. Mom, that's awesome," Ginger gushed.

"Why, thank you, lovey." Charlene always loved when we complimented her work.

"Alexia, you truly look stunning." I glanced in the mirror, because for some reason, I'd never thought of myself as anything above average.

"Thank you, Charlene, but if it wasn't for all of you, I think I'd still be an ugly duckling."

"Alexia, you've never been an ugly duckling." My mother pulled me into a deep hug, careful to stay away from all of Madison's work.

"Let's get this show on the road, shall we?"

Quickly, I ducked into the bathroom, since it would be an adventure to go later, and put on the necessary undergarments. I walked back in my bathrobe. It felt a little weird when I dropped the robe to the floor, leaving me in my matching white lace panties and strapless bra. Of course, no one said a word. With caution, I stepped into the fabric, which had been set in a hoop shape on the rug. Together, my mom and Charlene each lifted one side until I could hold the dress under my armpits. Charlene zipped it up, and the fabric became snug around my form. I held my breath, turning to the full-length mirror in the corner.

I gulped. "Wow . . . just wow. I don't know what else to say."

From the smiles in the room, no one else knew what to say either. How Charlene turned a 1960s gown into a 2010 masterpiece was beyond my comprehension. The fact that she had done this in less than a month was even more mind-boggling. Before me stood a gown like no other. The strapless lace bodice clung lightly to my skin and flared as it passed my hips into a flowing sea of satin. I turned to see that the back had been buttoned up in a scalloped shape to show the tulle layer underneath in waves.

Seventy-one minutes left.

"Kat, we're taking the cake over to the churchyard to meet the caterers," my father bellowed up the stairs.

"Hurry back; we need to take pictures before we leave."

"Alexia, we're going to pop downstairs to say good luck to the guys before they leave with your dad." Madison laughed when she and Ginger left my room.

"So, do you have any questions about tonight, you know . . . about . . . after you go back to the cottage?" I blew out a deep breath before I dashed my mom's hopes.

"No," I replied, not wanting to go there.

"You know you can ask me about anything you're unsure of?" I nodded. "Oh, I think I hear Alison and Brett. I should go and show them where we're taking the pictures in the yard. You're going to love the pictures; he takes the best photographs I've ever seen." Charlene followed my mother downstairs.

It was nice to have a moment alone to gather my wits. It didn't last long enough because Madison and Alison came waltzing in to put my veil in place. A few dozen bobby pins and a can of hair spray later, I walked out of my room.

Fifty-nine minutes left.

I smiled at the dropped jaws that greeted me when I sashayed down the stairs. It wasn't a greeting I had received before now.

"Alexia, you're breathtaking. Please follow me; we'll do the singles and family shots." Brett smiled and waved toward the back door..

Alison, Madison's older sister, and her husband Brett had been hired by my parents to take all the photos for the wedding. Brett had a very exclusive business, photographing the rich and famous. He usually didn't do weddings for the average person; however, he'd made an exception for me. Alison had always been the older sister I'd never had, and she would do anything for me, as I would for her.

My mom had been nice enough to let me plant an entire landscape just for the purpose of wedding photos. It had taken me two days of digging and planting to get it perfect. It had also helped to burn off the nervous energy from having a fiancé I still had yet to meet.

"Kat, everything is perfect at the church. The boys are staying to oversee everything, and Charlene, your husband is looking for you. He said, and I quote, 'Tell my wife I need her here for the suits'."

"Right, I'm on it. See you all at eleven sharp."

As we got into the positions Brett desired, I noted that there were only forty-seven minutes left. Once he was in the zone, Brett's camera never stopped flashing. Amazingly enough, just when we finished, an antique 1947 Rolls Royce pulled up.

My parents helped to maneuver me and my dress into the back seat and then got in as well, sitting on either side of me. Brett got in the front with driver while everyone else drove off in the rest of our cars. We arrived at the church with five minutes to spare. Brett ran off to take a few other shots before he returned as planned to photograph me exiting the car. Huddled in the backseat, we found we didn't have much to say. Therefore, I sat quietly between my parents with shaking hands and waited for the time to pass. Through the tinted windows, I could see Joey, Johnny, Madison, and Ginger pacing. I had to admit that the girls really looked good in their ice-blue, satin, sleeveless gowns. What could I say about the men in their double-breasted pinstriped suits? They looked hot!

It was then that I realized I had no idea who Justin had picked for a best man. My arrangement with my friends was simple; Ginger got to be the maid of honor, and in exchange, Madison got to be the godmother to my first child, if I had one. The decision was simple because we'd flipped a coin. When Johnny made his way into the church and shut the door, I wondered if he had the honor of being the best man or whether Justin had flown someone in.

I took one last deep breath before nodding to my father to open the door. The hot breeze stung my lungs as I stood up with the help of my dad's hand. All morning I'd been so excited to get here, but now that the time had arrived, I just wanted to go back and hide in the car.

"Okay, Alexia, it's time. Just let me unhook your train and drop your veil." Ginger attacked me from behind while Madison attacked me from the front.

"Dad, I'm really nervous," I whispered.

"Don't be; he's not. I saw him this morning, and he was more worried that you wouldn't come than about getting married." I smiled just knowing he'd be waiting for me.

"Really?"

"Yes, he wasn't sure if you had received his note. Johnny was given a free pass this once, but if I find him sneaking notes to your mother I'll have to whup that boy."

Slapping his arm, I played along with his joke. "I did get it, and I don't think Mom's his type." I giggled.

"Good, then let's get this show on the road before he runs out here to get you himself."

"Oh, no! I forgot his ring." My dad just smiled, placing it in my hand.

"Thanks, Dad. That was a close one."

With tiny steps, we walked through the outer doors and waited to the side. When the music started, the doors opened, allowing Madison and Joey to start walking up the aisle before they shut. My hands started shaking again when the doors opened long enough for Ginger to disappear. With a few steps, we were in place, waiting for the doors to open one last time. A gust of air signaled the doors opening; with one deep breath, we started the seventy-five-foot trek.

Even though I knew everyone was staring at me, I refused to look anywhere but at the young man waiting for me at the altar. His smile drew me in like a moth to a flame. I giggled when I felt my bouquet shaking in my hands. My father patted my trembling hand that rested on his arm. Each step closer sent my heart racing, a staccato beat throbbing in my chest. A single tear slipped from my eye. Seeing him awaiting me pulled on my soul, demanding I hurry, dragging me toward him. The awe-filled whispers pushed my feather-light steps forward faster. The slow pace was killing me; I wanted nothing more than to run the rest of the way.

Justin stood regally, his broad shoulders squared and his hands crossed in front of his waist. He showed no signs of the nerves that plagued me. The smile gracing his lips grew wider with each pew I passed. His hand stretched out to receive mine when we joined him at the altar. When I was close enough to see his deep blue eyes, I knew he was the one; he had always been the one, even in my dreams.

Justin chuckled nervously when my father placed my hands in his and pulled out a long white ribbon from his pocket. I sighed, feeling the warmth of his hand on mine. He tightened his fingers, locking me to him forever. My eyes fluttered shut until my father's voice broke through the haze wrapped around my thoughts. With my mother by his side, they said the words I'd waited eighteen years to hear.

"With these ribbons, we bind more than just your hands; we bind your souls, life spirits, and futures as one." They wrapped the ribbon three times around our wrists, securing my soul to his.

James and Jane stood up, joining us for their portion. "From this day forth, you will be a single entity, one united pair. You will remain forever faithful to one another and to our church." James also wrapped his ribbon around three times.

Still bound, I turned to my mother to raise my veil. Once the lace was behind me, I turned bashfully to look at Justin for the first time unobstructed. I couldn't help but gasp; he left me breathless. His pearly white smile, chiseled cheeks, and sapphire blue eyes stole my breath away. With one grin and a twinkle in his eyes, he guided me two steps closer to stand just inches away.

His smile broadened, and he mouthed, "You are mine to love."

I smiled, blushing, mouthing back, "I've been waiting."

After our fathers shook hands, the parents all took their seats, leaving us at the altar with Minister Jeff. As Minister Jeff began speaking, he removed the ribbons and placed them in his pocket.

"Welcome friends and families of Les Portes de l'Ange community. Les Portes de l'Ange is French for Gates of the Angels. We're a tight-knit community, with our religion binding us together forever. Today, Justin and Alexia are embarking on the first of many wonderful adventures together, the one of holy matrimony.

While Minister Jeff continued, I found myself lost in Justin's mesmerizing eyes. It seemed like we were both hypnotized, because his eyes never left mine, not even for a second. If I hadn't heard Johnny's whisper of a chuckle, I wouldn't have even noticed he was there as the best man. We were forced to look away from each other when Minister Jeff handed us each a card to read from. Justin took a deep breath and began.

"I, Justin, take you, Alexia, to be my wedded wife. With great joy, I receive you into my life, that together we may be one united couple. As is Christ to His body, the church, I will be to you a loving and faithful husband. Always will I perform my headship over you as Christ does to me. I promise you my fullest devotion, my tenderest care. I promise I will live first unto God then to you. I promise that I will lead our lives into a life of faith and hope in the Lord. No matter what may lie ahead of us, I pledge my life to you."

When he finished, it was my turn to read. "I, Alexia, take you, Justin, to be my wedded husband. With deepest joy, I come into my new life with you. As you have pledged to me your life and love, so do I happily give you my life, and in confidence submit myself to your headship as to the Lord. As is the church in her relationship to the Lord, I will be to you. Justin, I will live first for God and then for you, obeying you, caring for you, and ever seeking to please you. I have been prepared for you, and I will forever strengthen, help, comfort, and encourage you. Throughout life, no matter what may lie ahead of us, I pledge to you my life as an obedient and faithful wife." Together we looked at Minister Jeff for him to speak.

"Justin, will you take Alexia to be your lawful wife, love her, honor her, and keep her in sickness and in health, forsaking all others, and keep only unto her so long as you both shall live?"

"I do," he vowed, a grin gracing his lips.

"With this ring I thee wed, with my body I thee worship, and with all my worldly goods I thee endow. In the name of the Father, and of the Son, and of the Holy Ghost."

I gasped when he slipped an enormous diamond-covered wedding band onto my finger.

"Alexia, will you take Justin to be your lawful husband, love him, honor him, and keep him in sickness and in health, and forsaking all others, keep only unto him so long as you both shall live?"

"I do," I vowed, knowing it to be true.

"With this ring I thee wed, with my body I thee worship, and with all my worldly goods I thee endow. In the name of the Father, and of the Son, and of the Holy Ghost." Justin smiled wider when I slipped on his diamond-encrusted wedding band.

"You have declared your consent before the Church. May the Lord in his goodness strengthen your consent and fill you both with his blessings. What God has joined, men must not divide."

Unified, everyone pledged, "Amen."

"By the power vested in me by God and the State of Minnesota, I now pronounce you husband and wife. You may kiss the bride."

Slowly and sweetly, he leaned in and brushed a kiss on my lips for the first time.

CHAPTER 6

JUSTIN MCNEAR'S RUMORS AND REPENTING

Staring into the depths of her deep emerald eyes, I knew my dad had found what I'd been searching for all along. Seeing the eyes that had haunted my dreams in person humbled me. I hadn't done them justice in my drawings. Minister Chan was right when he'd said in our retraining that I needed to trust my parents to find the right woman for me. They had indeed found the perfect woman I desired.

When I leaned in to kiss her lips for the first time, it physically hurt to keep it quick and emotionless. Deep in my chest, I wanted to claim her soft, pouty lips as my own. I admitted I'd kissed two girls before Alexia, but they had both felt wrong; they were quick and unfeeling kisses. However, with Alexia, it felt right. It was the first time in my life that I wanted to kiss someone, and I wanted massive amounts of it.

Hand in hand and smiling, we walked back down the aisle as husband and wife. I was in such a daze when we passed our family and friends that I barely saw anyone's faces. The only thought my mind would entertain was that I needed to be alone with my wife. I needed to stare into those gem-colored pools and lose myself in them forever. These thoughts started my feet moving faster until I was practically dragging her down the stairs into the meeting room where we would be taking our pictures. As soon as we entered the room, I spun around and pulled her into my desperate embrace. Seeing her smile back when I placed a deep kiss on her perfect pink lips had me begging for more.

"I have waited my whole life to kiss someone like that," I whispered against her nose with my forehead resting against hers.

Before it could go any further, we heard giggles and chuckles coming from the doorway. The wedding party had arrived, thankfully before the parents had. In what could only be described as nothing short of a whirlwind, we were pulled apart, hugged, kissed, and passed on to the next person in line.

Brett introduced himself and set to work. Every time they separated me and my wife, I suppressed a growl. I wanted to wrap myself in her and stay there forever. My patience had started to wear thin by the time Brett declared himself done; I almost cheered when it was over.

With the pictures finished, I thought I'd get a chance to talk to Alexia, but instead my father took me aside. "Justin, I know you wanted to see this earlier, but I didn't want it to cloud your judgment," he whispered, passing me our contract.

"Thanks, Dad, but it won't change anything. You chose perfectly." I grinned, taking the contract anyway.

"I'm glad to hear that son." He clapped me on the shoulder and returned to my mother.

Before we needed to go outside, I headed to the men's room for a quick peek at what was expected of me. Deep down inside, I prayed it said something about having children. Once I found an empty stall, I sat on the closed lid and started reading.

The American contracts were much like the English ones. It stated all the usual things, from our living arrangements to how much money my parents would pay. My father was correct; they had doubled all the amounts to be handed over after proof of the consummation had been completed.

That one thought made me cringe. As if I wanted to hand over a towel with my wife's virginal blood and my semen on it. I would do it because it was required, but I didn't have to like it.

Skimming lower, I did discover the child clause had remained intact. We indeed were expected to produce children. Unfortunately, it didn't say how many or how soon. I could only hope she wanted them sooner rather than later. It was funny; I'd always wanted kids for as long as I could remember.

At the bottom, there sat the standard no-divorce clause. Well, she was stuck with me now. I knew it went both ways, but I doubted there would be anything I'd find out about her that would make me want to throw away everything my religion stood for.

After folding the contract back up, I tucked it in my pocket for safekeeping. Before I could exit the stall, the outer door opened, and the sounds of men's voices stilled my movements.

"Poor kid, I bet when he slept with her he never thought she'd trap him." A man chuckled sarcastically.

"Talk about a shotgun wedding. I bet he didn't know what hit him," another man snickered.

"Yeah, well, you don't get married at eighteen and in a month unless you're trying to do it before she starts showing." The first man laughed again.

"We better get back before they introduce them. We don't want the boss getting pissed at us."

When I heard the door shut, I sank back down. My stomach churned while I digested what they had said. My breath hitched in my throat when I tried to breathe for the first time after hearing those God-awful words.

She was pregnant by someone else. Before I could stop myself, my fist hit the metal door with enough force to rattle it open.

How could they do this to my family? How could she do this to me? We had a deal! My father would insist on nullifying the wedding immediately if he heard about this. I closed my eyes, taking a few deep cleansing breaths.

Did I want out of the marriage knowing this? Just the thought of losing her hurt more than the betrayal itself. No, I didn't want to lose her. My hands were shaking as I raked them through my hair, trying to figure out a plan of action. Maybe no one knew? If that was the case, then why tell anyone? Everyone could keep on thinking it belonged to me, and no one would be the wiser except for her parents, but as long as I accepted it as mine, they wouldn't tell anyone. The best I could hope for was that her family had kept this secret behind closed doors. It would be even better if her parents didn't know.

The only glitch in my plan was the dreaded proof of consummation. How could I produce that when she didn't have a hymen to break? If they knew about the pregnancy, they must have a way for me to get through that loophole.

"Justin, you in here? We need to go, dude," Johnny bellowed before he shut the door again.

Still feeling sick to my stomach, I made my way to the sink and splashed my face with cold water since it would be a long day. I tried my best to smile when I made my way back to Alexia's side. It turned out to be a daunting task. When she snaked her arm through mine, I did my best not to flinch. It was hard when I was suffering from visions of some strange man pawing my bride. I had to swallow back the bile that threatened to escape when I envisioned him taking her virginity in the backseat of a car.

"Justin, are you okay? You look a little green around the gills." If she only knew how close to the mark she'd hit.

"I'm fine," I ground through my clenched teeth.

Once we were introduced, we headed to the table for dinner. Just the thought of food made me want to run for the loo. When the champagne arrived, underage or not, I took two. However, I was horrified to see Alexia take one as well. After downing my two in four gulps, I took hers, too.

"No drinking for you," I demanded in a whisper.

"Um, okay, that's fine," she muttered.

I could see my behavior had left her confused, but there was nothing I could do about it. The aching in my core made it impossible to think clearly. I scanned the room to see if any of the men were looking at her, but no one stood out.

When the waiter walked by with more champagne, I took another two flutes and downed them, too. By the time our first dance arrived, I'd drunk eight flutes of champagne. My brain had finally started to feel numb from the alcohol.

I could barely hold her when we waltzed around the dance floor. Confusion once again graced her beautiful features. If I didn't get a grip on myself, everyone would notice my aversion to her. That problem was answered when her friends arrived.

"Come dance, Alexia." They giggled.

"Justin, do you want to come?"

"No, you go," I slurred, watching them all take off to dance.

With my hands dug deep into my pockets to prevent me from hitting someone, I stalked off toward the beach. I wished I could say it wasn't enlightening, but it was. The enlightenment came in the form of yet another overheard conversation.

"Man, he's one lucky guy. That's one fine piece of ass. I wouldn't mind tapping that." My temper boiled over; I'd reached my breaking point.

Before the other kid could say anything, I ran up and sucker-punched the repulsive jerk square in the face. Neither of them knew what to say when I went off.

"You will never talk about my wife again! Is that understood?" I sneered inches from his face.

"Yeah, I got it," he grumbled, rubbing his throbbing jaw.

"Justin?" Alexia's voice chimed behind me.

Before they could disgrace her further, I grabbed her by the elbow and towed her back to the reception. I didn't stop until I reached the table where her dinner now sat cold.

"Eat," I demanded, lowering her into her seat.

"Okay, but I wish you'd tell me what's going on." She looked concerned.

"Later, eat . . . now." If I had to watch her every move, this was going to be a long pregnancy.

"You're not eating?" She peeked up, fluttering her eyelashes.

"No, I'm not hungry." I didn't want to tell her it would come right back up if I did.

When the waiter made another swing by, I grabbed two more flutes. This didn't go unnoticed, and Alexia called me on it. "You've had a lot already."

"Yeah, well, I'm drinking for two." I chuckled, inebriated.

She didn't understand my little joke. However, I was spared having to explain it when they called us up to cut the cake. Drinking before you try to feed your new wife probably was a bad idea. The minute I shoved cake up her nose and across her face, I knew I'd be in trouble. "Revenge is so sweet," was the only thing I could think when she took hers by shoving my whole head into the remainder of the cake and muttered, "Jerk."

She ran off to the loo before I could say I was sorry. With cake frosting dripping from my face, my cousins dragged me off to the men's room to clean up. We all burst out laughing when I looked in the mirror. The icing completely covered my face; she had even gotten it in my ear. Once all the frosting was gone, my cousins let me have it.

"What were you thinking?" Johnny glared.

"Is this your plan to avoid your first night together? You do realize you will be sleeping on the couch tonight, right?" Joey enjoyed a laugh at my expense.

"Maybe."

They both looked stunned. "Why would you want that? What, she's not attractive enough for you?"

"No! Of course not! I didn't mean it that way," I trailed off, half-hearted.

"Then, how did you mean it?" Johnny cocked his eyebrow.

"It's nothing . . . just wedding night jitters, I guess."

"Lay off the alcohol, if you know what's good for you." Joey pounded his fist into his palm.

I just shook my head; one fistfight a night was my limit. I decided that if I wanted to make it out of my wedding reception in one piece, I'd better get a grip on my anger. That was easily accomplished when I walked by the ladies' room and heard Alexia crying. Nothing sobers you up like a helping of guilt. I had ruined her wedding day.

"I can't believe he did that! I knew when his mother said he didn't know that they didn't tell him because he wouldn't like me. Can you believe I actually thought he did when he sent that note?" Her anguished cries tore at my heart strings.

"Lexie, it's probably just the alcohol. You know men can't handle their booze." I could still hear Alexia sobbing.

"Yeah, Lexie, that's probably it." Madison didn't sound convinced.

Johnny shoved me outside to where the reception was still going full swing. I lowered my head in shame when I noticed my father glaring at me with an anger I'd only seen when I'd buggered up in a major way. When I turned around to hide my embarrassment, I found myself face to face with my bride, and she looked heartbroken. Just then, a slow song started, so I took the opportunity to grab Alexia by the hand and drag her to the dance floor. I sighed into her hair once I'd wrapped my arms around her waist. I knew at that moment that it didn't matter. She was the only thing that mattered. As the song played, we swayed together, and her body slowly relaxed against me, for which I was thankful.

"I'm sorry about the cake," I whispered into her ear.

"You're forgiven." She huffed into my chest.

The sound of a clanging glass brought our attention to the crowd, who had found our dance interesting. When someone clinks their glass, you kiss the bride. Slowly and sweetly, I placed my lips against hers. The taste of the frosting lingered on her lips, and I let myself get lost in them.

I broke it off when I heard that plonker Crazy Eight whooping from the side of the dance floor. It hadn't taken me long to figure out why they called him that: he was a lunatic. His future wife would have her hands full.

Hand in hand, we walked around and thanked everyone for coming. Sadly, none of my friends from England had been able to make it. If I were a betting man, I'd say their parents had forbidden it.

Finally, the time arrived for us to leave, and the nervousness in the pit of my stomach grew again. Together we dashed through a shower of rice to get to my car. Once we were inside, I pulled away and headed for our cottage. I held the steering wheel in a death grip, letting my anxiety get the best of me. Suddenly, worry overtook my rational thinking. What if she didn't want to consummate the wedding? What if I wasn't as good as the guy who had knocked her up? What if she'd continued seeing him in private?

It was still light enough out to find the cottage without any help. Alexia flinched when we came to a quick stop on the gravel driveway. She didn't wait for me to help her out, so I joined her at the front end of my car, and together we walked to the door. When I swept her up into my arms, she released a sharp gasp. I carried her over the threshold and placed her on her small feet once inside.

Without a word to me, she went into the loo. I took a deep breath and went to our room before removing my suit jacket and tie that dangled untied from my collar. My breath hitched when Alexia walked out of the bathroom wearing a royal blue silk chemise with spaghetti straps. Seeing it cling to her glorious body made me want to tear it off like a Christmas present.

The downside was that I knew in a few months it wouldn't fit anymore thanks to *him*. I would have been the happiest man on earth if it didn't fit because she was heavy with my child instead of someone else's. That was the moment when something snapped in my head, and everything came out rather bluntly.

"Alexia, why didn't you wait for me? That child you're carrying should be mine! Who knows about the father? Don't answer that. If I find out who got you pregnant, I'll kill him! I forbid you to ever see him again! From this moment on you will tell everyone it's mine! Is that understood?"

I lashed out.

"Justin, I'm not carrying a child!" She sobbed, dropping her head into her hands.

Her confusion baffled me. "But . . . they said you . . . we had to get married *before* anyone found out." I was more confused than ever.

"Who said that?" she gasped, tears rolling down her rosy cheeks.

"The blokes from your father's firm." I shrugged.

"That's why you were acting like that earlier? You thought I slept with someone and got pregnant?"

"Yes. Are you saying you didn't?"

"Yes, I'm saying I didn't. I saved myself for marriage, unlike other people in this room," she insinuated.

"Didn't they tell you why I went to the revirgining retreat?" *She thinks I'm not pure?*

"No one needed to tell me, but yes, Joey and Johnny said you dated outside our faith," she muttered, looking at the floor with her arms crossed over her chest.

"I did, but I never did anything more than kiss them." My soul begged for her to see the truth.

"So, you didn't either?"

"No, they wanted to, but I couldn't do it, so I went home and repented." I took a few steps closer to her delightful form.

"I'm sorry. I thought you had . . ." I couldn't take the separation anymore, so I pulled her into my arms.

"I'm so sorry, too. I should never have believed those awful things about you," I mumbled against her lips, finally letting go of myself.

"But – you were – going to – raise – someone else's – child – to be with me?" she panted in between my kisses.

I cupped her face to look into her emerald eyes. "I would do anything to be with you," I told her in all honesty.

With opened-mouthed kisses, I moved across her cheek and under her ear. "I have seen your eyes in my dreams since I was eight years old. It has always been you," I whispered into her ear before sucking her earlobe into my mouth for the first time.

She whimpered at the sensation. "I dreamt of you, too. You were always there in the background, reminding me of who I belonged to." My heart raced, and my chest puffed out with pride at her words. She did belong to me.

I urgently captured her lips in mine and traced her lower lip with my tongue, begging for permission to enter her mouth. When she parted her lips, I slipped my tongue inside. Since it was the first time I'd ever had my tongue in someone else's mouth, I wasn't sure what to expect, but when she followed my lead and met me halfway, I thought my heart would burst. It was amazing to feel her smooth tongue slip around mine. I moved my hands into her curled locks and pulled her even closer. The feel of her body against mine had my brain in overdrive, amongst other parts.

With a new purpose, my hands finally rubbed over the slippery fabric down to her curvy sides. Feeling brave from the alcohol, I moved my hands to her back and allowed them to stray down so I could grasp her firm bottom in my hands. She couldn't deny my need for her once I pressed myself flush against her. I wanted her, and I wanted her to know it. Alexia started to unbutton my shirt, exposing my skin for the first time. With slow caressing strokes, she explored my chest and stomach. I couldn't stop my moan when her fingertips grazed across my nipples. She pushed the shirt off my shoulders, letting it fall to the floor.

Alexia mewled when my hands started sliding around her sides and onto her stomach. I hesitated, looking at her nervous expression and silently asking for permission to proceed further up. With her lower lip between her teeth, she closed her eyes and nodded.

Slowly, I grazed my way up to her covered breasts. She released a sharp breath the first time I cupped them in my hands. I watched in awe as her nipples made themselves known, straining against the shimmery fabric where my thumbs massaged them in soft circles. They felt just right nestled in my hands. Even clothed they were perfect; the right size, firmness, and weight for my large hands. Deep in the pit of my stomach, I ached to see them in the flesh.

I breathed out when Alexia started fumbling with my belt buckle. When she lowered her face to accomplish her task, I did the same, resting my chin against the crown of her head. Once the belt was unbuckled, she moved on to the button and zip, I held my breath waiting for her reaction to my desire for her. When she squirmed back I thought it might be bad sign, but when she tugged my slacks down, I realized she had just needed the room to remove them. When they slipped to the floor, she looked up, showing her shyness. The pull was too much to resist, so I wrapped my hands in her hair again and pulled her back into a desire-filled kiss.

The time had arrived for my turn to help her out of her one piece of clothing. With that in mind, I hooked my fingers around the spaghetti straps, sliding them off her shoulders. The silky material just ghosted down her soft flesh and floated to the floor. For a moment, I froze in place, gawking at her body. The light flush she radiated told me I was the first man to see her so vulnerable.

"You're so beautiful," I finally mumbled when my speech returned.

Her little fingers trembled, reaching out to do the same to my boxers. With each breath I took, it became harder to exhale while I waited to see what she thought of my naked body. My eyes fluttered closed when she gently examined me first with her fingers, then her palm. I gasped when she wrapped her fingers around me for the first time. The sensation she caused felt like a cascading waterfall. My body shuddered, and then the burn in the pit of my stomach started pushing outward, spreading through my entire body.

I opened my eyes to see her smiling at my reaction to her touch. Since two could play that game, I moved one of my hands that were resting on her hips and found her soft curls. With one finger, I rubbed along her fold, only to discover it was already moist. Her soft moan didn't go unnoticed by my ears. My head screamed to claim my wife; thankfully, I remembered that we needed to be in bed before it went any further.

"Alexia, is the bed ready?" I implored.

"Yes," she breathed against my chest, causing me to shiver in excitement.

I groaned when she stepped back to fold down the linen, exposing the consummation towel. Even that couldn't distract me from the stunning creature crawling into our bed before me. I patted her bum playfully, causing her to giggle and fall onto her backside. She looked nervous about what was going to happen next. I smiled, moving onto the bed at her feet and trying to get her to relax. She blushed and hid her face behind her knees. On my knees, I crawled until my thighs were against her shins, and I lifted her chin with my fingers.

"Alexia, have a little faith in me to know I won't hurt you," I vowed, sincere.

"I know," she sighed, parting her knees so my hands would fit between them.

Her worry lines faded when I leaned in, capturing her lips with mine. I admit I was scared out of my mind. She couldn't know that, though, because if I was a nervous wreck, then she would be, too. As the man, it was my job to make her feel secure and safe; I wanted to do that for her.

I nudged her knees open with light pressure from my hips while I leaned my body closer. When I started nuzzling and moaning into her neck, she relaxed enough to drop her knees to the bed, giving me the opening I needed. I moved my hands to her hips to steady us both. Kissing my way across her rosy cheek earned me a morale-boosting whimper. Once in position, I locked my eyes onto her emerald pools to ensure she was indeed ready. She bit her quivering lip, nodding her acceptance.

Through my calm exterior, I managed to hide my quaking insides. Just the feeling of my tip at her entrance had me panting. Painstakingly slow, I pushed into her intimate walls an inch at a time.

It was hard to resist the urge to just push myself deep inside her all at once. My body fought against me. The anticipation tried to win out, but I managed to control myself.

There was no mistaking the moment when I took her virginity because of her sudden intake of air. "Oh," she uttered, grabbing and holding my hips to still my movements.

Clenching my eyes shut, I muttered incoherent thoughts. "Alexia . . . oh, I . . . never . . . I'm sorry," I begged when I paused for her to acclimate to my intrusion.

The sensation of being engulfed inside her was beyond description; it was heaven and hell all at once. It felt uplifting, but at the same time the heat threatened to singe my sensitive flesh. She hissed through her parted lips.

In an effort to take our minds off of the burning between our legs, I pulled her into a deep, passionate kiss that threatened to sear my lips off my face. When she broke off our kiss, I could already feel the lubrication flowing downward.

When she ground against me, I lost it and started moving, slow at first. The pace quickened when she joined me in my motions. I knew I hadn't hurt her any more than necessary. A burning feeling in the pit of my stomach forced me to move even faster. I knew when she gripped my shoulders tighter that she was ready, like me, for our first release as husband and wife. For me, it was my first climax ever; I could only hope it was hers also.

"Justin!" she screamed, letting it rock her glorious body.

With the tightening and relaxing of her intimate walls, my body could no longer resist. Her climax forced mine, and it overtook me. "Alexia!" I groaned while my body shuddered against hers.

Together we panted against each other's sweaty flesh. She was so beautiful. Her skin shone, flushed from our consummation. Reluctantly, I withdrew, and after looking down, I saw the unneeded proof of her virginity pooling on the towel. When she moved off the towel to go to the loo, I rolled it up and placed it in a Ziploc bag to be presented to our parents.

When she came back dressed, she joined me on her knees next to our bed for our nightly prayer. She looked to me to lead the prayer.

"Dear Lord, thank you for the blessed union you have granted us today. And with Your blessing, we pray that our efforts to be fruitful are answered. It is in Your name that we strive to live better lives. We do this for you. Amen." I looked up at my bride. "Alexia, are you all right? I didn't hurt you, did I?"

"No, I'm a little sore, but that's to be expected." She blushed again.

"It will be better next time, I promise."

"I thought this time was pretty great," she mumbled, looking at the floor.

"Why, Alexia, is that a compliment?"

"Yes." She stifled a yawn.

"Let's get to bed." I helped her up.

Together, we climbed back into our marital bed. I pulled Alexia closer so we could snuggle. After our first experience and the stresses of the day, I needed it as much as I was sure she did. It was a comfort when she rolled over so that her face rested on my bare chest. When she drifted off in my arms, I thanked God again for sending me my dream girl.

CHAPTER 7

ALEXIA MCNEAR'S EMBARRASSMENT AND EXCHANGES

The early morning sun shone through the window, warming my face. I opened my eyes when two strong arms pulled my body into a warm embrace. I leaned into the safety they brought along with them. His breath fanned out across my back, reminding me of what had happened the night before. There were no words to describe how he made me feel; so safe, wanted, well cared-for, and happy. When I rolled over and glanced up, Justin's eyes were already open, and he looked back at me with a slight smile playing on lips.

"Are you okay this morning?" His face was full of concern.

I ducked my head to hide my pink cheeks. "Yes," I breathed.

"That's good. I was a little worried you might be sore." His cheeks flushed.

"No, you were very gentle." My cheeks flamed hotter as I remembered the way he'd touched me.

My eyes fluttered shut when he stroked my cheek with his fingertips. "So beautiful," he muttered in a whisper before I felt his soft lips brush against mine. After only a few seconds, I felt like my heart would beat out of my chest.

The loud screeching of the alarm clock caused us both to jump a little. I giggled when he tried to shut it off with one hand and ended up knocking it to the floor. He just groaned, pulling away to retrieve it.

"We should be getting ready. We have the breakfast at my parents' in an hour." I slid off the bed to get showered.

"I'll make some coffee. Did your mother happen to stock the medicine cabinet with aspirin?" I could see by the way he held his head in his hands he had a hangover.

"Yeah, I'll get them for you." I knew it was terrible, but it served him right for drinking so much yesterday; but then again, he had thought the unthinkable. However, that was no excuse.

I couldn't help but watch when he walked down the hall to the kitchen in his boxers. With a quick headshake, I tossed aside thoughts of dragging him back to bed for another go.

Once I'd collected my clothes for the day, I headed into the shower. The hot water was just what I needed to relax my tightened muscles. Who knew sex would be such a workout? Then again, a little exercise never hurt anyone. Thankfully, today I'd be wearing just a white peasant skirt and a baby blue tank top with white sandals, so I'd be comfortable.

The smell of coffee wafted down the hall when I went to bring him his Tylenol. I needed a few, too, for a different reason. Just thinking about what we had to do today made me think that I might need to drink the whole pot of coffee by myself. Really, what were they going to do with the towel anyway, show it off? I blushed at the thought of someone besides our parents seeing it.

"Alexia? What's wrong?" I guessed my face had shown my fear.

I sighed. "Why do we have to show it to them?" I whined, looking up and pleading for him to find a way out of it. He hesitated for a minute before putting his cup down and coming over to me.

"I know it's an awful tradition, but it's in the contract. Please know I don't like the idea any more than you do, but if it's required, then we do it." When he wrapped his arms around me, I couldn't help but feel safe.

He was right, of course. We did have to do it; at least it gave me comfort that he did not want to either. I sighed and shivered at the thought. It was enough to make you feel like you had been born in the dark ages.

"I don't know; maybe I can get our fathers to do it with just me. Would that make you feel better?" I nodded quickly. Just the thought of not having to be there made me happier.

"I'll see what I can do. Once we get there, I'll take my dad aside and ask him." As payment for the favor, I handed him the bottle of Tylenol. He smiled and popped two tablets with his coffee.

"Thank you." He flashed me a grin before heading off to get showered and dressed.

By the time he'd finished, I had everything in my bag and was ready to go. He looked rather sexy with his hair tossed to the side and wearing green khaki shorts with a white polo shirt.

On the drive over, we talked about the honeymoon we would be hearing about this morning from my parents. I think it surprised Justin to hear that we were leaving the confines of our community.

When we arrived, I was quite horrified to see extra cars in the driveway. "Why is Minister Jeff here?" He just shrugged his shoulders and led me up to the front door with his hand on my lower back.

I took a deep breath and opened the door. Before us stood my parents, his parents, the minister and his wife, the entire church Council, and their spouses.

"Alexia, Justin, congratulations! Come in," my mom gushed.

"Um . . . hi everyone," I muttered, turning crimson.

We were quickly passed around and hugged by everyone present. Since I had never been to a post-wedding breakfast, I'd had no idea who would be here. Lesson learned: always ask about something you do not know.

"Mom, why is everyone here?"

She just smiled and answered, "To see the towel, of course." I gasped at her and looked for Justin, who seemed to be having the same conversation with his dad.

"You can't be serious? This is a private matter!" I raged in a hushed voice.

"No, dear. The Council is always present when the towel is handed over and the transactions are completed. It keeps everything above reproach later."

Smiling, she led me across the living room to where Justin was still talking to his parents. Justin placed his arm around my shoulders and whispered in my ear, "I have to do it in front of everyone."

I nodded.

He slipped his free hand around his back to receive the Ziploc baggie I passed him from inside my handbag. The whole room gasped when he held out the white towel safely sealed. All of a sudden, everyone started whispering. I didn't understand what was going on until Justin's father started yelling at my dad.

"She wasn't pure?" What? Not this again.

"She most certainly was! Right, Alexia?"

"Why are you all yelling? Of course my bride was pure!"

"But . . . the towel is still white!" Minister Jeff stepped forward before it could come to blows.

"Oh . . . I . . . um . . . rolled it up. Was I supposed to do it differently?" Poor Justin looked like he was ready to faint along with me.

"No, son, it's fine. It is just here we fold it so it is showing, that is all. Just unroll it for everyone to see and then we can all relax and eat." Eat? I was ready to throw up.

After a quick glance at my beet red face, Justin removed and unrolled the towel. Everyone was quite pleased as they gawked at it. Justin looked like he was turning green again. Quickly he rolled it back up and put it back in its bag before handing it to his dad. The man actually patted him on the back for a job well done. I was beyond horrified. I felt as if I was going to faint.

"Alexia, are you all right? I am so sorry I screwed that up. Do you need to sit down?" Justin pulled me closer and held me tighter.

Turning my face into his chest, I wanted to cry at that point. "I am so embarrassed they did this to us." I was really fighting not to let my tears fall in front of everyone.

"Me, too, but it's over. Now we move on with our lives. Okay?" The best I could manage was a nod.

"Justin and Alexia, we have a surprise for your honeymoon. You're going to Aruba next week with the two other McNear couples." Oh my gosh! Our parents were so sneaky. Safety in numbers. They knew we couldn't be led astray when there were two other faithful couples with us.

"That's great, Mom. I'm sure they'll be as thrilled as we are." I hoped my smile looked natural, because on the inside, it was a grimace.

Everyone moved to the dining room, happy and chatting about the completion of the first marriage of the season, while Justin and I took a moment to sit on the couch.

"Was that as awful for you as it was for me?" Justin asked with a hint of concern.

"Um, yeah, why does everyone think I wasn't a virgin? First you, then the Council. Do I look like a girl who is easy or something?"

He took my hand and rubbed it. "No, never. People just always believe the bad stuff."

"Well, it can't get any worse than this, so let's go eat."

He helped me up and led the way.

Everything was going great, the food was wonderful, and everyone was chatting, until I started choking on a grape after my mom mortified me again. "So, Alexia, with Justin's past you must have had some awesome sex. Did he show you how to use your mouth to please him?" Yep, that grape went straight down and stuck in my throat.

After the third whack on my back, Justin looked me over, relieved. Of course, Patty wasn't thrilled when the grape landed in her drink.

"Katrina, I hate to break this to all of you, but I've never had sex before, never mind a – um . . . mouth – that . . ." Justin was suddenly flustered when everyone gasped at him, including his parents.

"But you dated outsiders. You mean you didn't . . . never?" He just shook his head.

"No, I couldn't. I kissed a couple of them, but never anything more than that." Everyone smiled at his admission, even me.

After another hour, we decided to head back to the cottage before anything more humiliating could happen. I sighed once we were inside the door. The cottage just felt like home.

"Alexia, come here, I have some things to cheer you up." I sat with him on the couch.

From under the table, he pulled out a beautiful, shiny, pink paper bag. He looked so nervous that I wondered what could possibly be in there.

"First, I'm very sorry I wasn't here to do our tying ceremony before the wedding. I bought this to celebrate it." He held out a black velvet box.

I smiled brightly when I saw a platinum charm bracelet with a heart-shaped locket attached. "Justin, it's beautiful, but you didn't have to." I stroked the bracelet.

"Yes, I did. But, there's more. This is for missing your graduation." He handed me a smaller box.

Inside was a matching charm of a graduation diploma. "It's perfect!" I caught him off guard when I planted a chaste kiss on his lips. Adding the charm to the bracelet, he clasped it around my left wrist.

"Thank you." He sighed. "This is for missing your birthday; I really would have liked to have been there." He handed me yet another small velvet box, only this one didn't hold a charm; instead, it held a pair of large diamond-studded earrings.

"Thank you; they're so lovely." I grinned.

"May I have the honor of seeing you wear them?" I nodded with a smile and started removing my grandmother's pearls.

He surprised me when he got down on his knees in front of me and started fumbling with the box. He smiled, leaning in and slipping the first one on. I couldn't help but sigh when he shifted to put on the other one. Once the earrings were in, he surprised me again by kissing my earlobe before kissing right below it. If I had been a cat, I would have been purring at this point. I threw my head back when he kissed around my neck to my chin and moved up to my lips.

His tongue sliding across my lower lip told me he wanted more, which I granted. I moaned when he grabbed my hips and pulled me against him while still kneeling between my thighs. When I tilted my head, he moved one hand into my loose hair. Shivers ran up my spine when he groaned into my mouth. In my desperate attempt to get even closer, I slid both my hands into his hair and arched my back.

I shrieked when the front door swung open and in strolled the twins with Ginger and Madison. "Hey, we're here to entertain your hubby while you ladies leave for the dress appointment, which judging from that position, I would say you forgot about." Joey wiggled his eyebrows as everyone laughed seeing us wrapped around each other.

Justin smoothed out my skirt and mumbled something I only caught the end of, "– – – – blockers." I was about to ask him to repeat it, but he shook his head. I guess I wasn't meant to hear it.

"Just wait until next week, and we make sure you prats are never left alone," Justin chided them as he righted himself.

"Nice try, cuz, but we will be on our honeymoon, so there!" Joey bellowed.

"Oh, like say, the island of Aruba," Justin taunted smugly while flashing and fanning himself with our airline tickets.

"Oh! No way! Are you serious? That is just the best news ever!" Madison and Ginger jumped on the couch and tried their best to suffocate me with love.

"The best," Joey grumbled, no doubt wondering if Justin would make good on his threat.

"So, Justin, how was the couch last night?" Johnny chuckled, but gasped when I turned every shade of red possible.

"Nicely done, Lexie. You made an honest man of him. So, no more straying, pal!" Johnny leered at Justin, who just held up his hands to surrender.

"Actually . . . about that, yeah . . ." He cleared his throat, so I decided to save him.

"Justin was a virgin, too. He only kissed the outsiders." I giggled at his slight embarrassment.

"You went through the retreat for kissing? Are you crazy?" Joey gawked.

"Hey, she's worth it. If I had known about her sooner, I would have swum here to find her." I tell you, the grin on his face said it all: he really would have.

"Let's go, Lexie. My mom wants us there ASAP. Bye, guys. Have fun!" Ginger waved, dragging me out the door.

When they started giggling as we got into my car, I couldn't help but ask, "What's so funny?"

"The look on your face when we busted in. I really should have had a camera for that one." Madison was laughing so hard she looked like she would wet herself.

"Just wait until next week. You won't be laughing then," I retorted.

"Hey, you wouldn't!" Ginger gulped first.

"Trust me, you don't want to get on my bad side about this," I warned as we left my driveway.

Knowing all the shortcuts came in handy, and I had us at Charlene's in less than ten minutes. It was a long day with having both brides trying on their dresses. Thankfully, most of the stuff we needed to do for their wedding was long done, and only the last-minute things were left. When Charlene asked if I wanted to stay for dinner, I politely declined. I had a new husband at home who I still knew so little about.

When I walked back into the cottage, there was no mistaking the smell of food cooking. Peeking my head inside the kitchen, I found much to my delight Justin standing there in nothing but a bathing suit and pulling a tray of lasagna out of the oven.

"Where did that come from?"

Justin just grinned and replied, "Your mom popped it in and told me to take it out in an hour."

"So, I gather you went swimming today?" I openly ogled him when he leaned over to place the tray in the center of the table.

"Yeah, after we moved the last of their stuff to their new homes. I won't lie, I'm glad they won't be too close." He laughed.

"But still close enough," I chortled at his mock shocked look.

"Why, Mrs. McNear, I didn't know you liked having people walk in while we are making a child," he playfully teased.

"Yeah – no, we'll just have to do the unthinkable: lock the doors." I covered my mouth with my hand and gasped.

"Let's try that tonight. I would love to see the look on their faces when they show up tomorrow." He grinned and accepted the dish I passed him.

As he scooped out lasagna for both of us, he asked, "You did know that they asked me to be an usher for the wedding, right?"

"No, when did that happen?"

"The week before I went to the retreat. It was sort of the reason I went into the retreat. Even though I was happy they were getting married, I wanted the same for me, so I asked my dad to arrange for me to attend. I even missed the last two weeks of school so I could go."

I couldn't help but feel a little sad. I had been so self-centered; I'd never thought about what he had given up. "I'm sorry, Justin. I never realized what going to the retreat cost you."

"Don't be. If I hadn't gone, your parents probably would have never agreed to my father's offer, and we wouldn't be sitting here right now." He took a bite and groaned, "Wow, this is really good."

"Yeah, my mom's a great cook. I'm unfortunately challenged in that area."

He smiled and nodded. "I guess we'll be buying a lot of already prepared food."

"Ginger is going to teach Madison and me. I hope you're not upset that I can't cook."

"No, I think I can handle it until you learn; that, or we can pay her to cook for us." We both cackled.

The rest of dinner was quiet, and when it was done, I cleaned up so that he could shower. Once the kitchen was clean, I headed to our room. There in the middle of our bedroom stood the most beautiful sight I could imagine: Justin in nothing but a towel wrapped around his waist.

I actually wanted to lick the water droplets from his toned chest. When he lifted his arms to brush his hair, the towel slipped off and landed on the floor. He made no move to retrieve it, but when he turned around, I got the shock of my life.

"See something interesting, Mrs. McNear?" Like an idiot, I stood there staring at his endowments.

He closed the gap between us in two strides and didn't hesitate to wrap himself around me. Eagerly, he kissed me with the same passion as he had that morning. The best I could manage was to pant like a dog on a hot summer's day when he started kissing down my neck. The kissing only stopped long enough for him to peel off my tank top. He sucked in a quick breath when he saw I was braless. With open-mouthed kisses, he started moving over my collarbone and down my chest.

He looked so innocent when he peeked up, looking for permission to put his mouth on my breast for the first time. I bit my lip and nodded unable to stop the shiver that ran through me when he suckled me. When he sucked harder, I felt my peak harden against his tongue. A moan escaped my parted lips as his tongue swirled around it once. I slipped my hands into his hair and pulled him closer.

His hands had no problem slipping my skirt to the floor. I lifted one leg up to his hip, hoping for a little more friction. He moaned into the crook of my neck as he lifted me up and walked us over to our bed. On his knees, he pulled us to the top and gently placed me down with my head on the pillows. By this time, my heart was racing, and my breathing was erratic with anticipation. He had said this time would be better than the last, and I was anxious to see that.

"Roll over, Alexia." I wasn't sure why, but I obeyed anyway and lay on my stomach.

With his hands, he pulled me up by my hips so he was pressing his manhood against my butt. As he sucked below my ear, he ground against me. This small act had me whimpering and Justin panting. I trembled against him, feeling his breath fanning out across my shoulders. One hand caressed my butt cheek while the other pushed between my shoulders until I was on all fours.

My head dropped so my hair spanned across the pillows below me. His hand that had pressed me down gently glided across my flesh, sending shockwaves through my extremities. Hearing him moan at the sight of me washed away any lingering insecurities I had about being exposed. Every touch, every breath, and every utterance set my body aflame.

His magic fingers swept along the secret area where only he would touch. My body belonged to him, and I knew it. With a secure grip, he held my hips while he pushed in, groaning. When he had completely filled me, I moaned out at the sensations he invoked. It was as if my body knew who its master was, and I would be hard-pressed to deny it.

Cautiously, he pulled back, then pushed straight in again. I bit my lip to hold in the lust-filled rant that threatened to give away just how much I was enjoying the physical attention he lavished on my body. With each thrust he grew more confident, and when a rhythm formed, he allowed himself to utter incoherent thoughts.

"You're mine to love . . . so deep . . . so perfect . . . Alexia," he panted like a prayer to the good Lord.

The coil in my stomach tightened when his hands gripped harder on my hips and his movements became more erratic. I remembered what that meant from last night: he was close to his finale, but so was I.

"Ohhh . . . um . . . yeah . . . I . . . um, please . . . I can't stop," he groaned with the desperation clear in his voice.

"Ahhh . . . Justin, I want . . . I need . . . now please," I moaned in reply.

That was all the encouragement he needed to quicken his pace, trying to drive us both to the brink of insanity. A slick layer of sweat coated our skin when he finally lost control and just let go. Together we chanted each other's names as we rode out our release.

He pulled me with him as he collapsed on the bed, never disconnecting us. There he held me, whispering in my ear, "Don't move. My dad says the longer we stay connected, the better our chances of conceiving."

I was too worn out to fight the logic. They had more experience in this area; if they said so, we would do it.

Tonight he whispered our nightly prayer as I drifted off to sleep in his arms, still intimately connected to his body.

CHAPTER 8

JUSTIN MCNEAR'S TWO WEDDINGS AND THREE HONEYMOONS

Saturday morning I found myself back on the beach where I had first met Alexia. Joey and Johnny were slightly stressed over their wedding today.

"Come on, Justin, you have to give us some pointers. I don't want to look like an idiot," Joey begged again.

"What kind of pointers can I give you? Do you want to know how to almost ruin your wedding day? Or better yet, how about the best way to fight with your new bride so she won't sleep with you? Because if that's what you want, then I'm your man." I chuckled.

"Funny, dude. Seriously, I want Madison to think I'm suave when I make love to her for the first time."

I smirked. He had no clue. "Joey, I was far from suave. I was the everyday fumbling fool you're going to be." I think that's the first time I've ever seen him pout.

"I've heard stories from the outsiders about their girlfriends using their hands and mouths to, you know . . . Have you heard about that?" Johnny looked hopeful.

"Yeah, I heard about that, too, and no, we haven't done that stuff. At the retreat, they said it was a waste of our seed. Their opinion is that if you're trying for a child it should all be released within the womb."

"Well, Madison and I are going to wait on trying until she finishes school, so tell me what you do know." I took pity on them and told them what little I'd heard when we were in sessions.

"All right, there was one guy at the retreat that was caught with his fiancée's mouth on him." I took a deep breath and scanned the area for anyone who might be able to overhear us. "He said she licked him like a lollipop and sucked on him like a straw." I shrugged not sure if they found that helpful.

"And?"

"He said he'd never felt anything so good, but he'd never had intercourse so . . ." It was difficult to imagine anything feeling better than being intimate with Alexia.

"He didn't lose his contract?"

"No, since they had never had intercourse, and she was the one he was contracted to, they were just both required to be retrained at the retreat." I winced, thinking about what they did to us during the retraining. It was the worst part of the retreat.

"Sorry, Justin." Waving it off, I really didn't want to think about that again.

Together we walked back from the beach to the church. Eagerly, we assumed our positions, with them at the front and me by the door waiting for the car procession to arrive that would be bringing Alexia to me.

Joey and Johnny gave each other a once over to ensure their suits were pristine, while I did the same.

It was hard to believe that it had been a week since I'd been here to take my own vows with Alexia by my side. In just that short amount of time, I had started missing her when she wasn't around, and this week had been nonstop running in different directions. With the exception of our nightly intercourse, I felt I hadn't had enough time with her.

Thankfully, we would be flying off to our honeymoon tomorrow night, and I could take some time to get to know her better.

Brett arrived before the procession. "Hey, Justin, they're five minutes behind me. Is everything ready?"

"Absolutely. The caterers have everything set up, the band is ready to go, and the guys are inside with the guests."

I'd never been one to check out men, but you couldn't help noticing Brett was one handsome bloke. His long, straight, blond hair and grey eyes really made him stand out in a crowd. Just as long as he didn't make a play for my wife, I could see us being friends. He and Alison would definitely make beautiful babies.

"Great. Oh, before I leave, I have the proof shots from your wedding. I'll leave them with Katrina for you all to see when you get back from Aruba," he rattled off while he took a few shots of the church.

"Cool. That should make Alexia very happy."

"You just better keep her that way. You don't want to be on the receiving end when Madison and Alison are pissed off; it's not a pretty sight." He looked like he knew from experience.

Before I could vow to never let that happen, the procession arrived. I smiled when Alexia stepped out, looking breathtaking in her short, lavender, satin dress.

I quickly approached and pulled her into my embrace. "You look stunning."

With her teeth firmly holding her lip hostage, she appraised me as well. "You look very handsome," she gushed.

When Madison and Ginger exited their cars, I couldn't help but notice that their gowns were as different as their future husbands were. Madison wore the latest style that was all the rage: strapless and covered in layers of tulle with sequins and pearls hand-sewn onto it. Ginger's was elegantly plain. Her shoulders were also bare, but she had three-inch sleeves that wrapped around her slender biceps. There were no ribbons, sequins, or pearls. It was just a constant flow of satin from her breasts to her toes.

Even their hairstyles were very different. Madison had hers all curled with pearls scattered around, while Ginger had gone with a traditional twisted french braid.

Quickly, we arranged ourselves in the order we were to enter. Alexia held my spot while I escorted both mothers inside.

Once Alexia and I marched down the aisle, we watched as the rest made the same journey. We were seated across from each other in the pews when the ceremony began. After hearing the same speech last week, I spent my time staring at my wife and wondering again how I had gotten so lucky.

When the nuptials were completed, we headed to the beach for the neverending flashes from Brett's camera. Unlike most photographers, he used a 35mm camera instead of the new digital type. It was no wonder why the rich and famous paid him a fortune for his services. He did a phenomenal job.

Katrina's double wedding cakes were, as expected, spectacular. No one even blinked when Crazy Eight shoved cake up Madison's nose, but she made sure to return the favor and then some. Johnny and Ginger's exchange was as soft and sweet as their relationship.

There was no doubt that both couples already loved and knew each other very well. I couldn't help but wish that Alexia and I could have had the two years they'd had to get to know each other.

Unlike at our reception, I never took my hands off my wife. We ate, danced, and talked all night long, as we should have done at our own wedding.

Before they left, I pulled the twins aside. "Listen, when you get home and are ready . . . go slow. It hurts them for a few seconds, so don't lunge right in. Trust me, your wives will thank you in the morning." They both nodded with widened eyes.

Alexia and I left shortly after they did; we still had our nightly ritual to perform. Only tonight, when we walked into the cottage, it was Alexia who attacked me – not that I minded having my beautiful wife paw at me.

In her eagerness to begin, she leaped into my arms and knocked me backward onto the settee. I hummed in pleasure when she latched her lips onto mine. She moved her legs up until she was straddling my hips. This new position allowed her to push my jacket off and unbutton my shirt.

The shifting of her weight on me made the stirring in my trousers quite evident. When she kissed me again, her tongue begged for entrance, which I happily granted. She moaned in my mouth when I slipped the zip to her dress down. Thanks to her pivoting to a seated position on me, my grinding against her was made easier. That mere act caused me to groan in return.

I had never seen Alexia so aggressive with our sex life; I liked it a lot. With one swift motion, I slid her gown over her head and onto the floor. A gush of air escaped my lips when I saw she was wearing a pink-laced bustier with matching panties. She shyly ducked her head down to hide her flushed cheeks.

I was on the verge of losing my mind when she reached between us to undo my trousers. Her leaning position gave me a perfect view of her cleavage. She arched her back and mewled when I lifted my hips to remove the offending material. My slacks never made it all the way off before she glided onto me.

Rational thought went out the window at that point. I didn't care if it wasn't a recommended position for conceiving; it felt too good to be wrong. Every time she rocked her hips, I pushed up to meet her. I had never felt more connected to her than I did at that moment. The feeling of being so deep within her walls had me begging for my release.

"Ohhh . . . please . . . now . . . can't stop," I panted.

"Wow . . . so deep . . . need more . . . please." Her chants pushed me even deeper.

"Anything . . . for you," I moaned and forced myself not to explode.

Seeing her bouncing on me was my undoing. "Ah, Justin . . . oh . . . ahhhh!"

When she clamped down on me, I let loose. "*A – lex – i – a*," I roared.

She giggled when she collapsed into my arms. I stroked her locks and replayed what had just happened in my mind. When did my kitten become a tiger?

"Where did that come from?" I laughed.

"Alison," she sighed, now that she was exhausted.

I kissed her softly and reveled in the intimate connection between us. As we had done every night that week, we stayed in that position until I could no longer physically manage it. We never moved for the rest of the night. If I had to sleep on the settee, at least she was with me.

The twins, like us, were tortured at their breakfast.

Our flight left at twelve-twenty Sunday afternoon from Minneapolis-St. Paul International Airport. Thankfully, our parents arranged for a livery service to drive us there.

The entire flight took seven-and-a-half hours. Alexia spent every second of that time clinging to my hand. She gripped my fingers so tightly that my knuckles were white from the pressure. I felt so bad for her; it was her first time flying.

Once we landed, we headed to retrieve our luggage and found the hotel's van waiting to pick us up. I chuckled watching Alexia stare out the window, awestruck.

I leaned in to ask her something that I had been wanting to since the moment she'd seen the first palm tree. I'd hoped now that she'd had a small taste of the world, she might entertain the thought. "Alexia, my friends from England are getting married in mid-August. I was hoping you would like to accompany me. I'm in the wedding, so I have to go. Would you be willing to come with me?" I tried to be patient, waiting for her to answer.

I knew her answer when she grinned. "Yes, I would love to go. Do you think they'll mind? They don't know me."

"They're going to love you," I reassured her. "When we get home, we'll book our flights. My dad has already cleared my time off."

"Um . . . Justin, I was hoping to take some online courses when we get back, but if you're opposed to it, I could withdraw." She nervously chewed on her poor unsuspecting lower lip.

"What kind of classes?" Suddenly an unexpected fear started welling up in my chest. Was she going to be like Madison and work away from home?

"Art classes . . . I – well, I like to draw and paint," she mumbled.

"Really? I think that's wonderful. You know, I've never told anyone this – well, except for Krista – but, I like to draw, too. When we get back, maybe you could show me some of your work." I smiled, relieved when she grinned at me.

"You've already seen some of it."

"Really, where?" Now my curiosity was piqued.

"Our bathroom. All those leaves; I painted them."

"Wow, you're very talented. It would be a crime not to pursue your art further."

When Alexia shrieked, I looked up to see that we had pulled up in front of the Tiki Village hotel. She looked like a kid in a toy shop as her eyes darted everywhere, a grin plastered on her face.

After we'd checked in, we made our way to our rooms, since it was late and time to settle in for the night. With all our nightly rituals complete, she settled in against my chest, and we drifted off to a peaceful sleep.

Alexia looked so beautiful with the sunshine beaming on her creamy skin. I slipped out from under her and made my way to my suitcase. We had made plans to spend the day on the beach with everyone, so I retrieved my trunks and headed into the kitchenette to make some coffee. It was a good thing I got up first, since Alexia was the only woman I knew who could destroy a pot of coffee without even trying, even the prepackaged kind.

Once I'd started on my second cup, I heard Alexia shuffling about in the bedroom. Still, I remained where I was, staring out the window and watching the waves roll in.

She blushed when I turned to see her ogling me.

My jaw dropped in an instant when I saw her new bikini. That damn thing should have been illegal in all fifty states, and a few other countries as well. I'm fairly certain there was a passage in our Bible forbidding the wearing of that skimpy, white excuse for swimwear. I think my dental floss would have covered her better.

"You don't like it?" she asked when I found myself unable to speak.

I finally managed to clear my throat. "I wouldn't say that exactly." I shrugged and envisioned myself flossing with it.

"Then what?" she asked as I sauntered over and pulled her closer to me.

"Well, I was thinking it would look better on the floor next to mine."

She laughed as I wrapped myself around her and slid my hands up to the ties. I groaned when a loud bang rattled through the room. Alexia wiggled out of my hold and went to open the door, revealing Crazy Eight. From his devilish expression I knew this was going to be a long week.

"Let's go, guys." He motioned toward the elevators.

"Hey, Joey, payback's a real bitch. You know that, right?"

"Owww, I'm really scared." He pretended to shake his hands.

Before I could reply, Alexia grabbed my hand and dragged me out the door. The lift had just opened when we arrived, and between the six of us, it was officially full.

My first retaliation against Joey came when he left his coffee unattended to revisit the buffet. They really shouldn't leave salt on the tables where it can find its way into an unsuspecting cup of coffee. Ginger was less than thrilled when he spat it all over her.

Alexia managed to keep a straight face throughout the entire ordeal. To make up for it, I told the ladies to make an appointment for a spa visit on me.

I laughed as we exited the restaurant and headed toward the beach. Ginger and Madison ran straight for the water, giggling, while Joey and Johnny chased them in. While I went to save us a few chairs, I watched Alexia gazing down in awe at the picturesque shoreline.

She was so lost in the view before her that she didn't see that every male on the beach was drooling over her. Just then, a familiar feeling reappeared as I looked around at the men ogling my wife: jealousy. When I looked to the left, then to the right, there was no denying they were checking out Alexia.

I ran up and whipped off my shirt. "Put this on!" I rather harshly demanded.

"Did I do something wrong?" She looked so baffled.

"No! It's all the dogs on the beach!" She looked around.

"Why are they staring at me?" she asked, letting me shove the shirt over her head.

"Because they want what is mine!" I sneered.

"Oh, but . . ." It finally dawned on her what they wanted. "But I don't want them," she purred to me and started rubbing my bare chest.

I grabbed hold of her hips and pulled her flush against me. After I kissed her in a very dominant and possessive display, I moved along her cheek until I reached the soft flesh of her neck. She groaned in surprise when I latched onto the sensitive skin with my mouth and started sucking – softly at first, then harder. She didn't resist; instead, she wove her fingers into my hair and held on tight. Her slight moan spurred me on to mark her as mine for all to see.

I pulled back and chuckled at my handiwork. "You are mine to love," I cooed in her ear.

"Always." Hand in hand, we waded out to where the others were just starting to play chicken.

"Hey, Justin, you going a little caveman there?" Johnny pointed to my wife's neck.

I just laughed and dragged Alexia under the crystal clear water, only to resurface with my head between her legs. With an iron-tight grip, I held her ankles so she wouldn't slip off my shoulders. Once we were all ready, the war began. Ginger was the first to fall; that left Alexia and Madison to fight it out. Alexia bested Madison quickly, so as payback, Joey grabbed my shorts; it was either my shorts or Alexia. Yeah, she went down.

Joey knew I was about to kill him, so he scrambled away to save his own trunks. Johnny had his back, which was a big mistake. In the end, they both lost their shorts and refused to leave the water.

I watched as the girls discussed Alexia's deep purple hickey. When they all giggled and looked at me, I smiled and shrugged. The ladies demanded their husbands' swimsuits so they could blackmail them into giving them one, too. I graciously obliged.

Alexia tried to walk past me, but I grabbed her by the waist and pulled her backward into my embrace. "Does it hurt?" I kissed it softly.

"No, but . . ."

"But what?"

"It felt really good," she breathed as I rubbed her stomach, where one day my children would grow.

"Maybe tonight I'll give you another one." I wiggled my eyebrows.

"Or maybe I should give you one." She laughed.

Together we watched, laughing, as Madison pouted and stomped her way into getting Crazy Eight to mark her, too, but not before taunting him. Every time he'd reach for the shorts, she'd pull them away. Ultimately, I suspected both of them knew he was planning on giving her one all along, but they just enjoyed the game.

Ginger had a much different approach, and for good reason. Watching her and Johnny was like watching a debate. She held her fingers up one at a time, telling him each reason why felt she needed a hickey while he tried in vain to argue against each point. She won; she always did.

In the end, mine was better. It was twice the size and twice as dark as theirs.

By the time dinner rolled around, we'd decided to just eat at the buffet in our swimsuits. After Alexia's second trip up, she caught me staring at her with a smile across my face. At first, she must have thought she had something on her face because she wiped it. I couldn't help but lean in and chuckle. "I can't wait to see you eat once you're pregnant."

For the next week, I made sure anything Alexia wanted was hers. It didn't matter if it was food or jewelry; anything she wanted I granted her. It felt wonderful to watch her smile whenever I would do even the littlest things for her.

The six of us spent our days basking in the sunshine, and the two of us spent our nights basking in each other's bodies.

She looked the picture of happiness. Her face glowed, her laugh was infectious, and my heart started to open up to her. I couldn't tell her that I had started to develop feelings for her yet. It was too soon, but one day I would tell her when the feelings had started to change for me.

As the week came to a close, I hated the thought of returning to reality and all the struggles that came with it. We were so happy and carefree with no judgmental eyes upon us. It was paradise. That was when I decided that we would have to escape back here again one day.

CHAPTER 9

JUSTIN MCNEAR'S MY WIFE'S BIGGEST FEAR

How did it take two weeks for me to see Alexia's biggest fear? I have no idea. All the signs were there, begging to be noticed, from the night I missed our introduction to the day on the beach during our honeymoon. Was I so blinded by my happiness that I didn't see what she really needed?

I finally had a wife – for whom I already had started to develop feelings – and a home I was looking forward to working on. No one in Minnesota sneered at me in passing as they had back in England. My family, after hearing my admission at the breakfast, looked at me with a new respect. Even my cousins had become as close as my friends back in England had been. Happiness, which had always eluded me, was finally mine.

The honeymoon was more than we could have hoped for. Relaxing on the beach soaking up the rays of sunshine every day had us energized for our nightly activities. As the sun set, we walked the stretch of beach outside the hotel hand in hand and talked about every little thing we could think of. We spent the entire week getting to know each other in more than just the physical aspect, but we did that, too. My favorite part was watching my new wife laughing until she cried.

I thought I had a good grip on her needs. Well, that was until we came home, and before I knew it, everything had spiraled out of control.

After spending my first full day at the dealership – even though I had managed to sell an SUV – I was anxious to get home to my wife to spend some quiet time alone.

Honeymooning with two other couples hadn't allowed for a lot of alone time. Sure we had some, but not enough.

At first, I drank in the peacefulness of the cottage, basking in the harmonious hum of the nature that surrounded it, but it was quickly snatched away when I entered the bedroom to change out of my black, double-breasted, Armani suit. There, softly sobbing on the bed, was my new bride.

"Alexia, what's wrong?" I knelt next to the bed and swept away the hairs that were stuck to her tear-soaked face.

"I am so sorry!" She sobbed, but allowed me to lift her so she was sitting with my arms around her waist.

"What are you sorry about?" I stroked her cheek with my fingertips. What could she have possibly done to warrant such a reaction?

"Please don't hate me." She sucked in a quick breath. "I started my cycle today." She wept even harder. I sighed, letting her words sink in. Alexia hadn't conceived a child that month.

"Alexia, I don't hate you. It's only been a few weeks. We haven't even been trying for a full month yet. Please don't be discouraged by our failure." On the outside I portrayed a strong husband, but on the inside, I was just as crushed.

The desire to procreate was embedded in us from birth in our faith, but it was something we both wanted, as well. The arrival of her cycle meant to her she had failed, but the truth was that we had failed as a couple.

"Maybe I did something wrong? Maybe I didn't pray hard enough? I don't want to be like Brett and Alison."

I pulled her onto my lap and held her tightly with her head against my chest. I needed to be held just as much as she did, so when she wrapped her arms around me, I melted into them. I clenched my eyes shut and fought the urge to release my own tears. Alexia had told me about Brett and Alison's two-year struggle to try to conceive a child, which unfortunately still hadn't happened yet. That was not something I wanted either of us to go through, but if we did, we would face it together.

"No, Alexie. Let's just give it some time. You cannot think negatively about this. They talked to us about this at the retreat during my third week there. They told us it doesn't always happen right away, and God would decide when it's right for us. We need to have faith in Him, and when it's time, we'll be waiting for it." I spoke with more conviction than I felt as I stroked her soft, red, silky hair.

"Everyone is going to be unhappy it didn't happen. Right? I could go see a doctor and get some advice."

"No, of course not, they'll be praying for next month just like us, and you know the rules on seeing a doctor." I hated to remind her of that, but something told me if it came to that, I'd be sneaking her off in the dead of night to a fertility doctor.

Thankfully, her sobs had quieted down, and she nodded her acceptance. For the next hour, I sat there cuddling her and rocking us both. I should have warned her about this; I had received instruction at the retreat that she had not.

As I put all the pieces together in my mind, I finally saw it, like a puzzle finally fitting together. She was always afraid she would disappoint me, disappoint everyone.

One of these days, I was going to have to talk to her about what happened at the retreat, but today was not that day.

"Are you hungry? I could try to cook something." Alexia smoothed her hair, trying to look presentable.

"No, I don't want you to worry about dinner. I'll go pick up some takeaway and a film, and we'll picnic on the living room floor. Does that sound nice?" I wiped away the last of her tears as she nodded.

Even in this state, she was a beautiful woman, too beautiful to be this heartbroken. Seeing the distress in her emerald eyes hurt me so deeply, it went to straight to my soul.

When she shuffled off to the loo, I headed out for food. Takeaway wasn't something we generally did on a regular basis since the wives were expected to cook, but I knew cooking was not her forte. Plus, I thought I needed to figure out a plan to keep this from happening every month.

Once in the car, I headed back toward the main gate. The only restaurant inside the community was a diner; it would do.

I glanced at the menu. A few things stuck out, so I ordered Alexia a chicken salad sandwich with a bowl of soup, and for myself a steak and cheese sub with chips.

While they prepared the food, I ran to the video box to rent a film. There wasn't much available, since all videos needed to be approved by the

Council. In the end, I found a comedy that I hoped would cheer her up. Everything was ready when I went back to the diner, so I ran in and out.

Alexia looked much better when I walked in the front door. She had showered and put her hair into a messy ponytail. The pajamas she wore were mine, but I didn't mind; she needed to be comfortable tonight. Honestly, they looked better on her than me, and I liked seeing her in them. She had even placed a blanket on the floor for us to eat on. Alexia took the bag and went to sit on the blanket while I went to change.

By the time I returned in a pair of sleep shorts, the film was ready to roll, and the food was set out. She just smiled when I sat across from her and started eating. Honestly, I wasn't paying attention to the film; I sat with my back against the settee while she sprawled out on the floor.

From my position, I watched as she allowed herself to relax. It was a good thing she wasn't watching me assessing her glorious body. That would have been embarrassing, because I was thinking about sex with her when we weren't trying to have a child. Right now, she thought we were having sex just for a baby, but truth be told, I was attracted to the woman more than I was willing to admit.

Halfway through the film, I noticed Alexia had fallen asleep on the floor. I didn't have the heart to wake her, so I went to the bedroom to retrieve our pillows and another blanket. Once our makeshift bed was made, I lay down on the floor with her. In a matter of seconds, it seemed as if gravity pulled her to search out my embrace. I helped her along in that venture and held her close. She sighed contently and snuggled against my chest. That, of course, did not help with the urges.

Thankfully, the rest of her cycle passed by without any more episodes. I had a new understanding about marriage because of that night. Just knowing that she counted on me to see to her happiness made me realize I needed to provide more than a good financial life for my wife. She needed emotional support as well. I wanted to provide her with anything and everything, and if that meant having twenty kids, I would do that for her – for us both.

Even though it was against the rules, I did do an Internet search on fertility and pregnancy. There was a lot out there, but my time was limited, so I tried to remember as much as possible.

The best times for us to conceive were ten to fourteen days after the first day of her cycle, so on those days, even though we connected every night, I made sure we were together every morning before work.

Without telling Alexia, I went to church every day and prayed for her to get pregnant and for her to be happy with me. Minister Jeff had taken up sitting with me and helping with my struggle.

He understood our plight better than most. Throughout the years, Minister Jeff had counseled many couples, and since he knew how important it was to start off our marriage right, he was more than willing to help on the spiritual side. Hearing him explain how our feelings would blossom through the pregnancy and delivery spurred me on to make it happen.

Chapter 10

Alexia McNear's Confessions and Confusion

The first week of our marriage was wonderful beyond belief as we learned the little things about each other; things that you wouldn't notice but needed to be told about a person. Nothing deep, just things like favorite colors and our childhood friends. Justin stared off when we discussed our friends; I think he'd really missed having his friends from England here for the wedding.

Every night we barbequed on the deck to cover up my inability to cook without mutilating the unsuspecting meal. Justin liked doing the manly thing. With him in charge of the meat, I set the table, prepared the side dishes, and had everything ready for him. He always chuckled at me when I peeked around to see if I could figure out how it was supposed to work.

"You will not need to know this, Alexia." Justin wiggled his eyebrows and laughed.

"How come?" I twittered, surprised.

"This is man cooking. And I am the man . . . aauuggghhh." He pounded his chest like an ape. My giggle turned into a full gut-wrenching laugh. He was too cute for his own good.

In the end, Justin was right; I did buy mostly prepackaged food. Of course, my mom was there to tell me which ones were better than the rest. To me they all looked the same. Justin never complained when I unloaded the grocery bags. It was one of the reasons I was so insecure about us. He didn't say anything to tell me how he felt. I had no idea if I was doing anything right in his eyes. Was I or could I make him happy?

After Ginger and Madison's weddings, it was time for our long-awaited honeymoon. My nerves were a little frayed by the flight, but the beauty of the island was not lost on me. To make me feel more comfortable, Justin held my hand the whole way to the hotel. I reveled in the security it brought.

Justin, in true form, made it one of the best times in my life. He insisted on buying anything I looked at. I tried to tell him I didn't need any of it, but he played his husband card, quoting, "It's my duty to see to your happiness." What if I didn't need possessions to make me happy? Did he ever think of that?

His initial reaction to my new bikini was unexpected but definitely not unwanted. When he wanted to remove it to try for a baby, I'll admit that I wanted to do it for a whole other reason. Unfortunately, our lovemaking was interrupted. That was a major downside to honeymooning with two other couples. As much as I loved my friends, we needed to figure out our lives, and they weren't letting that happen. I tried to keep in mind that they had no idea how it felt to marry someone you did not know, but I didn't think they would get it.

His jealousy on the beach the first day was something I had never seen before. He nearly knocked me over trying to shove his shirt onto me. I didn't understand how he could have felt so threatened. He should have known I belonged to him forever. Didn't he know that? I knew I did.

Knowing that I belonged to Justin, I never entertained the idea that someone else would think of me as being pretty. Just as long as Justin did was enough for me. It was all I could do not to melt into his arms when he locked his lips on my neck and started sucking. I had never felt anything so arousing than when he marked me. Deep down, I was hoping he would do it again; it left me feeling so dominated and wanted.

By the time we ate dinner at the buffet, I knew how he felt. A table full of teenage girls never even bothered to hide their drooling over my husband. In retrospect, I suppose I couldn't blame them; Justin was beyond desirable. The only thing that made him more sought-after was the glow of his sun-kissed skin from our hours on the beach. By our last day, I wanted to lock him up and throw away the key. Yeah, I would definitely be talking to Minister Jeff about my jealousy.

It wasn't until I woke up after he left for work on the first day back that the loneliness crashed over me. Luckily for me, the girls and I had cooking lessons to distract me from missing Justin. Ginger was ready for the torture to begin when she bounced in with Madison right behind her. In the end, she was very patient with me. She took the time to teach us how to do everything, from measuring to storing the food for later. Ginger taught us the special marinade she discovered, and I couldn't wait for Justin to grill the steak tips I had marinated for him.

With everything stowed away in the freezer, I headed for the bathroom to clean up. That was when I saw it; one pink stain on my panties. That could only mean one thing: I had failed Justin. The tears of disappointment stained my cheeks as the realization hit me. I'd never realized how hopeful I had been until my monthly cycle reared its ugly head.

Ginger and Madison found me sitting flabbergasted on the toilet. "You got your period." Madison plopped onto the side of the tub.

"Justin's not going to be pleased. I thought I did everything right. I don't understand it."

"Oh, Lexie, I'll go make you some tea and toast." Ginger marched off while Madison led me to my bed.

We always had our cycles at the same time, which meant theirs were on the way. At that moment, I knew I had let everyone down, especially Justin. The contract clearly stated we were to try to conceive a child in the first year. We weren't allowed birth control of any kind as part of our beliefs anyway. Justin had tried so hard this month to get his child into my womb, and I had failed him. My heart broke every time I thought about it.

I curled up in bed with Madison until Ginger arrived back with my lunch. Together we snuggled and waited for the time to creep by.

Justin was unaware of what had happened when he came home from work. Even though he wore his casual demeanor, I could tell he was disheartened with our news. Justin's tone never wavered as he promised everything would be all right. As usual, I found myself confused again. After all the energy we put into trying to make a child, he acted as if it there wasn't a problem.

One of these days, I was going to have to figure out the riddle of Justin. He must have wanted a child because he kept trying. Maybe it was because it was in our contract? Maybe he just wanted sex with his wife? I had more questions than answers.

In the end, we fell asleep watching a movie while having a picnic dinner on the living room floor.

For the next month, everything fell back into place, and Justin doubled his efforts to conceive a child. I never told him, but I enjoyed the closeness it brought with it. I knew what everyone had said about the slow process of falling in love once the vows were made, and it seemed I was not immune from it.

At Alison's suggestion, I headed to Small River the day before the dreaded cycle was due to arrive. She always kept a home pregnancy test under her bathroom sink. Even if my monthly did arrive, I would need a test eventually.

Driving the familiar stretch of road, I turned on my favorite CD of gospel music. The solitude of the car allowed me time to think. Of course my thoughts were of Alison and the child we'd been trying to conceive. I cried with her the day she revealed her heartache over the struggles to have a baby. She wanted nothing more than to have a little one, a perfect mix of her and Brett. My hopes and dreams mirrored hers now.

By the time I passed the bridge leading into Small River, my food shopping list had been forgotten, replaced with images of a baby lying in my arms. I never made it to the store.

"No!" I screamed, holding my hands up to block my face as a black, Chevy truck barreled through the intersection, running the red light, and impacting against my Mercedes.

In a flash, the Mercedes crumpled around me. The sounds of tires screeching came to a halt, only to be replaced with the sound of shattering glass.

Thank the good Lord I had been wearing my seatbelt, because without a doubt I would have flown through what remained of the windshield. It was bad enough that I smashed the side of my head into the driver's side window, shattering it in the process.

The other driver staggered up to my car, looking rather haggard. He reeked of alcohol and started ranting about it being my fault as he staggered around looking at the damage to his truck. Petrified, I looked at all the bystanders; they seemed appalled by his behavior. When he started yelling at me, the cops had finally decided it was time to stop his lunatic behavior. Still pinned in the car when they arrested the man for driving under the influence, I had no alternative except to wait for help.

Only thinking about Justin gave me the willpower to keep my eyes open as the firefighters and paramedics fought to free me. Cutting away the airbags, the EMT's allowed me and everyone else to see the damage. The blood was the first thing that caught my attention; the crimson fluid flowed down my neck and pooled in my cleavage. There was also a three-inch gash on my thigh. A whimper was the best I could manage as the blood soaked into the cotton of my skirt. I winced when I tentatively touched the gash behind my ear.

"What's your name?" The female parametric flashed a bright light in my eyes.

"Alexia Cr . . . McNear," I finally squawked, almost using my maiden name.

"Hi, Alexia, my name is Darlyn. Can you tell me where it hurts?"

"My head, arm, and thigh." I shivered, crying.

My body couldn't stop trembling; it was uncontrollable. I was scared, and every part of my body ached. For the first time since Justin and I had been married, I hoped I wasn't pregnant. There was no telling what the damage would be. I didn't think I could handle crushing everyone's expectations like that, but particularly Justin's and my own.

"How about your chest or stomach?" Darlyn gently pushed on my abdomen.

"No, but we're trying for a baby," I babbled, trying not to let the darkness pull me under.

"It's okay, Alexia. We're going to take you to the hospital to be checked out. Who's your doctor?"

"Dr. Michaels. I live in Les Portes de l'Ange." I whimpered, rubbing my stomach.

I heard the other paramedic calling ahead and arranging for Dr. Michaels to be at the ready. It was common knowledge that, due to religious beliefs, anyone from The Gates wasn't to be touched by anyone other than Dr. Michaels. He had handled it on all our medical records so we never had to explain it.

I won't lie; when they touched my arm, it felt as if it was on fire. The moment they pulled me from the wreckage, the pain doubled. Crying the whole way, I whined every time Darlyn touched me.

A flood of relief washed over me when we pulled up to the ER and Dr. Michaels was waiting outside with his nurse. I knew Donna from the years she'd worked at the clinic inside The Gates. She wasn't a member, but she knew of our lifestyle and was nonjudgmental, protective even. Not many outside our community understood our lifestyle, but those who did were loyal about keeping our secrets.

"Alexia, we've got you now. Your parents are already on their way." Donna stroked my cheek.

"Justin?"

"Your parents are calling him. We don't have his number here," Dr. Michaels answered while he pushed my gurney inside.

Once we were in a private room, Donna started pulling off my skirt so the doctor could see what he was working on. She also had to cut off my shirt, leaving me rather exposed. No one other than Justin was supposed to see me so vulnerable.

"Alexia, I know you just got married, so I need to know if you and Justin are actively trying for a child." Biting my lip, I nodded.

"Yes, my cycle is due tomorrow." He nodded, pursing his lips in thought.

"Okay, Donna, run a pregnancy test STAT. I need to know before she goes to x-ray." I was caught off guard by the harshness of his voice.

As if I needed another hole in my body, she made a new one for the IV and blood draw. She ran out the door the minute she had what she needed, leaving me with a nurse I didn't know to start my IV.

Shivering on the bed, the new nurse quickly covered me so that if anyone came in, I would be decent. Dr. Michaels was hard at work cleaning out the gashes while we waited for Donna.

Donna dismissed the nurse when she came back in. She handed a paper to the doctor before she slipped back out of the room. This time when she returned, she had Justin hot on her heels. If I could have walked, I would have run into his arms. There was no hiding my relief when he rushed into the room.

When Justin had first arrived at The Gates, I'd never had the chance to inform him who my doctor was. I grew up with Dr. Michaels's son Ryan. I knew he ran our clinic, too. Dr. Michaels, with the help of Minister Jeff, handled our health needs.

Granted, Minister Jeff had no medical training, but he was aware of our spiritual restrictions as far as medical treatments. It was not that we were not allowed treatments; we just believed God wanted to handle most of it. Dr. Michaels's knowledge in the old scrolls put him second in command in our community, just in case anything happened and Minister Jeff was unavailable.

As Justin rushed in to see me, I could see the worry etched on his face. Silently, I prayed he wasn't upset about the car; I hoped he was worried about me. Since our wedding in June, my attraction to him had done nothing but increase. The fact that now the feelings were changing from simple attraction to those of a loving nature were staggering. We knew this would happen over time, but still it was strange to experience it.

CHAPTER 11

JUSTIN MCNEAR'S WORRIES

The day before her cycle was expected again, I found myself sitting in my office praying it wouldn't come this month. I cringed when my mobile went off, and the caller-ID said 'Katrina Cross.'

Could it have arrived early? Why else would she call me at work?

I flipped it open and answered warily. "Good afternoon, Katrina. What can I do for you?"

"Justin, you need to meet us at the hospital in Small River." Her voice cracked.

"What's wrong? Is Alexia okay?" I held my breath and waited for her response.

"There's been . . . an accident. Alexia's car was struck by an oncoming car." She sobbed over the line.

"I'm on my way!" I leapt out of my seat and bolted for the door.

My dad overheard my part of the conversation and followed me out. After I explained what little I knew, he hopped into the first car on the lot and drove me there. Of course, he called my mum, who also ran out of the house to meet us there.

I dashed from the car and ran into the ER the moment the car stopped. Scanning the room, I spotted Katrina and Chris. You could see how scared they were, and this only made me panic even more.

"Where is she?" I asked anxiously.

A nurse approached us before they could answer. "Sir, are you Alexia McNear's husband?"

"Yes. Where is she?" I demanded.

"She's in here with the doctor." When she spun on her heels, I followed her down the corridor. She stopped and opened the door, revealing Alexia.

When Alexia saw me entering the room, she looked me straight in the eyes and reached out her left hand to me. She looked so fragile, lying there with blood-soaked gauze pads on her head, arms, and one thigh. The doctor seemed to see we needed a moment before he filled us in on her diagnosis.

He was right; I did need a moment to look her over and compose myself. There were a lot of cuts and bruises, but everything looked superficial. Emotionally, she looked as if she would break if someone said the wrong thing to her.

"Mr. McNear, my name is Dr. Michaels. I'm sure you have many questions, so I will do my best to answer them all." I nodded, but never diverted my eyes way from Alexia. She gripped my hand tightly, and I stroked her forehead, which had no signs of injury.

"First, your wife is going to be just fine. Her cuts and contusions will heal. However, the fractured radius will take a little longer. You probably don't remember me, but I was at your wedding. Alexia has told me you two were actively trying for a baby?" I could see he was looking for a confirmation, so I nodded.

"I see. Well, I don't want to get your hopes up, but the initial pregnancy test did come back positive. I want to do an ultrasound to ensure everything is still okay." I could see Alexia was already smiling with a glimmer in her eyes.

"Um . . . well, you see . . ." He cut me off before I could tell him about our religion. Just because he attended our wedding didn't mean he knew about it.

"Justin, I live in Les Portes de l'Ange." He smiled sympathetically. I breathed out easier.

"The rules stipulate that it can be done if there is a chance of loss of life or medical necessity. Your wife was just involved in a major accident. I have already spoken with Minister Jeff, and he agrees that it is necessary." Alexia begged me with her eyes to allow it. How could I deny her the proper care she needed?

"Do it, but please don't tell our parents yet. It's one thing if we're heartbroken, but I don't want them to be, too, if this ends badly." He nodded his understanding and slipped out of the room.

"Alexia, how do you feel?" I whispered into her ear.

"Scared." She sniffled. I knew she was crying.

"Will you pray with me?" I asked, hopeful.

"Yes," she breathed, obviously in pain, both physical and emotional.

Together, we prayed for the child she now carried in her womb. We had just said, "Amen," when Dr. Michaels reentered the room pushing what I could only guess was the ultrasound machine.

"This will only take a few moments to warm up. Minister Jeff is with your parents, and he has agreed to wait on the announcement until we know the outcome." Alexia and I both took a deep breath and exhaled slowly together.

"Alexia, if . . . we'll try again. I promise." She nodded, understanding I couldn't say the part about losing the baby.

"Since she isn't far enough along, we don't expect to hear the heartbeat yet. This will be an internal ultrasound, so I will be inserting the probe vaginally. We should be able to see if everything is where it should be."

He took a moment to prepare her by arranging her feet and lifting the sheet to expose her intimate parts to him. I won't lie; I didn't relish the thought of him touching Alexia's private area.

Alexia hissed as the probe entered her. I cooed in her ear, trying to get her to relax.

Suddenly, the room was filled with a rapid, repeating, whooshing sound. We both quickly looked at the doctor for an explanation. He grinned before explaining it.

"It would appear you're further along than we thought." I was baffled.

"That can't be; she had her cycle last month."

"I don't think she really did. Sometimes a woman can have implantation spotting or a mini-cycle, per se, during her first month of pregnancy. It's the body's way of discarding any built-up cells that had gathered before the impregnation." I'm fairly certain Alexia felt the same relief I did.

"The heartbeat is very strong, which is a great sign. If everything is where it should be, this is about where we should see the fetus. Hunh . . ."

"Is something wrong?" Alexia crooked her head toward the doctor.

"Wrong? No. It would appear there is more than one fetus. You're carrying twins, my dear. Congratulations! They both look very healthy for this stage of development." I released a shaky breath and looked to see if Alexia was taking the news well.

She took the shocking news wonderfully. Alexia even moved her injured hand and rested it on her still-flat tummy. I knew before she was even able to get the words out that she would worry about me.

"Alexia, this is the best news I have ever received, next to you that is." I nuzzled my face into the crook of her neck, hoping that one day she would feel as I did.

"Justin, we really did it." She glanced up, smiling.

"Does this mean they'll be fine?" I had to be sure there was no chance of them being lost later.

"Well, nothing is ever one hundred percent certain, but from all these readings, I would say yes. They look as though they will be just fine. Of course, mommy here will need a cast for her fractured radius and quite a few stitches, but all in all, they should be fine." I finally allowed myself to feel the excitement of the news.

"So, she's what, six weeks gone?"

"Six weeks and one day." I grinned, knowing it happened on our wedding night.

Alexia giggled after I kissed her heatedly. "Go tell everyone the good news, and come right back. Please?"

"Right back, I promise!" I nodded and strutted out of the room, feeling quite proud of myself.

Everyone looked anxious when I entered the waiting room. Suddenly they were all asking questions at once. "Calm down, everyone." Every couple in the room clutched each other's hands.

"Alexia is doing well. She broke her arm and will need stitches, but she's going to be fine; actually, better than fine." Minister Jeff took that as his cue.

"Folks, Dr. Michaels called me to come here. Alexia is with child." Everyone looked as if they were ready to jump out of their own skins.

"But the accident?" gasped Katrina.

"Katrina, they weren't harmed, as best as the doctor can tell from the ultrasound." I cocked my eyebrow and waited for someone to catch on to what I was saying.

"They? As in more than one?" my mum screeched.

"Yes, Mum, we're expecting twins!" I rushed up, grabbing her in my arms and whirling her around.

"I can't believe it, son. It only took you two months to get her pregnant." My dad patted me on the back.

"Actually, it happened on our wedding night. The doctor said she is six weeks along."

"Alexia had . . . is that possible?" Chris pondered.

"Yes, it is, and it doesn't mean there is anything wrong." When our parents started hugging each other, I left them to celebrate, and I went back to sit with my wife.

Dr. Michaels had just finished stitching the cut behind her ear when I walked in. Seeing her beam at me made me realize Minister Jeff was right about the bonding process that happened after a child was conceived. My feelings for her were indeed growing, and from her reaction to my entrance, so were hers.

Twenty-seven stitches and one cast – that ran from her wrist to her armpit – later, we finally left the E.R. I made sure to have all the facts from the doctor before we left. For the next month, she would need to rest as much as possible. Also no lifting, strenuous exercise, and no intercourse – yeah, that one wasn't good news – but a relaxing trip to England for two weeks was allowable as long as I watched her closely. From today on, that was my every intention, but it wasn't just me.

Thanks to my dad having the forethought to have my car brought to the hospital, we could go straight home. By the time we got home, the cottage was packed with family and friends. Everyone beamed at us when we entered; congratulations were gushed when we walked into the living room. Alexia managed a small smile as I carried her weakened form through the living room and off to our bedroom. Her mum followed with a pitcher of water and a bottle of Tylenol.

She undressed with a little help from her mom. She slid a light cotton sleep dress over her, and I couldn't help but look affectionately at her tummy, which now housed my future children.

Once she was safely tucked away in bed with her mum watching over her, I slipped out to see everyone. Ginger and Madison were chomping at the bit to see her, so I motioned for them to go ahead. I heard them all giggling, so I knew she would be entertained for a while.

"Justin, we need your schedule. We're going to coordinate our schedules so Alexia is always attended to." My mum had everyone's calendars in her hands.

"Just work; the rest of the time I'll be here." She was satisfied with that answer and went to hunker down at the dining room table.

Katrina joined her to arrange the planning of our meals. As if the house wasn't full enough, Minister Jeff and his wife Patty showed up and jumped right into the fray. They also brought us a casserole for dinner. It was so crowded, I slipped out and joined Krista on the back deck.

"Hey, it's a little crowded in there."

I nodded my reply. "Yeah, but they just want to help."

She frowned slightly and sighed. "That's the problem; there's nothing for me to do. She's carrying my nieces or nephews, and there's nothing I can do to help." I could see her point.

"Okay, squirt, I have something you can help me out with. How would you like to go to England with us and help me take care of her?" I raised my eyebrow as an invitation to her.

"Are you serious?" she shrilled and jumped into my arms. Right then and there, I knew I would be buying another airline ticket.

The second I released her, she raced inside to tell everyone in a shrill voice that could shatter every window in the house. The smile my mum gave me told me it was the right choice.

CHAPTER 12

ALEXIA MCNEAR'S DISCOVERIES

It was a little embarrassing arriving home to a full house, but seeing everyone looking at us with such affection, it was hard not to feel the love they were radiating.

For the first time in my life, I felt shy about my mom seeing me naked when she helped me into my night gown before putting me to bed. Usually when she would tend to me when I was feeling under the weather, it hadn't bothered me, but now I felt different. It was strange; I knew she knew we'd had sex, but now she was seeing me after he had changed me. I would no longer be the child she remembered; I was now a woman with children of my own growing in my womb.

Watching from my bed when Justin left the room, I had to wonder: was he avoiding me? I pushed the thought from my mind when Ginger and Madison bounced in, looking a little too happy for their own good. Together we sat on the bed, and I filled them in on everything.

"Alexia, do you have any idea how lucky you are? Alison has been trying for years," Madison gushed, all dreamy-eyed.

"Well, Justin has been hard at work. I just . . . ." I turned away when a tear slid down my cheek.

"Alexia, why are you crying? I thought this was what you wanted?"

"I do, but the question is, does he? I mean I know he wanted for me to be with child, but he never said why. Is it for the success of our marriage, or that stupid clause? I just wish he would tell me what he's thinking."

"Oh, you need to stop that. I have seen how that boy looks at you. And don't tell him I told you, but I've seen him spending his lunches at the church." Ginger wagged her finger at me.

"Why is he spending his lunches at the church?" My retort rushed from my lips before I could soften it.

"Don't know, but I'll bet it has something to do with your now-full womb," she replied.

Rubbing my stomach, I pondered it. Maybe he was consulting with Minister Jeff. However, that didn't answer the questions that were still rattling around my brain. If anything, it added more to the growing pile.

I heard the shrieking from the living room, and I could tell Krista would be joining us on our trip to England. Not long after, my mom delivered my dinner and kicked Madison and Ginger out, after a lot of protesting on their sides.

For the next couple of days, a new pattern started. I was never home alone. Everyone took turns staying with me; well, almost everyone. Justin seemed to be avoiding me. He left before I woke up and didn't come to bed until after I had fallen asleep. It was starting to tick me off.

On the third night, I woke up to see the alarm clock flashing 2:03am. Searching around, I discovered Justin wasn't in bed. Before I could think about why he wasn't there, I needed a bathroom break. It was the only time I'd been allowed out of bed. Normally, I had someone to walk me, but since I was alone, I ventured out by myself.

Being nice and gentle, I slipped out of bed and into my robe. Limping, I made my way down the hall. The bathroom door was opened a crack, and I could see Justin's naked reflection in the mirror.

His face wore an expression of pain and anguish. I found that confusing. Gasping, I heard the slapping of flesh. Was his expression pain? Or pleasure? Definitely pain.

In horror, I watched on as slapped his hardened erection with his hand. From the sound, I knew it hurt.

Justin heard my gasp, and his head snapped up to see me watching. He groaned and croaked out, "Alexia, what are doing up?"

"Justin, why are you hurting yourself?" Pushing the door open, I tried to approach him as he attempted to slide away.

He sighed and slumped down onto the closed lid of the toilet. "You weren't supposed to see that." I could see his eyes were starting to glisten with tears wanting to escape.

"But I did. Please tell me?" I whispered.

Looking away, he finally answered me. "At the retreat, we went through training to resist the urges to touch women, even our wives, unless it was to procreate." Locking my eyes on his, I knelt on the rug at his feet.

"They told you to hurt yourself instead of having sex with your wife?" I seethed.

"Alexia, I can't . . . we can't . . . you can't." I cupped his cheek with my good hand.

"There are other ways," I whispered, taking comfort in the feel of our first contact in days.

"No, I just need to learn more control. Please go back to bed, because you being this close is not helping the urges." He whimpered, now avoiding eye contact.

A plan started forming in my mind. When he threw his head back and a disgusted look formed on his face, I made my move. With his eyes closed, he never saw me leaning forward. The moment my lips wrapped around his erection, his eyes shot open, and he jerked, trying to escape. Thankfully the back of the toilet foiled his attempt, so I grabbed him with my good hand.

His lifted his butt in another attempt to run, but that only served to push him further into my mouth. "Alexia – no – you shouldn't . . . oh, that feels too good," he mumbled halfheartedly.

Remembering Alison's instructions, I bobbed down further each time and stroked up as I moved back to the top. Hearing him whimper, pant, and moan gave me the confidence to continue. Justin had a death grip on the toilet lid as he tried not to move.

"Oh . . . you – shouldn't . . . stop before – no – don't stop," he mumbled as he slipped his hands into my hair, careful not to touch my stitches.

When his hips started to wiggle, I doubled my efforts. Alison said she did this to Brett when she was cycling. I prayed Justin wouldn't be upset that I didn't stop when he'd asked. I knew he wouldn't ask for something like this, but I didn't want him to hurt himself over something like wanting to have sex with his wife.

"Alexia, don't stop. Please." I hummed so he would know I wasn't going anywhere.

"Holy cow!" He convulsed, releasing in my mouth.

Peeking up, I saw the most peaceful smile playing on his lips. It made me tingle from head to toe. He jumped when I struggled to stand up.

"I shouldn't have let you do that. It was wrong." Justin helped me stand, but I kept my head down.

I couldn't look at him; I thought I was doing something nice, but now he seemed even more disgusted. By the time I took a drink from the cup on the sink, a few treacherous tears had slipped out.

"Oh no, Alexia. I didn't mean you were wrong; I meant it was wrong for me to let you do that. I should be able to resist the urges until you're feeling better." His words didn't make me feel any better.

"I need to be alone," I muttered and pushed him out the door still without looking at him.

Seeing the expression of revulsion on his face was something I could without. I let loose sinking down onto the toilet. The last few days had been more than I could handle, and this was just the end of my ability to hold back the pain.

Clutching my chest, I fell apart, letting everything come out. Every tear I shed stood for a small piece of the pain and confusion I felt. There was no way I could hold back the strangled cry that ripped from my lips. In my frustration, I even slammed my cast into the wall behind me.

Once I was all cried out, I finished what I had come in here for in the first place. After washing my face, I opened the door to find Justin standing there waiting for me, leaning against the wall with his arms crossed over his chest. Without a word, he stepped in and scooped me up and headed for our room.

"Alexia, I'm sorry made you feel bad about that. It truly felt wonderful, it's just the training . . . they."

I shushed him with my fingers. "What did they do to break you so badly?" I needed to know what he had endured to become my husband.

Slipping into bed next to me, he hesitated but then opened up. "They um . . . well, they would have us masturbate." He shuddered. "Then they would hit us until we went soft again." Justin looked away from me, ashamed. He started to sob.

"Hit you? What do you mean? Oh my gosh! I can't believe they would do that to you." I pulled him over so he could cry it all out against my chest.

"Minister Mark said if I couldn't control my own body, I couldn't control yours."

Anger swelled inside me that I had never experienced before. My chest heaved as I struggled not to scream. How could someone intentionally cause someone that kind of pain and humiliation? "He was wrong," I choked.

I held him until he slipped off to sleep. He rolled us both over so my head was now on his chest, and I allowed myself to join him in some much-needed rest.

A new routine started after that night. Justin would come to see me the minute he walked through the door. He would sit with me on the bed, rubbing my flat stomach as we talked about our days.

When dinnertime would arrive, he'd bring in two plates, and together we would eat. I laughed when he came home bearing a small TV for our bedroom. That was a first; I'd never had a TV in my bedroom before.

Mocked By Faith

CHAPTER 13

JUSTIN MCNEAR'S GOING BACK TO HELL

Two weeks after the accident, I escorted Alexia to the clinic to remove her stitches and have her cleared to fly to England. We never spoke again about my retraining, but I'd noticed something between us had changed. Since my confession, we'd grown closer. A small amount of relief came from being able tell someone about a portion of what I had gone through while at the revirgining retreat. I couldn't tell her everything; it would hurt her too much. You could tell when Alexia was thinking about it: a sudden flash of fire would flicker in her emerald eyes. It scared me that my confession tore at her heart; that should only be my pain to bear.

Another change in her behavior since my confession was that she started touching me in my sleep. Twice since that night, she'd found me wanting her affections, and twice she'd refused to stop rubbing my need until it was satisfied. It left me thankful and confused at the same time.

The second she wrapped her tiny hand around me, I melted into her touch and let her have her way with me. Alexia's eagerness to please me warmed my heart. I wished she didn't feel the need to please me; I'd rather she wanted to please me. One good thing did come out of it. Whenever I wanted to touch her – be it her arm, leg, or waist – she seemed to move closer to me. That was one thing I enjoyed to no end.

Unfortunately, as soon as she was done, the guilt would grow in my chest and threatened to suffocate me. Alexia snuggling against my chest lessened that pain somewhat. The running of my fingers through her long locks of hair seemed to calm me enough so I'd fall back to sleep. Soon she would figure out that I was attracted to her and didn't want to have sex just to conceive children; that was, if she hadn't realized it already. How could she miss the fact that she was already pregnant?

The trick I'd used at the retreat wouldn't work at home. Before the retreat, I'd never been physically stimulated by any female. Therefore, when they demanded for us to harden, I couldn't until I'd pictured the green eyes from my dreams. When they struck us with rulers, all I had to do was envision any other female, and my desire melted away.

That was where the problem came in. Now I couldn't avoid the green pools of my dreams, since they belonged to my wife. How would one avoid that? Easy answer – you didn't.

I'd thought about talking to Minister Jeff about it, but I couldn't seem to bring myself to. Alexia had tried her best to tell me there was no shame in what I had gone through, but she didn't understand because I hadn't told her everything yet. I knew I was going to have to come clean to her one day, which wouldn't happen in the near future. Seeing the pain in her eyes over what I'd had to endure to get my contract for marriage to her would eat me alive. I couldn't and wouldn't hurt her like that.

With me behind the wheel of Alexia's new Mercedes SUV, we drove to the clinic with a few minutes to spare before her appointment. It was definitely more relaxing taking her to the clinic in our own community. I'd be the first to admit it; I didn't enjoy the thought of her being anywhere near the outsiders.

Tenderly, I helped her from the vehicle and cradled her into my side. I loved being able to touch and hold her. That was one thing I was grateful had come out of the accident and my confession. Inhaling deep, I savored the scent of her perfume when her hair tickled my nose. The light, warm breeze made her tresses float like butterfly wings. She was always so beautiful with the sun shimmering off her silky skin and a smile playing on her lips.

She tried to fight my assistance when the time came to go in but I won and she allowed me to guide her in with my arms safely wrapped around her hips. She'd have to get used to me tending to her; I was not about to stop lavishing my attentions on her. Alexia would have to learn that, in my eyes, she deserved to be worshipped.

She grumbled when I held the door for her. "Not an invalid here," she pointed out.

"Deal with it, darling," I chuckled, following her to Donna's desk.

"Good morning, Alexia. How are you feeling?" Donna asked, smirking since she'd heard our dispute.

"Very good. Thank you for everything at the E.R. You were a blessing." Alexia turned on the charm, no doubt hoping it would help her cause.

"It was my pleasure. Mr. McNear, do you have your medical records for us today?"

"Actually, no. My mum has them for you. I'll remind her to drop them off."

"That would be great. Why don't you two follow me to the examination room? Dr. Michaels will be right in." Alexia nodded and followed her.

"Alexia, just relax. Everything is going fine. I can't see him holding you back from the trip." I caressed her lower back.

"I'm not worried about going. I'm worried about him saying there's a problem with the twins," she confessed in a whisper.

"Don't be. God is in the driver's seat here. You know that," I reassured, keeping my eyes trained on her.

I spoke the truth; our faith believed God made all the decisions, especially when it came to procreating. He could give it, and He could take it away just as easily. There would be very little Dr. Michaels could do if we encountered a problem. All we could do was pray and hope for the best outcome.

"Hello, Alexia." Dr. Michaels entered the room, reading her records.

"Good morning, Dr. Michaels," Alexia replied with a sugarcoated voice.

"Have you had any spotting? Cramps?" He peered up to see her answer.

"No, everything feels fine." She smiled, looking all too innocent.

"Well, that is good news. Now, let's have a listen, then we can remove those stitches." He'd already pulled the monitor from his pocket.

Alexia lay back and lifted her light gray T-shirt. Relief washed over her delicate features when the machine started humming with the same whooshing sounds we'd heard in the ER. I would never grow bored of hearing that sound. Each beat was a gift from God, and I made sure to thank Him every chance I had.

"They still sound strong, so I think a trip to England is in your immediate future." He smirked.

With that out of the way, we moved onto the stitches. Alexia hissed and winced with the extraction of each black stitch. I clutched my hands into fists; it was all I could do to not slug him every time he hurt my wife. Granted, they needed to come out, but did it have to hurt? If I was overreacting about stitches, I could only imagine how much of a basket case I'd be at the delivery.

Alexia nuzzled against my chest when he started on the ones in her thigh. She'd already told me she wasn't happy with having the scars on her body. I did my best to assure her I didn't care. However, I'd admitted that if I ever ran into the plonker that hit her car, all bets were off. I'd mangle him into a twisted pretzel without a moment's hesitation.

Alexia breathed a sigh of relief when the doctor announced that the torture had ended. Nudging her chin up, I scanned her face to see if she was all right. Big mistake. She batted those long lashes at me, and my insides crumbled.

"Ready to go home?" I breathed, mesmerized by her gem-colored eyes.

She must have known what she did to me since she did it so frequently. Giggling, she nodded and moved off the bed. Holding her close, we left the clinic and headed home to pack for our trip. For the first time since leaving, I was actually excited by the thought of going back to England. Not necessarily the community's reaction to me, but more the places I wanted to show my wife. Alexia glowed as we drove back to the cottage.

We both laughed when we walked in to see Krista already packing our bags. "Hey, squirt. In a wee bit of a rush, are we?"

"Rush? We leave tomorrow. I've been packed for a week." She grinned and rushed off, only to return with another armload of clothes. From the looks of them, they were mine.

"Alexia, relax on the couch and supervise. I have to get our passports and tickets." She grumbled, but did it anyways.

After retrieving everything from our recently-installed wall safe, I returned to see Alexia trying with one hand to fold our clothes into the trunks Krista had brought up from the basement.

"Alexia, do not make me confine you to the bedroom."

"Only if you're coming with me." She cocked her eyebrow, challenging me.

"Now that wouldn't be very much of a punishment, would it?"

The gleam in her eyes said it all: she'd missed our nightly rituals, too.

"Stay put while I get your clothes."

Seeing her stick her tongue out at me had me groaning as I made my way back to our room.

Once everything was packed in the two large trunks, Krista went to the kitchen to cook dinner. Since we were having something I'd already prepared with the help of Ginger, I knew she could handle it. I'd never seen Krista so in her element than she was at that moment. She finally had gotten her chance to help us.

We enjoyed a nice dinner together at the kitchen table for the first time in two weeks. Krista and Alexia couldn't stop talking about our trip. By the end of dinner, we were all laughing about the upcoming adventure.

Krista tucked herself into bed in the guest room when Alexia and I headed for our bedroom.

I prayed silently for a son when, the next morning, I had to wake up two grouchy females for our early flight. Even coffee didn't please them while they rushed around the cottage trying to remember everything. I could swear that Alexia growled at me when I told her to sit down and let me do everything.

We used the same livery service from our honeymoon to take us to the airport for this trip. I had warned Krista already, so she made sure to keep Alexia's mind off the flight. There were moments when I thought Alexia would tear my fingers off my hand. The perfect example came when the plane was jostled by turbulence. Alexia looked ghostly white, and she tried to crawl onto my lap. Not that I minded, but she would have been safer in her own seat.

Gawking out the window, she watched as we landed at Heathrow Airport. I had to restrain her from running off the plane when they opened the door. True to her word, Krista handled the bags while I rented a car for our two-week stay. Thankfully, we were able to stay in our old house since it hadn't been sold yet.

Driving through the gate to the community we had once called home, my mind flooded with the reminders of why Minnesota made me so happy. Aaron, the guard on the gate, wasn't so happy to see me. No great surprise there, since he all but threatened to kill me when the contract talks were called off. He took protecting his baby sister to a whole new level. Standing at six feet, four inches, he scared a lot of young men. As much as I would have preferred Alexia not to see him leer, it wasn't the case.

"Justin, why does he seem so mad at you?" She looked so bashful when she mumbled to me.

"Simply put?" Alexia nodded. "His parents were in talks with my parents when I left to search for love on my own." I smiled, letting her know she could talk about it.

"Oh, so his sister's feelings were hurt?" she muttered, looking down and fiddling with the hem of her shirt.

"Yeah, his sister wasn't too happy with me after that, but I think I needed to do it. If I hadn't, I wouldn't have found you. I think it was God's way of reminding me that I had someone else waiting for me." I tilted her chin up to show her my sincerity.

"You don't regret it? I mean . . . the way people here reacted?"

"Not one bit. Minister Jeff and I agreed that it was a test that I needed to survive in order to find my way back to His good graces. Does that make sense?"

"Yeah, it does. Just, it's so sad that people didn't understand the circumstances." She chose that moment to look out the window.

Mrs. Chesterfield was out walking her dog when we drove by. Again, she didn't hide the fact that she wasn't pleased with my reappearance. I should have warned Alexia when I'd asked her to come, but I hadn't wanted her to turn me down.

"That wouldn't happen to be Aaron's grandmother, would it?" she snickered.

"No, that is Mrs. Chesterfield. Her husband died right after they were married, and she never had children. She's on the Council here. The fact that no one would take me made her job more difficult." I chuckled, remembering all the times she chewed me out for running away.

My mum had called ahead and asked Minister Peter's wife Sonia to stock the house with groceries. It was nice not to have to worry about Alexia overdoing it with grocery shopping.

"Wow, it's beautiful," Alexia laughed when we pulled into the driveway.

"My mum was meticulous about keeping my dad happy." I couldn't help but smile. "You make being here bearable." An adorable blush crept across her cheeks.

"Come on, let's go inside. You two can compliment each other inside the house, you know," Krista chided from the backseat.

Laughing, I leapt out and jogged around the black rental car to open Alexia's door. As soon as I helped her to her feet, I went to retrieve our bags from the trunk. Krista was a great help carrying in the luggage, since I didn't want Alexia to lug anything too heavy.

With wide eyes, Alexia followed me into the foyer. The house in England was much grander than the townhouse in Minnesota. "Oh my gosh!" I grinned when Alexia took in her surroundings.

"It looked a lot better with furniture. For now, the bedrooms are the only rooms with any furniture in them, so you can count on spending a lot of time in there. But don't worry; I'll keep you company." I hugged her, cackling and wiggling my eyebrows.

"Oh, please! Let's get this stuff upstairs. I need to go see if my friends are around. I called and told them when we were getting in." Krista huffed, grabbing half the bags.

Alexia followed her, and I followed Alexia. I couldn't help but think I had the best view in the house. Whoever invented tight jeans was my hero as I watched Alexia wiggle her bottom up the stairs. Dropping the bags, I grabbed her and flopped us into the bed. Sonia must have made the beds as well, because they had been bare when we'd left.

Alexia's breathless laugh vibrated against my chest when I held her. Krista made a hasty retreat as she tsk'ed at us for snuggling.

"I'm going out," Krista called up the stairs.

"Have fun." I laughed, pulling Alexia closer into my hungry touch.

Nuzzling her neck elicited a beautiful moan from my wife's lips. "Alexia, I need you." Having her in my childhood bed did nothing but excite me even more.

"Um . . . yes," she panted when I started unbuttoning her pastel pink blouse.

While I sucked her earlobe into my mouth, I ground my hips against her butt cheeks. "Justin," she breathed.

"Do you realize how many times I slept in this bed and dreamed of you?" I slipped her blouse off her shoulder.

"Tell me," she whispered her voice heavy with lust.

"Night after night, I would lay here seeing those soulful, emerald pools in my dreams." I kissed the creamy flesh of her collarbone. "I always knew you were out there. I just needed to find you," I panted aloud.

Seeing her shiver while I unlatched her bra was a delight. I loved the way her body reacted to my attention. Ghosting over her side, I sought out the breast I'd just released. It felt heavenly in my hand when I caressed it. Her breast felt firmer than before, and her darkened peak hardened when my thumb caressed it. Arching her back, she pushed deeper into my hand.

Needing more, I slid my hand down her stomach, searching for her promised land. With one twist, the button of her jeans gave way to me. She shuddered against me when I inched her zip down.

There was no denying that she wanted me as much as I wanted her. This would be the first time for intimacy for her since we'd found out about the twins. The desire to please her the way she'd done for me spurred me on.

"We need to get these clothes off." I moaned into her neck.

Without a word, we each slipped out of bed and started to take off our own clothes. Alexia finished first and crawled back in bed in all her naked glory. With her lip locked between her teeth, she ogled me while I slid back in under the bedding.

"Come here, Mrs. McNear." I pulled her heated flesh against my naked form.

"I missed you." She whimpered when I rubbed my manhood against her stomach.

"As you can see, I missed you, too." I groaned when she grasped me in her hand.

Burying my hands into her hair, I placed a desperate kiss on her lips. When I finally released her lips, I licked mine. She always tasted like candyfloss. With slow, gentle strokes, she drove my need for her through the roof and up to the heavens. Grabbing her hips, I helped her hover over my greedy manhood A sigh slipped from our mouths when she slowly slipped down onto me.

I mumbled against her lips, "Home," causing her to giggle.

Together we set a slow and tender rhythm. We allowed our bodies to tell each other how good it felt to be together again. Neither one of us rushed to end the caring exchange we were enjoying. I reveled in the slow burn that began to spread from my stomach to my groin.

The constant mewling that rambled off Alexia's tongue made her sound like a kitten purring. My moaning and groaning had her quickening her pace while she moved above me. Kneading her breasts earned me a guttural moan when she threw her head back and arched her back.

As I made love to my wife, I knew I'd fallen in love with her, but I wasn't ready to share the revelation yet. I wanted to wait until she felt the same way about me. There was no need to make her feel awkward about not feeling as deeply as I did. We had a lifetime ahead of us to share our feelings, once we were on the same page.

Knowing I was quickly reaching the precipice, I flipped Alexia onto her back. Anchoring my hands on her hips, I took over, wanting Alexia to reach it first.

"Please, sweetheart, let go." I moaned into her mouth.

"Oh, Justin, I . . . I . . . um . . . oh – oh!" she gasped, unable to articulate correctly what her body was feeling in the moment of her climax.

Her lithe movements below me sent me free-falling over the edge of oblivion with her. "Alexia!" I grunted when I let go to join her in postcoital bliss.

Together we sighed and calmed down until we could breathe normally again. There was no better sight than seeing Alexia's afterglow. The way her skin flushed and shimmered with a light sheen of sweat was beyond compare. We never bothered leaving the bed. Instead, we said our nightly prayer and slipped off to sleep in each other's embrace.

Mocked By Faith

CHAPTER 14

ALEXIA MCNEAR'S MISSING HOME

Was it wrong to want to tear someone's face off? I supposed it was, but that didn't change the fact I wanted to do just that. The looks that Justin received from the community he'd called home for so long were purely appalling. These people were supposed to be his friends, and yet they acted like he was the scourge of the planet.

I'd be the first to admit I hadn't fully comprehended the amount of money Justin's family had until we pulled up to their former home. It flabbergasted me to see the sheer size of the house. We had nothing at The Gates to even compare it to. The enormous two-story red house was twice the size of my parents' home.

Sighing, I happily awoke in Justin's arms the morning after we'd arrived. The downside was that this moment of togetherness was going to end too quickly for my liking. He would be too busy all day, first with the pre-wedding preparations, and then with the actual wedding. I would be lucky if he could sneak over to see me along the way.

When my stomach growled, I realized we'd gone to bed without eating anything and I was ravenous. I jumped when I heard Justin's chuckle.

"Are my children hungry?"

Peeking up, I nodded. "They're not happy. I failed to feed them before bed." I laughed.

"Well, we don't want that, now do we? I think I should go find them something to eat before I have to leave. Paulie wants me at his house in an hour." I whimpered when he slipped out of bed, still naked from last night's activities.

Jumping into his jeans, he walked out, leaving me the whole bed to stretch out in. Krista grumbled something incoherently when she stalked by the door. Moments later, I smelled my second-favorite smell in the world: coffee. Of course, it was delivered by my bare-chested husband. Oh, the torture!

"Where are your prenatal vitamins?" he asked, handing me the steaming brew.

"In the carry-on." I grimaced, burning my tongue on my coffee.

Exasperated, I whined when he grabbed them out and handed me one. "I don't like them. They make me nauseous."

"You all need them. And have you considered that the pregnancy is what is making you feel sick?"

Forget the whining; I flat-out growled at him. "Of course, I know that, but they make it worse!"

"Now, love, there is no need to be upset." He leaned in and kissed me, causing my brain to forget what we had been talking about.

Did he just call me 'love?' Must be an English thing, because he'd never called me that before. Ever since that night I'd found him in the bathroom, he'd been calling me things other than my name. It wasn't that I minded, but it was new.

He seemed a bit more comfortable showing me affection. Up until now, he had withheld it. There had been times when I had to bite my lip to keep my mouth from telling him how I really felt about him. With each passing day, my heart swelled with love for him, but there was no way I was going to put that type of pressure on him so soon. It wouldn't be right to expect him to feel the same way. He would feel it when he was ready, and I wouldn't force him to say something he didn't feel because he thought he had to.

"What are you daydreaming about?" Justin whispered in my ear.

Feeling jumpy about being caught, I scrambled to deflect him. "Nothing, I . . . um, don't you have to get ready?"

With a quick kiss on my cheek, he slipped into the bathroom to shower. Once he was out of sight, I rubbed my tingling cheek. Justin had a way of awakening my flesh just by touching it. Sighing, I laid back when

Krista came in carrying a tray.

"Your breakfast is here. I hear my nieces or nephews are grumbling about their treatment," she chortled.

"Don't forget their mommy. Mommy gets no love." I giggled.

"I think mummy got more than her share of love from their daddy. Otherwise they wouldn't be on their way, now would they?"

I mocked offence. "Absolutely not! I blame it on the stork." We both laughed when Justin walked out in nothing but a towel.

"Yeah, let me know how that works out for you." She chuckled, running from the room.

"The stork, huh? I don't think my legs are that long." Justin grinned.

Who was he trying to fool? His legs were definitely long and lean, perfect to me. Chewing my lip instead of my toast, I watched while he dressed in his tuxedo. Dang, that boy was way too good-looking in the monkey suit.

To spare my poor lip from any more torture, I started chewing on my toast. I groaned when my stomach caught up to my mouth and realized there was food in the room. Hurling myself off the bed, I scrambled for the bathroom.

Crouching on the floor, I discarded what little I had in my stomach into the white porcelain bowl.

"Alexia?" Justin pulled my hair back. "Krista, grab a flannel," he bellowed while I dry-heaved into the toilet again.

"Is she sick?" The sound of running water made my mouth burn with want.

"Morning sickness, I hope," he whispered, sounding nervous while he pressed a cool, wet cloth to my forehead.

"I'm okay now. Can I have some water?" I moaned.

"Be right back. Justin, help her lie down in bed." Krista was gone before I could even entertain the thought of moving.

"I've got you." Justin grunted, lifting me from the floor.

Closing my eyes, I gave up on my ambition to move under my own power. When I opened them again, Krista had returned with a glass of water.

"Alexia, are you better now?" Krista's worry was clear in her voice.

"Yeah, sorry. I'll be fine in a few minutes," I mumbled, turning away and hoping they wouldn't see how embarrassed I felt.

"Alexia, don't do that. There's nothing to be ashamed or embarrassed about." Justin heaved a deep breath and hung his head. "Unless you're ashamed of carrying my children," he whispered.

Sitting up, I cupped his face in my hand and led his eyes to look at mine. "I'm not ashamed of carrying your children. It's my pleasure to carry them. I'm just sorry I'm making you worry about me, and not about your day." He didn't need to do that.

Pulling me into his embrace, he held me and gushed into my neck, "Thank you. I needed to hear that."

There was so much pain in his ocean blue irises when he thought I wasn't proud of my children's parentage. How could he think that I would be ashamed of their father? How much had he really suffered here?

I held him until he had to leave for Paulie's house. With one last kiss under my ear, he pulled away when a car horn sounded out front.

"See you there. Krista knows the way." He smiled, softer than before.

Krista and I were going to the ceremony alone. At least we had each other; Justin wasn't so lucky. Silently, I prayed that those he was with would treat him better than the few I'd seen so far.

An hour after his departure, I'd managed to get down some tea and toast without running for the bathroom. Krista and I were both dressed and ready to go only fifteen minutes before we needed to be there, which left us rushing out the door.

"Do you think Justin will like the dress?" I felt self-conscious, hopping into the car.

"Alexia, you look gorgeous. Green is definitely his favorite color on you."

"He never told me that. How do you know?" I stared at her for a moment.

She looked at me in disbelief. "You seriously can't see it? The boy cannot take his eyes off you. Well, his hands either."

I laughed with her, since it was the truth, but I didn't want to burst her bubble with the fact that he'd wanted a child in my womb, and now he was just enjoying his rights to my body. I wasn't complaining, since I also reaped those rewards; not to mention that we were also repairing the damage done at the retreat.

We found the church before I had a chance to ponder my relationship with Justin further. Pulling in, I found a spot not too far from the front of the building. From our parking spot, we could see Justin waiting out front and looking a little haggard. He kept running his hands through his hair until he spotted us. The grin that settled across his lips could melt anyone's unsuspecting heart. A sigh slipped from my chest when he strutted across the lot to where we'd parked.

Pulling me into his embrace, he gave me the once over with his eyes. "Alexia, how do you feel?"

"Better," I confirmed, proudly.

"Did you manage to eat something?" he asked, stroking my stomach with featherlight touches.

Blushing pink, I breathed, "Yes, toast."

"Toast is good." He chuckled, brushing my flaming cheek.

"This must be the missus." A deep voice rang from behind Justin.

"Yeah, Paulie, this is my wife Alexia. Alexia, this is Paulie, the groom." Paulie grinned, shaking my hand without the cast.

"It's nice to meet the woman who made an honest man of this thug."

My face must have shown how appalled I was by his statement.

"Alexia, don't get upset; he's only joking. He knows I never did anything." Justin punched Paulie in the shoulder.

Paulie, by all standards, was a good-looking guy. He stood only a hair shorter than Justin. His shoulder-length, pale blond locks flowed in the afternoon breeze. Unlike my green eyes, his were paler and mixed with a hint of brown around the edges.

"Sorry, I didn't mean any offence. We've always teased him about his indiscretions." I think that statement had my fury rising even more than the first.

"Why would you do that? That's not how friends treat each other," I snipped, praying my outburst wouldn't make Justin upset with me.

"Alexia, look at me." His breath tickled my ear. "From Paulie, it's okay. He'd never hurt my feelings. It's always been in fun, never malicious." Looking up, I could see he wasn't angry with me.

"I like her. Wish she was here when Abigail . . . never mind." Cocking my head in confusion, I looked to Justin for answers.

"The guard's sister." He huffed.

"Oh, right." I grimaced, feeling like I'd missed something bigger.

"Let's get inside before the bride shows up," Justin muttered, deflecting my questioning looks.

Krista refused to look at me as we walked into the church. The building there was exactly the same as ours at home. They must have brought the design to the States when the first settlers of our religion moved there.

Justin left me in a pew a few rows from the front and walked with Paulie up to another young man. I surmised it must have been Jonathan, bout whom I'd heard so much. He definitely fit the description to a T. His gelled, raven-black hair begged to be ruffled, and there was a hint of mystery in his sterling gray eyes. His form bulked over both Justin and Paulie.

It was a relief to see Justin being so well received by them, until I looked around and noticed very few were looking at him as kindly. Someone needed to remind Minister Peter to preach forgiveness to his parishioners.

When they moved into position, it was evident that the ceremony was about to start. Justin brushed his hand across my shoulder when he passed me, heading to escort in the mother of the groom.

It surprised me that she looked at him with gentle eyes. She seemed to care about him very much, and she showed no embarrassment having Justin guiding her to the front. A giggle erupted from my lips when he winked at me when he passed by. Such a flirt!

All eyes darted down the aisle to see the bride gliding in on her father's arm. I'd never met Danielle, but she looked breathtaking in her Cinderella wedding gown. Her curvy figure allowed her to wear a gown that would've made anyone else look hippy. What I wouldn't have done to have had a chest that voluptuous.

I was not ashamed to admit that I barely listened to the minister while he performed the ceremony. My mind was too wrapped up in watching Justin fidget. I couldn't help but wonder what had him on the edge of his seat. Then I saw her. A white-blond, curly haired bridesmaid was staring Justin down. Abigail!

The understanding of what they had been talking about in the parking lot finally hit me. She was here, was in the wedding, and expected to dance and partake in pictures with him. Anger, fear, and panic rushed over me. My heart raced, skin flushed, and my breathing hitched while I watched the exchange.

Krista must have noticed my reaction because suddenly she grasped my knee, drawing my attention to her. I could see her sharp headshakes, but I was too infuriated to understand what she was telling me "no" for. Jealousy is an ugly thing, but that didn't stop me from feeling it. Justin was mine, and just the thought that he had almost married her had me seeing red.

The churning in my stomach returned. I started to take long, deep breaths; it was all I could do not to retch in the pew. Clasping my hand over my mouth, I refused to let the bile escape. As the ceremony closed, I watched Justin take her by the arm. I slipped out the side door and ran for the trees that lined the lot. From the clanking of heels behind me, I knew Krista had followed me.

Grabbing a tree for support, I let my stomach have its way. Treacherous tears spilled down my cheeks when I let my emotions run wild. I'd always avoided thinking about Justin with other women, but I couldn't this time. Seeing it firsthand was more than my fragile heart could stand.

With my chest heaving, I gasped for air.

"Alexia, you need to calm down, otherwise I'm going to get Justin."

That so didn't help to calm me down.

"Alexia, what's wrong?" I shivered when Justin's frightened voice sounded from behind me.

"Justin, she freaked out in church. I tried to get her to calm down. As you can see, it didn't work."

"Alexia, look at me! What's wrong, love? Talk to me!" Scrunching my eyes shut, I tried to breathe at a slower pace.

"She . . . her . . . mine . . . home," I sobbed, dropping my head into my cast-free hand.

"No . . . no . . . no! There is no she or her. It's you and me." I tried to fight when he pulled me into the safety of his arms. "Please, Alexia? Don't do this. I'm your husband, not hers. She would never be my choice." Finally, I let him hold me close. "I'm sorry I didn't tell you that she'd be in the wedding. I really didn't think it would be an issue. She's married now, and so am I. I never loved her." He cupped my face in his gentle hands and forced me to look him in the eye. "Do you want to go home? I'll leave right now if it will make you feel better. Paulie will understand." The sincerity in his eyes had the guilt in me rising.

"Justin, is she okay?" a gruff voice asked.

"Yeah, Jonathan, it's just a case of morning sickness," he muttered into my hair.

"No way! Why didn't you tell us?"

Peeking up through my lashes, I laughed.

"I was waiting to tell you at the reception with her by my side." His gleaming grin washed away all my insecurities.

"Hello," I greeted Jonathan.

"Well, hello to you, too. I'm Jonathan. Justin's been raving about you. I see he wasn't lying. Congratulations to both of you. Take a few minutes; I'll tell them you'll be out shortly." He smirked, strolling away.

"See, even they know you own me. Do you feel up to going to the reception, or should I take you back to the house?"

I nodded. "I can still go in, I think. I'm sorry I freaked out, but can you blame me?" I prayed he'd understand.

With a smile, he put me at ease. "No, I don't. You saw how I reacted at our wedding when someone mentioned wanting you in a way that was mine." I did remember him hitting a young man on the beach; now I knew why he had done it.

Holding me secure in his arms, he helped me leave the cover of the trees. A few people were left in the lot, but mostly they'd all gone inside the meeting room.

Krista and I went straight to the bathroom so I could freshen up, while Justin went to take the wedding pictures. She waited outside the door talking to one of her friends while I went inside. Someone's crying reverberated in the tiny enclosure. While I washed my face, the unhappy woman emerged with her mascara running down her cheeks. Turning quickly, she tried to hide that she'd been crying, but I'd already seen the evidence.

"I know you don't know me . . ."

She cut me off before I could finish and heaved a heavy sigh. "I know who you are. Alexia, right? Justin's wife?"

"Yes, right. And you're Abigail?" She nodded. "Why are you crying?" Such a pretty face should never be tearstained. I decided not to hold her parents' actions against her.

After sighing again, she divulged something I was sure she hadn't told many people about. "How is it Justin came back from the retreat unscathed?"

"He didn't," I cackled.

"Robert's still a mess. He won't tell me what happened there, but I know it was nothing good." She sunk down on the tiny, white lounge behind us.

"It wasn't; it took a lot for Justin to tell me what happened. Talk to your husband about it. Make him tell you what happened. That's what helped Justin the most. The twins didn't hurt, either." I absentmindedly rubbed my stomach.

"Congratulations. We're trying, too. He's having problems in that department. It took three tries before we could consummate our wedding." Her embarrassment was etched on her delicate features.

Feeling her pain, I reached over and held her hand. The small smile she gave me told me she'd found some comfort in my gesture. "Don't tell anyone what I said. The only reason I said anything to you was because Justin was there the same time as my husband." I nodded my agreement. "I should go; they'll be looking for me to do the pictures." She rose, smoothing out her cerulean blue satin gown.

"Abigail, if you want to talk later, come find me." She smiled brighter and drifted out the door.

When I followed her out, I discovered Justin glaring at Abigail. Moving between them, I diverted his attention. "Alexia?"

"I'm fine; no more morning sickness." I rubbed his firm chest through his shirt. My eyes locked onto his, his warmth and heartbeat penetrating through my palm.

"She didn't upset you, did she?"

Shaking my head, I leaned in and kissed his lips. "Go take your pictures. I'll be waiting with Krista when you're done," I swooned after he kissed me with more vigor than I'd done him.

Clutching Krista's hand, we wove through the crowd, searching for our seats. I was surprised when Krista and I sat down at our table and found a place card for Robert Mills. Since he was sitting alone, I guessed it was Abigail's husband. He looked so uncomfortable; I felt for him. I felt uncomfortable, too.

"You're Justin's wife? We were at the retreat together," he mumbled.

"It's nice to meet you. I had a chance to meet Abigail earlier. She's great."

"Yeah, she is. She has the patience of a saint." He looked away.

"Robert, might I make a suggestion?" Without looking at me, he nodded.

"Talk to her about what happened. It helped Justin." He glared at me horrified.

"You know about the retreat?" he snarled under his breath. Demurely, I nodded. "I think the electroshock therapy was the worst." My hand flew to my mouth. Justin had never mentioned that part. "They take their retraining too seriously at the retreat," he continued in his hushed tone.

I decided to nod, letting him ramble on so I'd get all the details that Justin had held back. There was a conversation in Justin's future, and he wasn't going to like it. I couldn't fathom the atrocities Robert now described in detail. Visions of Justin's suffering entered my mind. I struggled but managed to keep my tears from slipping from my eyes. My chest ached for both of them; they'd suffered so much.

Krista remained oblivious to the conversation, thanks to the arrival of her friends. They had whisked her away right after we were seated. I would never want her to hear about the way her brother had been mistreated.

Robert clammed up when Justin and Abigail arrived at our table. "Come on, Alexia. Jonathan is ready to burst. If we don't tell Paulie, he is going to," Justin twittered.

Following him, I kept my discoveries to myself and forced a smile onto my face when we approached Paulie and Danielle. Justin had no idea how I seethed deep inside while he wrapped himself around me.

"Paulie, Danielle, this is Alexia, my expecting wife." He grinned into my neck and waited.

"Wait, she . . . you?"

Caressing our babies over my clothed flesh, he floored them. "Uh-huh . . . first try . . . twins." When they gawked, Justin wiggled his eyebrows.

"We're going to have a talk before we leave." Paulie poked him in the chest. "Congratulations, you're very blessed."

"Congratulations!" Danielle beamed. "It's so nice to finally meet you. Justin has said so many wonderful things about you." She stepped forward, hugging us together.

"And all of them are true," he spoke in my ear.

"It's a pleasure to finally meet you. Justin's told me so much about you both. The wedding was beautiful."

"Thank you. We're so happy you both could come."

"Danielle, your mother is looking for us." Paulie nudged his head toward the table that held the wedding cake.

They were ushered off to do all the required wedding traditions, like their first dance and the cutting of the cake. Justin and Paulie didn't have a private talk before we left, and Justin never caught on that I knew about the retreat.

Mocked By Faith

CHAPTER 15

JUSTIN MCNEAR'S MISERY

Seeing Alexia bolting for the small tree line near the side door of the church made my heart beat frantically in my chest. All I could think about was whether it wasn't morning sickness. What if something had gone wrong from her recent accident? That single thought had my feet running to check on her.

Krista looked just as flustered when, separately, we watched Alexia discarding the contents of her stomach onto the ground at her feet.

When the words slipped from Alexia's lips, I felt my heart skip a beat. How could she possibly think that I wanted Abigail? I knew I should've warned her, but I'd hoped it would go unnoticed. Being wrong seemed to be my trait in my marriage.

Pleading my case, I begged for her to see the truth. It crushed me when she refused to let me hold her. I knew that would be the one thing to calm her down, but she rejected me. All I wanted to do was embrace Alexia and show her the depth of my love for her. When she finally stopped struggling, I couldn't help but sigh and hold her until she felt like she'd become a part of me.

I'd never expected Jonathan to show up behind me. I had to admit that it was priceless to see the shocked expression on his face when I told him Alexia was suffering from morning sickness. The best thing that could have happened did: Alexia giggled. That small sound always made me weak at the knees, today being no exception.

After they'd introduced themselves, Jonathan left, practically dancing. There was no shame when I admitted to Alexia that even my friends knew she owned me, because she did. In every possible way, I would be hers forever. With care, I led her back to the church. The way my day had been going, my biggest fear was that she would fall and hurt herself, or worse, the twins.

Leaving her to wash up, I headed to the room where we'd be taking wedding pictures.

"So, when are you telling Paulie?" Jonathan laughed, clapping me on the back.

"When Alexia is there. I told you that already." I pointed to the photographer sitting in a chair. "Hey, what's the holdup with the pictures?"

"Abigail needed to use the loo." He shrugged.

Clenching my eyes shut, I tried not to flip out. I'd just delivered Alexia into Abigail's hands! My own hands clammed up and balled into fists. If she even upset her in the slightest, I'd lose all my attempts to stay calm. Stalking out of the room, I retraced my steps back to the bathroom.

The first thing I noticed was that Krista wasn't in there with her. That was an ominous sight. Unable to enter the room, I had to wait outside. At the first sound of screaming, I would tear down the door with my bare hands if I needed to.

It never came to that, since Abigail slunk out first. Just when I was about to go ballistic on her, Alexia exited. I would have lost it if Alexia hadn't interceded. Her ministrations against my chest forced my anger to dissipate. Once I was positive that nothing had transpired between them, I released my hold on her reluctantly.

My reward came in the form of a chaste kiss on the lips. It wasn't enough for the separation I'd soon have to endure. Crushing my lips to hers caused her to sway on her feet dreamily. Krista sighed, shaking her head before she dragged Alexia away and out of my reach for the time being.

I rushed off, hoping to get the pictures over so I could get back to where I wanted to be: by my wife's side. This time when I entered the room, the photographer was already in action. Abigail stayed off to the side, waiting for when we'd be needed. Taking advantage of my time, I decided to find out what had happened in the ladies' room.

Grabbing my chin, I tried to keep my voice hushed and neutral.

Honestly, I wasn't opposed to slamming the wall with my fist if it would get me my answers. "Abigail, what did you say to my wife?"

"What did she say I said?" She huffed, looking baffled.

"You know very well if she had said something, I wouldn't have to ask you."

"I asked her how you came back normal from the retreat," she whispered without looking at me.

Shocked, I demanded, "Abigail, please tell me you didn't tell her what happened there."

It had never occurred to me that someone else might tell her about the retreat. There was too much I didn't want her think about, especially in her condition. Why did everyone want to hear the disturbing tales of our incarceration?

"How could I do that when Robert won't even tell me what happened?" she retorted with her eyes blazing.

I gushed a heavy breath. "So Robert hasn't informed you about the retreat?" Relief washed over me when I realized my suffering was still my own.

Shaking her head, she whispered, "No, but he will if he ever wants to sleep in our bed again . . . Alexia said it helped when you opened up, so like it or not, he will talk to me." From the look of determination on her face, I believed her.

"Just remember, you might not like what you hear. If you push him to talk, you're taking on his punishment as your own. Please be sure you are prepared to hear the ugly truth." It was something I'd been trying to avoid at all costs.

Before she could answer, we were needed for pictures. That suited me just fine; I could get back to my wife sooner. Their photographer was good, but nowhere near as good as Brett. Before we knew it, all the pictures were done and we were free to leave.

Abigail and I froze when we saw Alexia talking to Robert. From the expression on her face, he was telling her something very interesting. Abigail seemed surprised by the way he blabbered to my wife. I needed to get her away from him before he said anything damaging.

A firm grip on my shoulder halted my advance. "You have five minutes to tell him, or I am going to announce it over the DJ's mic," Jonathan threatened with a twinkle in his eye.

"I'm going to get her now. Calm down, will you?" I chided, resuming my trek toward Alexia.

Our arrival had the desired reaction: Robert shut right up when he saw us. Taking care of the business at hand, I grabbed Alexia and diverted her away from Robert.

"Come on, Alexia. Jonathan is ready to burst. If we don't tell Paulie, he's going to tell the whole room," I twittered, grabbing her hand.

Even though she didn't fight following me, something was off with her. The pep in her step was missing, and her smile seemed uncomfortable. Hoping to put her at ease, I wrapped myself around her like a blanket.

Paulie and Danielle were shocked but overjoyed about our news. After promising to talk to him privately, I dragged Alexia to a quiet corner. I needed to get away from the disapproving looks. However, I had to admit they weren't as bad as they had once been.

It turned out that there was never time for Paulie and me to talk. We opted instead to talk the day before Jonathan's wedding. Paulie had scheduled their honeymoon to coincide with Jonathan and Amelia's, just like Alexia and I had done with our own honeymoon.

The days between the weddings were spent with me showing Alexia where I had grown up. We didn't have a lake, but there was a community pool that I took her to. Krista and her friends were there, too. Alexia seemed to relax around them, which only served to make me love her more. She'd truly accepted every member of my family. Krista and Alexia even took a small trip into town for some girl time. We also spent our evenings on the rockers out back, talking. I learned so much about her during our time there. Alexia enjoyed taking walks with me around the compound in the early mornings. All in all, the time there flew by without any more incidents or encounters of the unpleasant kind.

The day before Jonathan's wedding, Paulie picked me up so that I could leave my rental, in case Alexia and Krista needed to go somewhere. Luck was on my side when we left the compound and Aaron wasn't working. After driving into town, we found a quiet café to talk. No one else occupied the seats; we had our pick. The waitress arrived and departed in seconds to retrieve our coffees.

The café had outdoor seating; it was nice to sit and let my mind wander. Alexia dominated my thoughts, as always.

After my mocha latte arrived, I sat back, closing my eyes. I remembered connecting with her in my childhood bed. Something had been different about that time; an exchange had occurred, one I'd welcomed. I could've sworn I could feel Alexia was saying something with her body pressed against mine instead of her voice. Maybe it had just been wishful thinking.

"How much does she know?" Paulie's voice pulled me from my thoughts.

Lifting my cup, I took a sip before I answered. "Only about the rulers. If she learned anything from Robert, she's not telling. I do know something is weighing on her mind, but she won't admit it."

Paulie knew about everything that had happened. I had only spoken of it to him and Jonathan. At first they were furious; however, they'd agreed to keep silent. That was all I could hope for.

"Why are you hiding it from her? There's nothing to be ashamed of." He looked away.

"I'm . . . I don't . . . what if she doesn't see it that way? What if it's too much on her and she loses the twins?"

"Justin . . ."

My head shaking stopped him in his tracks. "I can't risk it. I won't hurt her. It would kill me to lose her, or worse, see her look at me differently."

"I watched her at the wedding when you two danced." Yeah, that got my attention. "She cares about you. If you wait too long, she may see it as a betrayal. It could do irreparable damage to your marriage."

Taking another sip, I tried to swallow down the lump that had formed in my throat. "After the birth, Minister Jeff said her feelings for me at that point should be in full bloom."

"Justin, have you told Minister Jeff about what happened?"

"Why would I do that?" I gasped, appalled at the idea.

"It might help . . . I – I . . . maybe he could help?" He shrugged.

"No, and that's the end of it. Why do you want me to rehash all of it? Is it not bad enough I lived it once?" My well-hidden anger seeped through.

"I'm sorry. I just wanted to help. If you don't want to discuss it, that's fine." He tried to smile, but I knew him well enough to know this wasn't the end.

After finishing our coffees in silence, we headed for a local jewelry shop down the street. Braley's carried only the finest pieces around. There I found an adorable charm of Big Ben's clock face. I wanted Alexia to remember this trip, in the event that we never came back. I also discovered a beautiful gold chain that matched the charm bracelet I'd given her the day after our wedding.

While we waited for them to be wrapped, Paulie floored me with his next statement. "Are you trying to buy her affections?" He cocked his eyebrow.

"Absolutely not. I'm hoping she'll see how much I care for her."

"And how do you feel about her?" I pursed my lips, deciding to tell him the truth.

"I love her," I admitted in a hushed voice.

He grinned. "I knew it. Have you told her yet?" I answered by shaking my head. "Justin, you can't keep hiding things from her. She'll say it back, I guarantee it."

Fighting the urge to wipe the smug look off his face, I put him in his place. "Of course she will, but she won't mean it." My growl certainly did the trick.

When the salesclerk Nickolas arrived with my packages, we made a swift retreat. Rushing through the raindrops that had started to fall while we had been inside, he let the conversation die out. Paulie must have realized my need for silence.

The quick ride back gave me the time I needed to plan how I wanted the evening to go. With it decided before we reached the house, I hoped Alexia would be happy. Paulie didn't complain when I asked him to pull over so I could bring home dinner: Chinese, one of her favorites. After a quick "see you in the morning," I hopped out and headed for the door. It was unlocked. Alexia never locked the door.

"Alexia, I'm back," I called up the stairs.

"I'm in the kitchen." I shook my head, smiling.

Walking down the hall, I investigated. "What are you doing in here?"

"Eating? Well, I will be once I find something I want." She pouted, looking in the refrigerator.

"How about a nice dinner with me?" I shook the bag, watching her eyes dance with delight.

"What's the occasion?"

I snatched it away when she reached for it. "Since when do I need a reason to bring my pregnant wife home dinner?" My taunting ended when she nearly tackled me to get at the food.

Releasing an evil cackle, she threw her head back and enjoyed her victory. It was short-lived; I chased her out of the room, down the hall, and up the stairs. Giggling, she dashed into the bedroom. Big mistake.

Stalking her around the bed, I reveled in the shocked look on her face. If she only knew how adorable she looked: her red hair swaying every time she dodged and weaved, hoping to avoid my grasp; the way her lips formed a perfect O when I got too close; and without a doubt, the way her bottom wiggled. When she tried to leap across the bed, it was her undoing. I pounced, dragging her down onto the mattress.

I grabbed her before she could bolt away. "Not so fast, Mrs. McNear. You're mine to love, and right now, I want to love you." To emphasize my point, I pressed my hardness against her.

"Oh, I see," she yearned, arching her back in search of more.

Without truly understanding why, our roughhousing had morphed into a slow, loving exchange. With the bag of Chinese food forgotten on the floor, I relieved my wife of the burden of her clothes. Searching out my lips, she let her passion run free. That was one thing I never wanted to change; she had always owned me, mind, body, and soul.

After making good on my promise and making love to my wife, we picnicked in bed. Hearing her sighing, content and rubbing her still-flat tummy, reminded me of what I had in my pants' pocket. Snagging them up off the floor from where I'd tossed them, I dug into the pockets and pulled out the two small, royal blue, wrapped tokens. Alexia eyed them carefully before snatching them from my palms.

"And what are these for?" She stroked the shiny paper.

"Mrs. Chesterfield, of course. I need to appease her jealous rage from seeing us together last week." I grinned while Alexia pouted. "They're for you, love."

"But, what did I do to deserve them?"

"Why do you have to do anything for me to buy you a present?" My feelings were beginning to be hurt as Paulie's earlier words came back to me.

"I'm sorry," she mumbled. "I didn't mean it that way. It's just, you buy me so much."

"Because I can, and I want to. Are those not good enough reasons?" I tilted her chin up with my fingers.

"Yeah, I just didn't get you anything." Her shoulders slumped.

"Are you serious? You want a list of everything you have given me since we said 'I do?' Because I have plenty of time to spell them all out. Do you want them alphabetically or by importance?"

"No, I get it. You're happy; you want me to be happy. I'm just saying I don't need presents to be happy." Once again, she fiddled with her gifts.

Pulling her close, I whispered in her ear, "Just open them."

When a smile crept across her flushed cheeks, she finally gave in and unwrapped the charm. "It's perfect," she hummed.

I slipped off her bracelet so I could add the newest emblem to it while she opened the chain. "Justin, it's beautiful, but you don't have to try to buy me. You already own me," she muttered my own reasoning back at me.

Reaching up, I pulled her down and locked our lips before pulling back just enough to mumble, "And you own me."

After clasping the chain around her neck and the bracelet back on her wrist, she cuddled against me, uttering our nightly prayer, and slipped off to sleep.

The following day, Jonathan's wedding flew by in a flurry of nonstop activity. I spent every moment that I wasn't doing wedding activities with Alexia. I kept a tighter rein on her at the wedding. Abigail wasn't going to get another chance at talking to her if I had a say in the matter. The night whirled by with us dancing, eating, and snogging. Everyone had been smitten with Alexia. She drew people in and captivated them, as she had me. The only difference was that, at the end of the night, she went home with me.

Before I knew it, the last two days of our trip had breezed by and we were rushing for the airport to head home. That was one thing that the trip had confirmed for me: Minnesota and Alexia were my home.

CHAPTER 16

ALEXIA MCNEAR'S DISARRAY

In the two weeks since our return from England, so many things had changed. With early September came the beginning of school, and with it, a lot of insecurities – mostly Justin's.

When my school schedule arrived, I knew he would be having issues with their requirements. I'd be required to take two on-campus courses. Pacing the cottage, I practiced how to explain that to Justin. He'd agreed to online courses during our honeymoon, but now with me being pregnant, I didn't see him agreeing so easily.

Justin still hovered, even after Dr. Michaels said everything from the last exam looked great. He couldn't stop himself from worrying.

Hoping to settle my nerves, I headed out onto the deck and walked down to the water's edge. The fresh air filled my lungs and instilled a sense of peace in my chest when I breathed it in. The soft September breeze blowing off the water caressed my skin in featherlight touches.

My serenity was short-lived when the sound of the sliding glass door drew my attention away from the serene beauty. "Sweetie, are you okay?" I hummed at the sound of his concerned question.

"I just needed to collect my thoughts before I showed you this." Pulling the letter from my pocket, I waved it above my head.

The clunking sound of Justin's Belvedere black dress shoes echoed behind me, his approach bringing with him his nervous breaths. Three months of marriage had taught me a few things when it came to reading his body gestures. With a slight tug, the paper slipped from my fingertips.

He slid down next to me, sighing, to read the letter.

"I see; and do you still want to go? Now? I mean, after the births you really won't have time for on-campus studies."

"When will there ever be time if I don't make time now?" Closing my eyes, I let him contemplate my theory.

"Honestly, I'd hoped we might have more kids . . . after . . . you know," he muttered.

Pursing my lips, I pondered his broken, unsure statement. I really hadn't considered having more children. In fact, I was still trying to figure out Justin's desire for the twins. If he wanted more, then it couldn't be about the contract clause, right?

"You really want more kids?" I whispered, almost afraid of the answer.

"Don't you?" He bowed his head, releasing a deep sigh. "I thought we both did."

I cupped his cheeks, causing his deep blue eyes to dart to mine. "I do, but you never said anything." I silently challenged him with my eyebrow cocked.

"We have a problem with communicating, don't we?" He blushed, his eyes still locked on mine.

"Let's work on that, starting now." I nodded, smiling.

Lowering his eyes to the water, he muttered, "Is it wrong to want you to be happy with me and our children?" Seeing him wince made me want to hold him, letting him know it wasn't wrong.

I hissed a deep breath before answering. "I am happy with you." I shrugged. "Are you happy with me?"

"Um . . . yeah, of course I am. Okay, the food's not the greatest, but I'm patient." He playfully nudged me with his shoulder.

"Since we're communicating, why are you holding back what happened at the retreat?" I knew I was pushing it, but I needed to hear about the atrocities from him.

"Alexia, please. I don't want you to wonder about what happened at the retreat," he groaned, his distaste evident.

"I don't have to wonder. Robert already told me." I shuddered out a heavy breath, fearing he would be upset with me.

"He what? Alexia, God, no!" His anguished cry echoed across the water, and I instantly regretted opening my mouth.

"Justin, please don't be upset with him. He thought I already knew," I pleaded.

Jumping to his feet, he screamed, "If I wanted you to know, I would have told you!" With that, he spun around and stormed off.

A shiver ran through me when he slammed the sliding door hard enough to make it quake behind him. His engine roared to life a few seconds after he'd barreled out the front door. There was no mistaking the sound of his tires peeling out on the gravel driveway.

Left alone, I clenched my eyes shut. Tears born of turmoil slipped down my cheeks. My hand fisted my shirt over my shattered heart. He didn't want me to know? He had no intention of ever telling me? I'd foolishly thought that he had opened up to our marriage. I had been wrong.

Never moving, I stayed frozen on the deck. As the hours passed, I watched the sky slip from a pale blue to pitch black. The moon reflected around in the sky above. Feeling the cool evening breeze nipping at my exposed flesh still couldn't force me to wander back inside. There was nothing in there I needed.

A sudden thought occurred to me: there was someone I could talk to. I quickly stood, and then I realized just how long it had been since I'd moved. Every joint ached when I stretched them. After a brief stop at the bathroom, I grabbed my black Coach bag and headed for the door. Stumbling in the darkness, I made my way to the car.

Justin had replaced my SUV after it had been wrecked in the accident with the same make and model. Climbing in brought back the memories of the fight we'd just had earlier that evening.

Moving on autopilot, I cruised toward the one person who might be able to comfort me. By the time I pulled up in front of his house, my tears had started falling again. He saw me coming and had the door open when I reached the stoop. His gentle smile faded when he drank in my appearance.

"Alexia, what's wrong?" His forehead wrinkled.

"I need . . . can we . . .? He left . . ." I sobbed.

"Come in and explain everything." He stepped aside, allowing me to pass by.

There was no denying the loving way he looked at me. It was his nature.

Clearing the lump in my throat, I started. "Minister Jeff, I apologize for intruding on your evening with your family." I whimpered, the emotions racing through me once again.

"You're not. Now, tell me what happened." He gestured for me to sit on the red velvet couch with him.

After a brief hesitation, everything started running from my lips. It took biting my lip to keep from spilling out about what Robert had said. I knew I should tell him, but I had no way of knowing if he was included in the sanctioning of what the retreat did to its charges. From the sadness in his eyes, he knew I was holding something back.

"Alexia, Justin wouldn't just storm away over you going to school. What aren't you telling me?"

Shaking my head, I huffed. "He'll be angrier if I tell you."

He sighed, frustrated. "Justin is a very private man. He's refused to discuss his experiences in England. You've seen how they treated him first hand. You know better than anyone outside of his family how they've looked at him, and that was the watered-down version. I've talked quite a bit with Minister Peter about how they shunned Justin. He's been trying to preach forgiveness to his flock, but progress has been slow. It's an ongoing battle for him to try to heal the community."

"It wasn't pleasant, but I tried to make him happier." I breathed, remembering all the time and energy we'd spent in his old room.

Minister Jeff grasped my knees, causing me to flinch. "Alexia, you and Justin have the most to deal with out of everyone in the congregation. Justin is determined to do anything and everything to make your marriage better. You need to be patient and give him space to do that. Can you do that for me?" Wringing my hands in my lap, I nodded.

Sniffling, I wiped away the salty tears that refused to stop falling. The whole experience had left me feeling weak and drained. When my eyes fluttered shut, I let them have their way. Slumping against the arm of the couch, I slipped into an uneasy sleep.

CHAPTER 17

JUSTIN MCNEAR'S RUNNING AND RAGING

The minute those words left her lips, the anger buried deep in my chest rushed forward. Robert had told her about the retreat! Bile threatened to creep up my throat while I tried to figure out how much he could have told her. My rage raced through me. I didn't even think about it before I hollered at her.

Jumping to my feet and fisting my hands at my sides, I ran, the urge to flee too great for me to resist. I stalked away from the only good thing I had in my life. Alexia.

With my world crashing down around me, I raced through the house and out the front door. I knew what I was running from, but I couldn't figure out why I couldn't stop myself from doing it. Even when I jumped into my car, all I could see were images of Alexia looking at me like the people I'd lived with in England did. She wouldn't learn to love me now. That dream had vanished the moment Robert had opened his mouth, letting his venomous words infect my relationship with Alexia.

Without thinking, I drove to my parents' townhouse. It wasn't until I found myself parked in their driveway that I realized I'd driven there in a rage-induced haze. Throwing my head against the rest, I clenched my eyes shut and let the misery wash over me.

The passenger door opened, startling me, and my mother slipped inside. Bordering on hyperventilating, I let her pull me toward her so my head rested on her lap.

"Justin, what's wrong?"

"He told her, Mum. He ruined it all! She'll never be able to see me as a man. I'll just be a broken boy to her." I cried.

"You're not making any sense. Who said what?" The way she stroked my forehead reminded me of the way she'd comfort me when I first came home after running away.

Before I could stop myself, everything fell from my lips. With the exception of a few gasps and sniffles, she let me pour everything that happened into her lap. I'd bottled it up so well, I'd really thought it would stay there.

The hours slipped by while I let her comfort and reassure me. I felt lighter than I had in months. With a renewed eagerness, energized and breathing easier, I wanted to search out my wife. I'd beg her to forgive me if I had to.

When I looked around, I spotted my father's car parked behind my mother's. The realization that my father must have walked by and seen us flabbergasted me. "I won't say anything to him. You can tell him when you're ready." Looking up, I noticed her face held the telltale signs of tears.

Wiping them away, I whispered, "I should go home. Alexia must be out of her mind with worry."

Grasping my hand, she squeezed it tightly. "Tell her, Justin. Alexia will see you as the man you are. She cares about you deeper than you know. I've seen it when she looks at you."

"I'm not ready, but soon; after the twins are born, maybe," I mumbled, starting my car.

"Okay, call me if you need to talk. I'm here for you, no matter what." Leaning in, she placed one kiss on my cheek before she left the car, and me, behind.

Flipping the car into reverse, I backed away, not waiting for my mother to enter the house. Passing the houses while I drove, I wondered how many families had dealt with the impact of the retreat. Abigail's comments came back to me. Like us, she and Robert had to heal from the same pain. Shaking my head, I let go of the feelings of anger toward him. He was just trying to survive the pain.

An uneasy feeling settled in the pit of my stomach when I pulled into the drive and found the cottage dark. My unease turned to fear when I entered the house, and the eerie quiet had me panicking. Good Lord! I prayed she was asleep and not out on the deck still. Flashing on the lights, I moved through the house. My heart crashed into my gut when I discovered that Alexia wasn't in our bedroom.

I ran to check the deck. A renewed anger swept through my body and soul when I realized she was gone. Racing back through the house, I finally noticed her car wasn't in the driveway where it should have been. Again the anger amplified, causing my fisted hands to shake. Lashing out, I punched the back of the front door.

Reaching for my phone to call her parents, it rang in my hands. "Hello," I grounded out.

"Justin, it's Minister Jeff. Alexia came over earlier. She's sleeping now, but I will send her home in the morning . . ."

"No! I'll be right over to retrieve her," I snapped.

"There's really no rush. It can wait until the morning."

"I said I'll be right there. Her place is at home. Trust me, you don't want to get on the wrong side of this," I snarled, hanging up on him.

My heartbeat pulsed in my ears as visions of her in the minister's arms played out while I rushed for my car. I didn't ever remember being that furious before. It was not that I didn't trust my wife; however, after the retreat, I didn't trust the minister. The fact the he was married and had a son the same age as my sister held no meaning for me. His gender meant he posed a risk to my marriage.

Gripping the steering wheel, I raced toward his house and my wife. My Mercedes ripped into the driveway, screeching to a halt just before he walked out to greet me. His face showed that he was well aware of my anger with the recent turn of events.

"Justin, you need to calm down before you wake Alexia. She was an utter mess when she arrived," he spluttered, blocking my entrance.

Inching closer to his face, I lost it. "What did she tell you?" I seethed.

"Justin, why won't you entrust us with the truth about your time at the retreat?"

"That is none of your business! If I wanted to share it, I would have. And when I am ready, Alexia will be the one I spill my secrets to. Now, I want my wife!" I demanded, pushing past him.

"Of course, and when you're ready, I'll be here to talk."

There on the couch in front of me lay my angel, my wife, and the expecting mother of my children. She had no idea how much power she held over me. One day she would know, but for now it'd be another one of my secrets. Would I really be able to tell her about the retreat? Would she ever love me if she knew?

I sighed, moving toward the couch. After shifting her cast and her other arm onto her chest, I roused her slightly. "Justin?" she mumbled.

"Your place is at home." I tried not to sound angry, even though anger didn't cover the extent of my true feelings.

"With you?" she breathed, almost sounding like a question.

"Yes, with me," I grunted, lifting her from the couch. "Close your eyes. We'll talk in the morning."

Holding her close, I strutted for the door. Minister Jeff held it open before he followed me to my car, doing the same for the passenger side door. He sent me one last hopeful glance before ducking his head, leaving me to settle in next to Alexia. Kissing her hair softly, the gratefulness of having her back comforted me, but things needed to change. She wouldn't be allowed to vanish again.

While I drove to the cottage, Alexia slept. It would have been better if we had talked it out. By the time I pulled into the driveway, my aggravation had reached an all-time high. If she needed guidance and rules to govern her life, she would have them. She'd hate them and me, but if it kept my wife from going to Hell, so be it.

When the early morning light crept through our bedroom window, I hardened my expression and waited to deliver the message my wife would consider cruel and unjust. If the generations of women before her could live with the rules we believed in, so could she. It was more than improper for her to be in the home of another man without her husband; it was deplorable.

This time, when she opened her eyes, there was no soft, snuggly Justin; she didn't see the gentle, easygoing man she'd married. Her eyes found me glaring at her. "Did you sleep well?" I fumed.

"Yes, did you?"

"Not a wink, since I came home to an empty house. I was just about to call your parents when the minister called. Can you imagine how it felt to to retrieve my wife from the home of another man?"

"You left first. You stormed away!"

I clenched my eyes, pulling away and leaving our bed. "You had no right to talk to Robert about the retreat. I bet you couldn't wait to spill it all to Minister Jeff."

"What? Why not? Why would it be so wrong to confide in Minister Jeff? Why won't you talk to me about it?" she sputtered.

Turning my back to her, I refused to answer her questions. Truth be told, I didn't know the answers. I knew from her shaky breaths that she found my silence disturbing. She had no idea what I was about to hit her with.

"You're not going to school on campus. It's apparent you have spent too much time with the outsiders. Cancel any plans you have to leave The Gates. From this moment on, anything you need from the outside I will provide, including your food shopping and such." Grabbing my clothes, I made a beeline for the door.

"Justin, wait!" She scampered out of bed.

Spinning quickly, I let lose "No, you listen; your corruption ends now! It's too late. This conversation is over." I left her standing in the bedroom looking baffled.

Making a beeline for the bathroom, I slammed the door behind me. The reflection I saw in the mirror was no longer my own. I didn't even recognize the man I'd become. My hands shook when I splashed cool water onto my face. Alexia moved about the house while I remained locked behind the door getting ready.

After a quick shower and shave, I dressed in my faded jeans and a white T-shirt. There was no way I'd be able to go to work today. By the time I left for the kitchen, Alexia had gone outside and started walking along the shore. Torn between staying and going to her, I was left struggling for what would be best for our marriage. The pull to follow her won out. I found her skipping stones into the water near the edge. Giving her the space she needed; though I didn't hide, I was behind her.

"Alexia, what are you doing?" My tone now softer than before.

"Nothing," she uttered, dropping the remaining stones to the ground.

Without another word, she skirted by me and headed home.

Grabbing my sketch pad and pencils from the tool shed, I ducked into the woods to the right of the house. I still hadn't showed her the pictures I'd drawn of her. Nestled in the trees, I watched her prancing around the house, oblivious to my watching. I plopped down on the newly fallen leaves, flipping the pad open and retrieving a pencil from the pouch. Pressing the pencil to the paper, I closed my eyes and drew. My feelings flowed through my hand as I gave myself over. It didn't surprise me when I opened my eyes and discovered I had drawn her again. My emotions were too much of a mess to try again, so I headed back and re-hid my pad in the shed. Once back in the house, Alexia continued to ignore me.

~*~

I wanted her to come to me on her own accord; I didn't know it would take two weeks before she'd be willing talk to me. For two excruciating weeks, all I received were one word answers muttered from her lips; every one of them tearing further into my heart. If the cost of keeping her meant I had to suffer for the rest of my life, I'd do it for her.

In that time, she had discovered my sexual need for her, but now she rolled away from me. She would shudder and move away if I touched her in any way, even stroking her silky hair on her pillow. Two weeks to the day of our fight, I crumbled. I couldn't take the hatred I saw in her eyes every time I tried to mend the bridge I'd burnt down with my words.

After saying our prayers alone for yet another night, I lay in the dark, letting the crushing pain envelope me. My chest heaved, forcing me to sit up and struggle to breath. I couldn't do it; I couldn't hide the pain. So, I let it go.

CHAPTER 18

ALEXIA MCNEAR'S MENDING BRIDGES

The last two weeks had been the hardest fourteen days I had ever lived through. I avoided Justin at all costs, only speaking to him when he asked a direct question, even going as far as avoiding my friends and family. There was no one I wanted to share in my pain. Every ounce of my energy went to holding myself together. On more than one occasion, I found myself slipping away to cry alone. The weight of his rejection hung heavily on my heart. Even after I cried myself out, I always managed to find more.

When Justin went to work, I spent my mornings in church. Minister Jeff finally gave up trying to speak to me about what had happened after the night I'd searched him out. Nowadays, he watched from a distance. His worry for me was etched on his weary features, though I found no relief in it.

Turning away from Justin nightly, I hid the fact that I wanted him to touch me. Even though I knew he wouldn't give in to his desires for my flesh; I missed the way he held me close, the way he would lead our prayers, and the way he'd once cared for me after my car accident.

I thought I had known what to expect from him, until I found him sitting on the edge of our bed in the dark, his head dropped into his hands and his shoulders shaking. The stifled sounds of his heartbreaking sobs overwhelmed me. Like it or not, I couldn't stay away from him any longer. I needed to try to show him that if he wanted me one day, I'd still be there for him.

Crawling up behind him, I wrapped my arms around him. "Justin," I sighed against his naked body.

"I've lost it all," he wretched.

Shaking my head, I clarified it. "You haven't lost anything."

His retort caught me off guard. "How can you say that? I've lost you, and any chance I had of us being a happy family."

My eyes filled with tears at his hidden fears, even if they were incorrect. "You never lost me. When you want us again, we'll be here waiting for you."

"I'm broken. You hate me now. I can see it when I look at you. You'll never want me again," he rebutted, his voice cracking under the strain of his emotions.

Rubbing his tense shoulders, I explained, "I've never hated you. I hated what they did to you. I always want you, both in my bed and in my life. You're my husband and the father of my children."

He winced, whining, "I need to tell you what happened, don't I?"

"I can't help you if I don't know," I whispered in a voice raspy from choking back my own sobs.

He nodded before he shared what happened, "Everything at the retreat went well until the week of retraining. It was the worst thing I've ever been through." Shaking his head, he sniffled. "The rulers were just the beginning. They – they . . . put these things around . . . oh, God!" He spun in my arms and buried his tear-streaked cheek into my neck. "They said we needed to learn to control ourselves. That every drop from our loins was made purely for procreation." His body rattled with a new vigor.

He couldn't continue through his sobs, but he didn't have to. Robert had described the trapping devises that had been placed on the men. Holding him tight, I hummed and rocked him.

Once he calmed enough, he continued, "Night after night, they made us stand facing the wall in the lavatory naked with our arms out in front of us. The first night, Robert dropped his arms, and they beat him. Can you believe they went as far as to kick him while he thrashed on the floor? I wanted to hit them, make them stop, but then they'd go after me. Maybe if I fought for him, I might have been able to do something . . ." He choked back a new round of gasps.

"And it wasn't just us. We could hear what the women endured. They were forced to sit for hours with an aspirin trapped between their knees. If they let the tablet fall to the floor, they were smacked across the face and forced to do it again. Do you know how helpless we felt listening to that night after night?"

I stroked his messy brown hair, trying to soothe away his pain. Nothing I could do would erase those memories. The best I could do was help him see that it hadn't been his fault.

"There wasn't anything you could have done, Justin. You were fighting for a chance at a wedding contract. Was it not God's word to take a wife, to be fruitful and multiply? You were only doing what God asked you to do." I kissed from his ear to his jawline, tasting the salty remains of his tears.

"Alexia," he moaned, capturing my lips in a heated exchange.

Dragging me by my hips, he pressed his desire against my stomach. "My touch doesn't repulse you?" he panted after pulling back.

Pushing my castless hand into his hair, I pulled his lips back against mine and mumbled, "Never. If you had fought them, we wouldn't be here, married, with children growing in my womb."

With open-mouthed kisses, he searched out my ear. "It's not wrong to want my wife?" It was a rhetorical question.

"No," I gasped, when he slipped his hands up my thighs, searching out what was hidden beneath my cream-colored silk chemise.

"You're panty-less?" Throwing my head back, I mewled when he stroked my intimate apex. It had been far too long since I had felt the connection between us. "I'm constantly being mocked by my faith," he panted. "It seems determined to keep you from me," he uttered, lowering the thin strap that held my nightgown in place.

Shrugging the strap off, I tempted him to let go. "No, Justin. The only thing keeping me from you is you. Stop pushing me away."

With his gaze locked on my exposed breast, he said the only thing I wanted to hear. "I promise, I need you . . . want to make love to you." He guided us back on to the mattress.

"Please? I've missed you," I begged.

My head lolled to the side when he attacked my neck again with his lips. Sucking and nipping, he marked the sensitive spot. My back arched as he slipped one of his fingers into my molten core. The moistness there sent him into a frenzy. Before I could react, his hips slid into place, and he glided into my center.

This time when he made love to me, every ounce of his passion shone through; the restraint he'd shown before in our lovemaking, now disappeared. My skin relished in the feel of his energy pouring from his body. In those moments of connection, everything disappeared, leaving only us behind.

With erratic hip thrusts, he released, spluttering, "I – I – I need you, forever." I surrendered any doubts I had for our future, knowing no matter what else happened, we would survive; we would be a family.

"Me, too," I screeched, my release rushing over me at the same time.

With our bodies spent, we folded in around each other, struggling to regain our normal breathing. In the quiet darkness, I let him know what I really thought about him.

"Justin, I want you to know, I've never thought of you as a broken boy. You're every bit a man." His sigh fanned across my damp skin.

Drawing lazy strokes on my stomach, he apologized. "I'm sorry I didn't tell you before. After being rejected by everyone, except those closest to me, I didn't think you'd be able to accept me if you knew. I don't ever want to lose you."

"You won't. Your past is like an old book; you've read it, now move on to the next one. I promise you this one has a happily ever after," I vowed, snuggling into his side.

"Alexia, can we talk more about this tomorrow night? I think I've had . . . too much. Maybe we can revisit you going to school next year. It was wrong for me to forbid you to leave The Gates." He hugged me tighter with a sigh slipping from his lips.

"Will you go with me tomorrow to have Dr. Michaels remove my cast?" A change of subject seemed like a good way to take his mind off everything he'd revealed.

"I'd love to, but after, I'm taking you out to lunch. Consider it a date." He chuckled for the first time in weeks.

CHAPTER 19

JUSTIN MCNEAR'S GIVING THANKS

The months slipped by, and before we knew it, Thanksgiving had arrived.
No doubts remained about how I felt for my wife. I loved her with every
fiber of my being. After our talk about what had happened at the retreat, I
didn't have to hide anything from Alexia, yet I still couldn't bring myself to
tell her I loved her.

As we walked into services at church, I no longer looked around to see
if someone was shooting me a despairing look. I held my head high and
escorted Alexia to the pew we always shared with her parents. Kat and
Chris greeted us with open arms before we all took our seats. My mum
waved from where she sat with my dad and Krista. Minister Jeff started his
reading of the scriptures while he walked from the back of the church,
lighting the pillar candles at the end of each pew.

He stopped and smiled at me. After I'd told Alexia about the retreat,
together we talked to Minister Jeff. I'll admit it had relieved me that he had
no idea of what had been happening there. You couldn't fake that sort of
reaction. For a minister, he had a fire in his eyes. I might not have been
raised at The Gates, but I was one of his flock. I only hoped he never
encountered Minister Mark.

He looked down to see my right hand resting on Alexia's baby bump
and my left hand wrapped around her shoulders. The tiny bump had just
arrived last week. With it came a new pride, knowing I'd created the tiny

souls that were due in mid-April. Their sexes meant nothing to me, as long as they were healthy.

Just when the minister reached the altar, a slamming sound from the front door dragged everyone's attention to the scene behind us. Alexia gasped when in staggered a very drunken Brett. The congregation sat frozen in place, unsure what to do about his inebriated state.

"What the hell do I have to be thankful for?" he slurred, waving his bottle of Jack Daniels in the air, spraying the few parishioners in the back who hadn't moved away from their seats quick enough.

A mortified Alison rushed through the doors with tears streaking down her cheeks. "Brett, stop! You're drunk. It's not their fault!" she begged, trying to wrestle the bottle from his hands.

Still he zigzagged forward, dragging her along. "You're damn right I am! This – this . . . He hates us, so why should we love Him?" he chortled. "We lived by His laws, and in return, God left us barren. Two years – two years of nothing but heartache!"

It all made sense now. They'd stop taking our phone calls after they heard about the pregnancy. Alison slunk back away from his poisonous words. Seeing her heartbroken expression, he moved to take hold of her, but it was too late. In his haste, he knocked over a pillar, sending the flame into a silk banner that hung below it. The fire flashed alive and quickly moved onto the newly-varnished wooden pew where it hung.

Pushing a frazzled Alexia into the arms of her father, I left her standing there in shock and rushed forward to the rising blaze. Minister Jeff followed me down the aisle, shoving the members out of the way. "Fire! Everyone out! Justin, they're going up too fast!"

"It's the lacquer! The fire is using it as fuel!" I bellowed over my shoulder.

"Move now! Hurry!"

Jumping up from their seats, some people ran, some were dragged, and a few refused to move from the only house of worship they'd ever known. By the time we reached the fire-engulfed pew, it had spread to the pews in front and behind. I choked, inhaling the black billowing smoke. The sickening smell of singed lacquer filled my lungs. In the chaos, I lost track of my family and Alexia.

Together, Minister Jeff and I kicked over the blazing benches. Just then, I saw my dad and Chris each dragging the fire hoses from their stations in the wall. Jeff tried fruitlessly to cover his mouth, but he'd already taken in too much. Neither one of us could stop the hacking as our lungs retaliated from the intrusion. Gasping for air, we stumbled back.

"Look out, Justin!" my dad shouted. Looking up, I saw the licking tendrils of flames spreading across the ceiling.

In my rush to get away, I tripped over the debris and fell into a pew that had not yet caught fire. The cracking sounds could have easily been mistaken for the crackling of the fire, but from the pain I knew my ribs had broken when I'd landed against the edge of the seat.

Wincing, I grabbed my side and righted myself just in time to see the water spraying from the hoses. I looked around, and thankfully, all of the attendees had run for safety. My eyes stung from the heavy smoke that filled the church. Minister Jeff latched onto my arm, and together we fumbled our way toward the side exit. Tears rushed from my eyes, trying to wash away the smoke and soot. The lights flashed once and then blew out. The only light left was the illumination from the blaze that now engulfed half the church. Stumbling over discarded items and Bibles, we made our way to the doors.

"Dad, let's go!" I bellowed, but the sounds of the high-pressure hoses drowned it out.

"C'mon, Justin. They'll be right behind us." Minister Jeff shoved me harder through the darkened sanctuary.

Struggling, I pled over my shoulder. "Dad! Now!" That time he heard me. From his stubborn features, I knew he'd fight the inferno until the very end.

By the time we burst through the still-open doors, neither of us could walk. Instead we dropped to our knees, crawling and fighting for any air available. Coughing, I choked on every haggard breath I took. The volunteer firefighters rushed in to help extinguish the blaze now that everyone else was out, and they were properly suited for the job. Dr. Michaels reached us before anyone else could. Flipping me over, he went straight to listening to my lungs. He must not have liked what he heard, because before I knew it, he'd pulled a small oxygen tank from his medical bag. "Justin, this is a racemic epi." A white mist billowed from the bulbous device below the oxygen mask

Turning to Minister Jeff, Dr. Michaels applied the same apparatus to his face. Our matching whistling breaths continued. My throat constricted;

it felt like I was breathing through a straw. A tightening in my chest prohibited proper breathing. My ribcage strained each time I tried to inhale as if it was trapped in a vice, and a tingling sensation in my lips made me lick them fruitlessly to alleviate it.

"Doc, I feel so cold." My teeth chattered.

"Justin!" I turned to see Alexia struggling to leave her mother's embrace.

Lifting my arm, I reached out to her. The moment her mother let go, she dashed to my side. Dropping to her knees, she grabbed my hand and cradled it to her cheek. I hated seeing the tears flowing from her beautiful, gem-green eyes.

"It's okay, baby. Don't cry," I choked.

"You could have died!" she growled with her usual tenacity. "You promised to never leave me . . ." Dropping her face onto my shirt, she whimpered.

When I groaned from the pain in my ribs, she jumped back. It didn't escape Dr. Michaels's notice, either.

"Justin, I need to check your ribs." Without waiting for permission, he ripped open my blue dress shirt, exposing my shivering body to the cold breeze.

Pain radiated from my side when he applied pressure with his fingertips. The intensity of the pain would have dropped me to my knees if I hadn't already been lying on my back.

"I think it's safe to say you have broken a few ribs. I'll x-ray and tape them when we get to the clinic."

Patty, my mum, Krista, and Kat knelt next to us and watched the flames swallow the once-majestic building. Minister Jeff and Patty sobbed while clinging to each other. The structure groaned when the flames burst through the last remaining windows.

"Lexie, your dad?" Kat gasped.

Alexia looked too baffled to speak; instead, she whimpered and shook her head. My mum and Krista also realized my dad was still inside. "I tried – to get them – to follow us," I croaked, the mask blocking my mouth.

In a single instant, everything shook as the building imploded on itself. Flaming embers, soot, charred pages of our Bibles, and the screams of the parishioners filled the air. A second before the fire rushed out the door, my dad staggered out a different door, dragging Chris with him. Still embracing each other, they collapsed just feet from where we lay. Grabbing Alexia's hand, I kept her from following Dr. Michaels to our fathers' sides. If they were too badly hurt, I didn't want her last image of them being that of a marred body. She looked so torn when our families rushed over.

Silence replaced the screams as everyone held their breaths and loved ones waited to learn the fate of the three firefighters who had gone in to help. The seconds seemed like hours. Clutching Alexia's hand, I squeezed it in support. When cheers erupted, we knew the firefighters had emerged and were all right.

The murmurs of love between our parents brought a smile to our faces. Dr. Michaels said our fathers were lucky and had only suffered from smoke inhalation. Stroking Alexia's cheek, I knew we'd heal. Together, we'd rebuild.

Alexia helped me struggle to my feet when parishioner Shamus O'Neil's bagpipes started playing the sweet melody we all knew by heart. His daughter Tayla placed her hand on his shoulder and started singing the words that would unite our sorrows and hopes for the future.

Amazing Grace had always been Alexia's favorite song. More than once, she had hummed it when we were locked in our two-week struggle after the devastating fight we'd had in September. Those moments had held me together. The words echoed parts of my life; I was lost then found, by the woman humming them. My saving grace would always be Alexia. Holding her tight, we locked gazes, and she sang it from her heart to me.

One by one, every member of the congregation joined in singing. The only exceptions were those of us who couldn't, but our loved ones sang loud enough for us. Each member reached out and grasped the hands of their neighbors, family, and friends.

Mocked By Faith

CHAPTER 20

ALEXIA MCNEAR'S SAYING GOOD–BYE

It was a long night at the clinic. In one night, I almost lost Justin, my dad, and his dad, not to mention the other members of the church I'd grown up with. Exhausted and emotionally drained, I slumped in a chair a few feet from Justin in his room at the clinic. I shivered thinking about how it had felt to be torn away from Justin's arms when the blaze started.

Seeing him rushing toward the fire, I had screamed out, but he hadn't heard me. Against my will, my parents managed to drag me out the side door. My last glimpse of Justin had been him scrambling into the throes of the fire, a man on a mission. Minister Jeff had screamed, "Everyone out!" I'd watched the younger members dragging the elderly with them, instead of pushing them to the side. In a time of panic, you'd expect a stampede; however, that wasn't the case.

Even after we had gotten outside, we'd helped everyone to safety, and the parking lot became the hub of activity for reuniting family members. Even though it had warmed my heart to see so many families embracing one another, I'd feared the worst when it came to my own. Locked in my mother's arms, minutes had felt like hours while we'd waited for them to come out.

Mr. Barkett, Mr. Crane, and Mr. Mills had already begun to bulk themselves up in their fire-protective gear to go back in. They were fully trained and usually had little reason to don their firefighter uniforms. Tonight had been an exception, yet they'd held the same stature and professionalism any paid firefighter would. The Gates sat so far out that, by the time the town's firefighters could arrive, there would have been nothing left for them to do.

Moving back to the grass, we'd waited as a family with the LeBlancs and the McNears. Everyone had shrieked when the windows started popping out. Flying glass had littered the yard. I'd gasped when Minister Jeff had dragged Justin out, and they'd collapsed on the grass just a few yards from where we stood. My mother had initially fought letting me go, until she'd seen Justin reaching for me.

Dropping to his side, I'd clutched onto him while the doctor assessed his breathing. Even I could tell it wasn't what it should've been. The wheezing, crackling, and labored breaths had sent my anxiety through the roof. Raking my eyes across his body, I'd confirmed that he hadn't been burned. Not that scarring would've made me love him any less, but I'd wanted to be assured of his complete recovery.

My heartbeat didn't stop hammering in my chest until our fathers had stumbled out a mere second before a superheated flash of flames had us ducking to avoid them. I'd understood how my mother felt when she scrambled to my father's side. The draw to be near your husband outweighed everything else. When my mother had nodded, I'd known my family would be whole again.

As a community, we mourned the passing of our church with prayers, songs, and sob-filled embraces. We were the first to leave to go to the clinic. Pick-up truck after pick-up truck carried Justin, the minister, the firefighters, and our fathers up the hill to where the clinic sat nestled in the woods. Sitting in the back holding Justin's hand, I watched the town's fire trucks arrive. I had been right; they were too late to do anything but extinguish the last blazing embers.

In the wee hours of the morning, Justin summoned me to his side with a few flicks of his finger. By the time I joined him, he patted the spot on the bed next to him.

"You need to rest." Nodding, I crawled into his bed.

"How are my children? Do they need anything?" His gravelly voice was full of concern.

"Just sleep," I whispered.

"Alexia, I know I've never said how much you mean to me, but you're my everything. You're all I thought about when we tried to put out the fire.

As long as I have you, everything else will fall into place. Please don't ever leave me." He stroked my hair.

"Never; you're my everything, too." I wanted to finish with 'I love you,' but it stuck in my throat.

"Sleep, love. In the morning, we'll deal with the rest."

I slipped into a fitful slumber after Justin muttered our nightly prayer. It wasn't a restful sleep. Every time he would gasp or wince, my eyes would shoot open. Dr. Michaels usually smiled at me, trying to assure me everything would be okay. I'd never seen him look so tired. Then again, he had a full house.

Brett and Alison were also brought in. She really didn't have any injuries to speak of, but he would now wear a reminder of what he'd done. The angry red welts running up both his arms would always be a symbol of the devastation he had caused. As much as I wanted to hate them for what had happened to my beloved place of worship, I couldn't. They had been left barren by the God they'd loved unconditionally. They'd never planned for it to happen, but the pain coupled with his alcoholism had devastated everyone in the community.

There were no words to explain the profound sorrow that blanketed my heart. Every aspect of my life had been housed in that one building. My baptism into my faith, every holy sacrament I'd achieved, my wedding vows spoken at the marble altar, were now just memories. My children would no longer receive their holiest moments in life in the same place I once had.

Watching Justin sleep brought me the comfort I needed. With him by my side, we could weather anything. Justin woke when Dr. Michaels came in one last time to check his breathing. A soft smile crept across his face when the doctor had finished.

"Justin, I think it's safe to say you can go home. I'll give you something for the pain. Those ribs will need a few weeks to heal. Alexia will take very good care of you." He patted Justin's leg before leaving the room.

"That I will," I hummed.

No matter how exhausted or brokenhearted I felt, I'd always care for the man I loved. A selfless man, who had thrown himself between his family and the fire that had taken everything we loved. Justin thought he'd been broken, that I wouldn't want him, but that was the furthest thing from the truth.

"Let's get you home." I helped him sit up.

Last night, Dr. Michaels had taped his chest after the x-rays had revealed he'd broken two ribs on his left side. Pointing to the now-empty chair, he saw a clean shirt folded on it. "Where did that come from?"

"Patty brought everyone something to wear home." I shrugged.

"It will do. Has anyone said how bad it got after we left?"

I wouldn't look him in the eyes as I shook my head. There was no fight when he wrapped his arms around me. Ducking under his arm, I led him to the front just in time to see our parents exiting. I stepped back, letting him rush into his father's extended arms.

"You crazy old fool, you could have died!" He sobbed.

"Like father, like son. I couldn't let you stay alone. It was our church, too. We had to try to save it."

With tears falling from my eyes, I made my way over to my dad, hugging him. We didn't need words; we just knew they weren't required. Sighing, I released him back to my mother. Justin, too, let go of his father and walked back to me. Something passed silently between the three men when they nodded at each other. Dr. Michaels delivered the medication, and we all took our leave of him.

Lost in our own pain, we made our way down the road leading to the church, Justin's discomfort clear on his face while he exerted himself. I had expected silence on the walk, but all that could be heard were sobs and uttered prayers. Taking the corner, I understood why. We froze when the devastating sight before us became apparent.

There was nothing left.

"Justin!" I wept, holding my hand to my mouth.

Pulling me further into his arms, he cried, too. Everyone did. Tears poured down my cheeks and onto Justin's shirt. My soul screamed to the Lord to give us back what had been stolen.

It had all been taken from us. Before us sat the mound of charred rubble that had been our beloved church. The still-smoking embers now mocked our faith. We'd never believed anything would bring down our church, but now we knew that anything was possible.

Clutching his borrowed shirt tighter, I begged, "Please take me home."

"I'd do anything for you," he vowed, placing a kiss on my salty lips.

Wiping the tears from his cheeks, I kissed his lips in appreciation. The salty mix tingled on my mouth. I led him to the car and settled him in. He usually insisted on driving, but not today. I'd be taking care of him this week.

And that's exactly what I did. Once home and in bed, I waited on him hand and foot.

~*~

Saturday dawned earlier than usual. Feeling the cold sheets, I discovered Justin was missing. I rushed from the bed in search of him. I didn't find him until I ventured out the back door and discovered him lying on the lounge chair. Panic rose in my chest when I saw the familiar brown sketchpad resting on his chest.

"Justin, why are you looking in my sketchpad? I don't . . . ."

"It's not yours; it's mine. I told you on our honeymoon that I like to draw. I'm done with keeping secrets. Life is too short to not live it fully. So," he sighed, "promise not to hate me?" He held it out to me.

"Why would I hate you . . .?" I gasped, flipping it open.

Looking over the water, he choked, "Because they're all of you, or parts anyway." Flipping the pages, I couldn't believe my eyes. There sat literally page after page of just my eyes. The first few pages contained a simpler version, but the further I ventured in, the more realistic they became. Finally by the end, he had started drawing full facial expressions. The last drawing in the pad was of me cradling my swollen stomach.

"Justin, they're beautiful. You did remember me. I wasn't one-hundred percent positive." I sniffled, tears seeping from my eyes.

"They don't do you justice. No, I never forgot you." He tugged on my hand, asking me to join him.

Scooting onto the side of the lounger, I wrapped myself around him, careful not to touch his side. He sighed into my hair before kissing his way down my cheek to my lips. My eyes fluttered shut when he locked our lips together in a passionate display of affection.

Pulling back, he whimpered. "I wish I could do more."

"I don't need more." I whispered.

"Why don't you call everyone to come over? We could use the distraction." He laughed then groaned, holding his side when he felt the pain.

Ginger and Madison were thrilled when I called and asked them to help me cook up a few weeks of meals. They also were in need of a distraction after the loss of the church. While we cooked, we reminisced about our first communions, confirmations, and wedding vows. More than once, we broke down and cried, holding each other. Madison carried a heavy guilt over her family's role in the destruction, but we never blamed any of them.

Johnny and Joey entertained Justin while we worked. The men dealt with the loss in their own way. Justin took out his heartbreak on a sketchpad, Johnny stared out at the water, and Joey cracked jokes. Their reward of a great dinner kept them happy.

By the following Friday, Justin was on the move again, slower than usual, but ready to resume life. Friday night, we held a community meeting in the cafeteria of our old school. When we walked in, everyone smiled and resumed their strategy planning. I joined the women at the refreshment table while Justin dug into the discussion on rebuilding. A smile crept across my cheeks when he pulled out the portfolio we'd brought.

"Once we have new plans drawn up, we'll have to start removing the debris. It's a hazard to leave it the way it is," my father cautioned.

"I have something I was hoping you would consider." With that, Justin opened the black leather case.

"What's that, son?" James's interest was piqued.

"They're drawings I made of potential plans. Pieces from the three churches in our communities all blended into one. I'll understand if you don't like them. I had a week in bed, and it felt right to draw them." Minister Jeff grabbed the first off the stack and ogled it.

"Justin, these are wonderful. I say we all pick our favorites, and then we can cut it down from there." Coming from James, that shocked me.

"Agreed, and Justin? Thank you. You've shown me over the last few months that my trust in you wasn't wrong. You're every bit a member of this community," my father praised.

Looking at me over his shoulder, Justin's cheeks flushed. Together they excitedly chattered about which renderings they liked best. In the end, it came down to the top three. By the time everyone arrived, the drawings were prominently displayed on a table at the front of the hall.

"They're beautiful," I gushed, slipping up behind Justin.

"Not as beautiful as you." Justin laughed, hugging me. "Come on, it's time for the meeting."

Minister Jeff led us in prayer before starting the meeting. The promised couples were hit hard by the loss of the building that would've been where their weddings should have been held. However, seeing the new designs that had been proposed, their eyes lit up with a new hope. By the end of the meeting, a design had been chosen. Everyone pledged anything they had, from time to build to the funds needed to do the work. Our church would be rebuilt, and in His name, our Lord, we'd worship the faith we loved.

Mocked By Faith

CHAPTER 21

JUSTIN MCNEAR'S MORE FORGIVING THAN ALEXIA

One week and one day after the planning meeting, the construction vehicles rolled into The Gates. We were lucky enough to have a construction company owner in our closed community. Since we were supplying the bulk of the laborers, Henry Atwood had agreed to do the job at cost; but even then, the costs would be astronomical. He'd agreed to pull all the men he had working on the shopping plaza where Madison and Joey's hair salon would be.

Kicking the debris at my feet, I couldn't help but feel devastated by the destruction that had been left behind. Nothing could be salvaged. Brett looked even more destroyed while Alison held him in her arms. His shoulders slumped in defeat, knowing everyone blamed him. He'd never intended his tirade to result in the loss of our sacred place of worship. Financially, his donation covered more than half the cost of the rebuild, but it brought him no peace of mind.

Alexia and I had never realized our happiness had tortured Brett and Alison. We should have, but we didn't. The joys of having twins fogged our judgment. We'd walked around flaunting something they were desperate to have. This morning, Alexia fretted over what to wear. She didn't want anything that would show off her bump. Even though I knew she wasn't ashamed of the twins, she feared she'd be rubbing it in the faces of those who didn't have them.

Looking around, I recognized the hate-filled glares that were upon Brett and Alison. They were the same ones I had received in England after my return. I'd never wish them upon anyone. When would people learn that inflicting more pain served no purpose?

Alexia's hand slipped from mine, and she began to walk toward them. Grabbing it back, I let her know I wasn't okay with her going to them. Instead, I held her in my arms, and we walked toward them together. Brett and Alison cringed when they saw us approaching, no doubt waiting for the onslaught of abuse to flow.

Without a word, I pulled them to us in one hug, letting them know we still loved them. Brett buried his head into my shoulder and poured his pain out.

"I didn't mean any of it! Alison's cycle started that morning, and I lost it. I can't give her what she needs. She's going to hate me for it one day — if she doesn't already."

"No, she won't. We'll find a way to make it happen. There are options, even adoption."

Alison clutched onto my wife, nodding.

"See, if she's open to giving a home to an unwanted child, half your battle is won."

His eyes drifted to his wife.

"Yeah? If we can't . . . you would?" he gasped.

"It would be ours. Maybe that's what God wants?" She looked at him with the same puppy dog eyes that Alexia used to melt me.

Looking over Brett's shoulder, I was surprised to see my family making their way to our sides, followed by Brett and Alexia's families. My uncle's family and their wives joined us next, each of us pulling more into our group embrace. Before we knew it, everyone else had merged in, including those who'd been glaring. Tears fell while we took comfort from one another.

Wiping away his salty streams, Minister Jeff proclaimed, "Let's get to work. We have a new church to build."

Moving away, Alexia and I followed our friends and families to start removing the charred remains. At my insistence, she manned the water and food table Patty had set up with donated sandwiches and baked goods. Wiping the sweat from my brow, the sight of my wife welcomed me every time I took a break. The pain in my ribs still nagged at me when I strained, but it was worth every wince.

With all the crashing, sawing, and grunting, no one heard the rumbling diesels until the two yellow school buses banked the corner and pulled into the lot. Everyone dropped what they were doing and started drifting toward them to see why they were there.

When Minister Peter hopped out of the first bus that had parked at the edge of the car park, cheers erupted. I didn't hesitate to rush over when Paulie and Jonathan followed him out. They were a sight for sore eyes. Our English community disembarked to the relieved sounds of their fellow worshipers.

My feet moved fast until I threw myself into their open arms. "We'll fix this, brother. It's what families do." Paulie sighed.

"I can't believe you blokes came." I gasped.

"You'd come for us, even after everything that happened. We love you, man!" Jonathan chuckled.

"Hey, Alexia. How are you?" Her tiny hands wrapped around my waist.

"Hi, guys. Sad," she answered, rubbing her baby bump, "but, okay."

"You're not serious!" I snarled, looking at the second bus unloading.

"He insisted on coming. Minister Peter tried to talk him out of it."

Snapping her head between me and the minister, Alexia gaped. "Is that . . .?"

With a lump the size of a grapefruit lodged in my throat, I nodded with my jaw slack. Before I could see the signs, she bolted in his direction. Forcing my feet to move, I raced after her with my chaps right behind me. Alexia reached him first, her body language screaming.

"You!" Her slap across his face drew the attention of everyone. "How could you?" she seethed.

"Who do you think . . .?" He raised his arm, and that was it.

"Touch her, and deal with me!" Minister Jeff bellowed.

"She hit me!" He actually looked offended.

"You lay one hand on my wife, and it will take every man here to peel me off you!" I roared, pulling Alexia behind me.

"So your wife has as little control as you did." He smirked.

"Talk about my daughter again, and it won't be Justin you have to worry about," Chris snarled, pushing us both behind him.

Cupping his reddened cheek, he bit back, "She hit me and you're defending her."

"After what you did to us, you're lucky it's only her hitting you," Robert sneered, getting off the bus behind him.

"What am I missing here?" Minister Peter looked taken aback.

"We'll talk about this in private," Minister Jeff grumbled, dragging Minister Mark away before a riot could break out.

I had one last demon to face. "Robert, I'm sorry I didn't help you at the retreat. I should have . . ." Without waiting for me to finish, he embraced me.

"There wasn't anything you could do. Abigail helped me see that." He patted me on the back.

"Okay, enough lovey crap." Crazy Eight cackled.

Pulling Alexia close, I devoured her lips. When she moaned, I slipped my tongue in. Her hands dug into my hair, tugging on it. An adorable whimper slipped from her lips when I ended it.

"What was that for?" she panted.

Whispering in her ear, I explained for her alone. "Seeing you stand up for me, yeah . . . what a turn on." I laughed.

She blushed rosy when I brushed her cheek with my fingers. Her swelling chest heaved when she sighed. My soul filled with pride, knowing I could send her reeling. Chuckling at her reaction to my closeness, I rejoined the men working on the disposal. Ducking her head, she grinned and made her way back to her station.

In a few short hours, we had succeeded in removing all the debris with the help of a backhoe loader. By dinner time, the ladies had rolled out the heavy-duty food. Pulling out blankets, we all sat about picnic style. It gave us time to catch up with Paulie, Jonathan, and Robert.

"Thanks to Alexia here," Robert pointed to my wife, "Abigail is due in early June," he boasted. "I took her advice and talked about what happened. Minister Peter was quite livid, but between him and Abby, I'm working through it all." His natural, relaxed smile proved it to be correct.

"Yeah, things are a lot easier now that I don't have to hide it anymore." I squeezed Alexia's hand in mine.

"I planned on calling you the night of the fire; we found out Danielle is due, too." Paulie flushed crimson.

"Congratulations!" I punched him in the shoulder.

Looking up, I saw Ministers Jeff, Mark, and Peter coming back from the school. Minister Mark looked defeated and irritated; not a very good combination. Snagging Alexia by the arm, I ensured she wouldn't attack him again.

"Robert, Justin, could we have a word with you two alone?"

Alexia hissed at them.

"Relax, love." Her eyes softened when she shifted her attention from them to me. "Nothing will happen, and if it does, Robert and I will handle it together this time."

Robert nodded his agreement and set his jaw.

"We got her. You handle this." Paulie slid closer, holding her shoulder after waiting for me to nod.

Alexia looked ready to rip Minister Mark's head off. Honestly, with her hormones, she might have. I grimaced, releasing a groan when I lifted to my feet. We followed the three heads of our church to the chapel in the school. It was hard to believe we'd all fit in there for Sunday Mass, not that we had any other choice. Then again, knowing the husbands here, we would have sat with our wives and kids on our laps to make sure everyone fit in the tight confines.

Just entering the room with the same man who'd made our lives hell had my heart pounding in my chest. I tried to look inconspicuous when I wiped a slight sheen of moisture from my brow.

No one spoke until the doors shut, sealing us in. "We've discussed this with the other two ministers at the retreat. Minister Chan will be taking over for Minister Mark permanently. He wasn't involved, correct?" Minister Jeff looked to us both to answer.

Shaking my head, I replied, "No, his portion of the retreat helped me the most. His teachings showed me that I needed to believe in my parents' ability to find me the right wife, and they did as he'd promised."

"Yeah, his preaching on why we should wait hit home, and once I returned, Abby and I didn't have any more problems holding off until our wedding." Robert blushed.

"Everything I did made you better men," Minister Mark retorted.

I restrained Robert before he pounced on him. "Better men? I couldn't even take my wife on our wedding night! Three days, that's how long it took to finally consummate our vows. Do you know how that felt? Abigail thought I didn't want her. Where were you when she cried for three days straight? Everyone in our community thought I was gay. Where was your brilliant training when I couldn't make love to her to get her pregnant?"

"Easy, Robert. Think about the baby and your wife; she wouldn't want this to escalate," I said. His struggling ceased.

"You're right. Sorry, Ministers, I meant no disrespect to you." His shoulders slumped.

"We understand what you went through. I've counseled Justin, and Minister Peter has coached you. We each thought it to be an isolated incident; now we know it wasn't." Minister Jeff paced the marble floor before us.

"Others have come forward. After calling Ministers Chan and Walsh, they have confirmed the accounts. We had hoped to discuss this at our yearly meeting, but it can't wait any longer." Minister Peter bore the shame on his features. "If I had known this didn't start and end with your retraining, Minister Mark would've been removed long ago. He's decided to go on a long holiday."

Glaring at Minister Jeff, Minister Mark snarled, "Really didn't have a choice in the matter, now did I?"

"You need to seek forgiveness; only God can grant you redemption." Minister Jeff retorted.

"Are we done here?" I asked. "I want to take my wife and friends home."

"Sure. How are your ribs doing?"

Rubbing them, I felt the twinge aching. "After today, sore, but it's worth the pain. Come on, Robert, you guys are crashing at my house." I slapped him on the back.

For three weeks, we had a full house. Alexia made sure to have Ginger cook up trays of food for us. She tried to refuse my money, but I insisted. My cousin Johnny didn't make any money as a student, so they needed it.

It was a bittersweet day when our English friends left to return home for the holidays. We were saddened by the void they'd leave behind but thrilled that the exterior of the new church had been completed. That also meant I'd be returning to work.

CHAPTER 22

JUSTIN MCNEAR'S CHEATING WAYS

With one week to go before Christmas, the push was on at work. We had a lot of customers who loved to give their families cars for the holidays. When Mrs. Aldean walked in, I thanked my lucky stars. She'd been in twice over the last two weeks looking at different cars for her husband Scott. Even though I'd been on hiatus working on the church rebuild, I handled her and her husband's accounts.

I never expected the thirty-something-year-old woman to have a sixty-plus-year-old husband. Most of the men working at the dealership said she was a hottie, a looker, a babe, and every other expression they could think of to describe the long-legged, platinum blonde woman with light green eyes, but Alexia held all my attention.

I greeted Mrs. Aldean enthusiastically when she proclaimed she'd decided on one car in particular. She wore a victorious, painted smile when I told her the car she wanted was indeed still on the lot. Since she'd already test-driven it, I showed her straight to my office.

The paperwork would be the longest part of the process. Once completed, the only thing needed would be the bank's approval. Leaving her seated in my office, I ran over to the finance department. They had no problem getting her approved. Of course not; her husband ran a billion-dollar company.

Now, I just needed to assure her that I'd have everything ready for a Christmas Eve delivery. Looking up, I saw my father watching me with a proud smile.

Since my wedding, he'd really loosened up on his demands on me. He'd even shown his pride in me on more than one occasion. Between my design of the new church and the long hours at both the dealership and the construction site, he looked at me in a whole new light. The fact that in three short months he'd be a grandfather didn't hurt either.

Seeing Alexia waltzing around the house was better than any other sight in the world. I loved seeing her heavy with my children in her womb; her round center was now the center of my existence next to Alexia herself. Every day, her protruding tummy grew.

I still hadn't told her "I love you," even though I could not deny it to myself. I loved her with every cell in my body. My soul screamed for her when she wasn't with me. One day, I'd finally say the words, then hope and pray she would say them back.

Reaching over my desk for the keys, I never saw Mrs. Aldean moving to stand behind me. When she grabbed my arse, I almost lashed out at her, but I never had the chance. The sharp gasp behind us made me spin in her unwanted embrace. My eyes searched out where the sound came from; in the doorway stood my wife with my lunch in her hands. Her expression of horror screamed that she'd mistaken the unwanted contact.

Before I could call to her, she dropped the plate to the floor, sending the food splattering onto the gray rug, and ran out the door. Jerking away, I tried to follow her to the lot. Mrs. Aldean reached out, only to come up empty. For a pregnant woman, Alexia sure could move. She jumped into her SUV and flew out of the lot before I could get her to stop. Standing there dumfounded, I had no idea how to get to her before she told the Council of my supposed infidelity.

Grabbing my phone, I called Alexia's cell. It didn't surprise me that it went to her voicemail. My eyes started to sting.

"Justin, I called Minister Jeff and explained everything. He's headed to Chris's to try to stop this before this gets out of hand," my dad said. When he wrapped one arm around my shoulders, I crumbled.

"Why, Dad? I love her; I can't lose her!" I whimpered.

"I know, son. Let's go find your wife and fix this. Mrs. Aldean's being handled by Kim. She'll explain her patronage will no longer be welcomed here. Her husband will be very interested to know why we can't sell him any more vehicles." I slumped into my dad's Lamborghini.

I couldn't stop thinking of what I could've done to prevent this. Nothing made sense anymore. I knew at that moment, I'd never be happy without my wife and children. Surviving without them wouldn't be worth the wasted breaths I took. In the span of one minute, my life had fallen apart, and there wasn't a thing I could have done to stop it.

Lost in my thoughts, I never saw us approaching The Gates. From the disapproving sneers, I'd say the guards knew what had transpired between Alexia and me – or at least parts of it.

We drove by the Crosses' first, but their driveway sat empty. The cottage was a whole other scenario. We found almost everyone we knew standing in front of my house. There wasn't a pleased look on anyone's face when Minister Jeff tried to explain what happened.

"Folks, you all need to relax. It's not what you think!" He held his arms up, trying to gain their attention.

Dashing from the car the moment it stopped, I tried fruitlessly to gain access to the cottage. My darling cousins were the first to greet me. No greetings were spoken, instead they met me with a left cross from Joey. Yeah, it stung, but nowhere near enough to stop me from getting to my wife.

"Alexia! Please? Nothing happened!" I struggled against their bodies to break free.

"Justin!" she shrieked from the cottage.

From the fear in her voice, something wasn't right. When she waddled out clutching her baby belly, I rushed through the crowd just in time to catch her when she collapsed to the ground.

"Alexia, I've got you. What's wrong, sweetheart?" Stroking her stomach, I knew before she answered.

"The babies," she whimpered, tears slipping down her cheeks.

"Dad, call the doctor." Her father made the mistake of trying to pull her from my grasp. "Don't! I never cheated on my wife! My father is my witness. The witch touched me, not the other way around!" I raged.

"He's telling the truth. You can ask every one of our employees. Mrs. Aldean grabbed him, and before he could tell her to stop, Alexia walked in." My father managed better than I did to keep his voice calm.

"Justin, I believe you," Alexia gasped, curled into a ball on my lap.

"Dr. Michaels said to bring her to Small River," Minister Jeff demanded, already moving to open the back door of his green Tahoe.

Cradling her to my chest, I followed him, crawling in with Alexia on my lap. A free-for-all ensued when everyone fled to their cars to follow us. Chris and Kat were unfortunately the last to leave the driveway. They'd been blocked in by everyone else.

"I'm scared, Justin," Alexia sobbed.

"I know, love; me too. Try not to think about the pain. Praying will help you think about something else." I started humming her favorite hymn in her ear.

Kissing her forehead, I never stopped humming since it seemed to comfort her. When I started rocking her gently, she joined me in the hymn. As on the way home, I didn't even remember the ride to the E.R. Nothing else mattered to me when I was wrapped around my wife.

I tried not to let her see my hands shaking from the fear welling up in my chest. Half my fears were that I'd lose my children, and the other half were that I might lose my wife. How do you survive after losing either?

Dr. Michaels stood outside the E.R. when we pulled up. Donna had a wheelchair ready. I tried to keep my hold on her shaking form, but in the end, they won and I had to let her go. However, I did keep hold of her hand.

We quickly settled into a room, and I lifted Alexia onto the bed. It turned out to be the same room we'd first heard our children's heartbeats. Kissing her hand, I continued to hum to her.

We both froze when the doctor pulled out the Doppler scanner, lifting Alexia's top. When the whooshing sound began, even I could tell the difference; the rhythmic beats were softer, slower than I'd ever heard before. Dr. Michaels sighed, confirming the change. Donna lowered Alexia's shirt as they both shook their heads.

"Donna, process the admittance papers."

She simply nodded, slipping out of the room.

"I'm sorry to say it appears at least one of the twins didn't make it. We still have one strong heartbeat, so I can only hope that the other may survive. Alexia will have to stay overnight to ensure she doesn't hemorrhage. I'm so sorry." My heart sputtered in my chest.

Alexia screamed out in agony, "No! Justin don't let them take it from me!" Cradling her shaking body, I held her as close as I could without hurting her.

"They aren't taking anything from you, Alexia. It's not in their power to do that." Clenching my eyes closed, I let my tears fall as well.

Ignoring my own tears that slipped uninhibited down my cheeks, I wiped away Alexia's salty streams. Looking at me through her tear-soaked lashes, she appeared so young and innocent to me. If I could have saved her from the pain, I'd have done it in a heartbeat.

"Alexia, Minister Jeff has agreed to another ultrasound. The chance you may hemorrhage is too great to ignore," Dr. Michaels explained, wheeling in the necessary machines.

"Why? Did I do something wrong? Are we being punished?" Alexia cried, trembling.

Pulling her tighter into my embrace, we clutched onto each other, anchoring ourselves together. Kissing her hair, I sighed and waited for the explanation I needed to right my mind. I prayed for there to be a medical reason for our loss and not a spiritual one. If I'd done something to cause this, I doubted I could live with myself.

With bated breath, we waited for the machine to hum to life. Closing my eyes, I prayed we were wrong, and they were both okay. Releasing a cleansing breath, I steadied myself for whatever came next. Alexia shook harder when the doctor approached with the wand in his hand.

"Breathe, sweetheart. Look at me!" She snapped her head to meet my eyes. "That's right; keep your eyes on me."

Her breathing sputtered when the gel touched her skin, but she held my gaze. The only sound in the room came from the ultrasound machine. When the doctor sighed heavily, I couldn't help but look up. I wish I hadn't.

"It would seem it's a case of TTTS or Twin-to-Twin Transfusion Syndrome. The recipient twin took the blood flow from the donor twin through abnormal blood vessels in their shared placenta. There's nothing we can do now." Moving closer to the bed, his sympathy written on his face, he tried to comfort us. "This wasn't anyone's fault. It can happen to anyone. The other twin looks very strong. Pray for them."

"So what happens to the baby we lost?" Alexia's weak voice whispered.

"It will have to be delivered when you go into labor. I'm so sorry." He patted her leg, turning to leave. "I'll send in Minister Jeff and your parents."

"He could be wrong. What if . . .?" Shaking my head, I silenced her.

Cupping her cheeks, I directed her to look me in the eyes again. "No, God has him now."

"It was a boy?" she sobbed harder.

"He's in the arms of the angels." I heard the door open, but never shifted my attention away from my wife.

The room filled with the sounds of sniffling, whimpering, and the strokes of comfort. "Justin, Alexia?"

Looking up, I nodded for the minister. He didn't need any more prompting before he moved in, holding our hands together. Our parents all wore expressions just as pained as ours. They'd lost a grandchild. We laid our hands across Alexia's stomach, praying collectively with Minister Jeff leading the way. His words brought no relief; nothing could.

The prayer group continued until Donna came in with a syringe in her hand. "This will help her sleep. It's been a very traumatic day for ya'll." My wife nodded her agreement, laying back.

With hugs and kisses, everyone left us to our pain. She didn't even seem to notice when Donna injected her. That's when I noticed it. The dull, lifeless gaze of Alexia's eyes. She'd begun turning her pain inward. Crawling into her bed, I cradled her lithe form.

"Both our twins need us. We need to love them both. It's no one's fault that this happened. God didn't want to take him, but he did when he passed. He'll always be ours." When I stroked her cheek, her eyes fluttered shut from the medication.

We were moved to a regular room in the maternity ward. In the quiet hours after visiting had ended, I ventured out in search of the chapel. The night nurse pointed me in the right direction. Lost in my thoughts, I strayed by the nursery. That was my undoing.

My feet couldn't move fast enough for me. Barreling through the door, I staggered up to the altar and crumbled to my knees.

"Why? Why are you doing this to us? You made doctors we can't see to help us. You gave them the knowledge and the desire to cure, but not us. How is that fair?" I cried, shaking from head to toe.

"It's not." When Brett placed his hand on my shoulder, I collapsed against him.

"What are you doing here?" I choked.

"I knew you'd need me once you let yourself feel the pain. Knowing you, you stayed strong for Alexia." He assumed correctly. "C'mon, let's have a seat."

When I turned to follow him, I realized we weren't alone. In the middle of the first pew sat Minister Jeff with his hands folded on his lap. Releasing a sigh, I joined them both on the pew and prayed with them. I prayed for what I had, what I'd lost, and what I hoped for in the future.

Mocked By Faith

CHAPTER 23

JUSTIN MCNEAR'S MELTING DOWN

After departing the hospital the following day, everything changed.
Alexia refused to talk to anyone, including me. She cocooned herself in our
bed, avoiding everyone and everything. The only times she left the bed
were to use the bathroom. Her movements were almost robotic, the way she
walked there and back or opened her mouth to be hand-fed. She ignored the
doctor when he came to check on her, as if he wasn't there.

I hired Ginger to care for her while I worked. I couldn't sit home
watching her lying lifeless in our bed. Each night Ginger reported the same
words to me. "Nothing's changed." She would sigh, patting my arm and
slipping out the door.

In the beginning, I spent my evening hours watching her staring at the
wall. The pain in my chest threatened to suffocate me. Seeing her
completely withdrawn broke my heart, not that it wasn't already. The loss
of my twin son had done that job. Finally, it became too much.

Christmas came and went without Alexia's notice. She never even
opened her presents. They still sat under the tree I didn't have the heart to
take down. I started attending Sunday Mass alone. Minister Jeff did what
he could, but nothing reached through the walls she'd constructed around
her mind and body. Soon, I stopped attending Mass altogether. If someone
attempted to touch her, she cringed away, so I took up sleeping on the
couch.

By New Year's, I couldn't take it anymore and started heading to local bars with a few guys from work. They didn't care that I was underage. As long as they bought the drinks, the bartender never bothered checking my ID. They could see the pain I suffered from. It started slowly, one drink to numb the pain. Before long it stretched into two, then three. In my numbed state, I even let women throw themselves at me. I never cheated on my wife, but I never stopped them from flirting. I just didn't care anymore. Next thing I knew, it was the night before Valentine's Day and I stayed out, closing Cleo's bar.

How I made it home without totaling the car baffled me. Staggering into the cottage, I never expect the sight that greeted me. There before me stood every member of our families. I drunkenly snickered at the nerve of them to intrude into my home.

"What do you think is so funny?" my father snarled, pinning me against the wall behind me.

"You, that's what's funny!" I gurgled.

"You're drunk again. You're always drunk! Ginger's not your slave. It's not her job to take care of your wife!" Johnny snapped.

"Yes it is, that's what I pay her for." I chuckled.

"We know you're hurting . . ." Madison tried to comfort me.

I fisted my hands at my sides. "You have no idea how it feels!" I bit back, my anger rising.

"Yes, I do!" I gaped at Chris's admission. "Alexia wasn't an only child. Her sister, Alicia, died at birth."

My brain fumbled over his words. They knew what it felt like to lose a child. They'd walked in my shoes. Even in my inebriated state, things made more sense. Alexia had lived with the loss of her own twin and now our son.

"Why didn't someone tell me?"

"It's not something we announce to people. She knows because we, of course, took her to see her sister's grave every year on their birthdays." Kat clutched Chris's hand. "Even as a baby she knew something had gone missing."

Looking around the blurry room, I realized everyone knew. From their bowed heads and solemn expressions, it would be hard to miss. My father let me go, and I slumped against the wall. Knowing I had abandoned my wife when she needed me the most had bile creeping up my throat. Burying my hands deep into my hair, I tugged on it, trying to pull it from its roots. I needed to feel the pain. I'd been running from it, and I knew it. It had to stop. I had to stop.

No one could stop the dam when it broke. "I want my son back!" I screamed, feeling the tears starting to trickle down my cheeks.

"We know you do. You'll always want that. Nothing anyone says will fix that. You've heard all the crap people think will make you feel better. Every time someone said, 'It's God's will,' or 'God wouldn't do this if you couldn't handle it,' and of course, the dreaded, 'She was sick and is in a better place,' I wanted to punch them, too. No one understands unless they've been through it." Chris crossed the room, grabbing me into his embrace. "The truth is, it happens, and no one knows why. Alexia has it worse than anyone. She has to carry the child in order to give the other baby a fighting chance to survive. Can you imagine how that feels? I can't."

Gripping his shirt, I let out everything I'd bottled up inside me. I screamed, cursed, and whimpered everything I had held back for the last two months. It flowed out so easily. To be honest, I never gave any thought to how it felt to be my wife. What she was enduring was beyond my comprehension. It took hours to wretch out all the emotions that washed over me. When I finally calmed down, one by one everyone slipped out the door. Their job was done; I'd sobered up.

Walking into our bedroom, I studied my wife's form. Moving to her side of the bed, I discovered she had her eyes open. Our screaming match must have woken her. I knelt on the floor beside her. She didn't move when I slid the blankets down to see just how much her belly had grown. Scrunching my eyes shut, I sighed, placing my hands on her very extended stomach. That's when it happened.

Under my hands, a sharp kick followed by the flesh rolling over, my unborn child awoke my insides. A gasp rippled through my chest. Reality rushed in, causing my heart to race. I hadn't just failed my wife, I'd failed my unborn child. My eyes snapped open when I felt the tiny touch of Alexia's hand over mine. She locked her gaze onto mine, allowing a hint of a smile to grace her lips. I'd missed that smile.

"Alexia, I love you," I confessed. "I have for," shaking my head, "so long."

A single tear slipped from her right eye, rolling down her pale cheek. "I love you, too," she whispered.

Wiping away her tear, I begged her, "I'm sorry I haven't been here to help you through your pain. I was selfish. Can you find it in your heart to forgive me?"

She sighed. "I was so lost without you." Leaning in, I latched my lips to hers and let my feelings pour into her.

Pulling back breathless, I stroked her hair and pledged, "I'll never let you go again. I'll fight for you, for us." Unable to stop myself, I slipped onto her side of the bed.

"I missed you," she groaned, wrapping her arms around me.

"Will you be my Valentine?"

"Yes," she hummed, drifting off to sleep in my arms.

Sunlight filtering through the window roused me around noon. The first thing I noticed was my wife snuggling against me. It had been so long since I'd felt her heated flesh against mine.

"Good morning, sweetheart," I purred in her ear.

"Justin, where were you?" She avoided looking at me.

Tilting her chin, I let myself get lost in her emerald pools. "Lost, like you. I couldn't bear to see your pain reflected back at me."

She wrinkled her nose. "You smelled like alcohol again."

Sighing, I admitted, "I hid behind the booze to numb the pain. It was wrong, and I am so sorry."

"Are you . . . are you going to come back to our bed?" she mumbled.

"Yes, and I'm not ever going to leave it again. I missed feeling you beside me, praying with you, touching you." Sliding my hand up her soft, creamy thigh, I knew she'd missed it, too.

Her moist apex greeted my fingers like a long-lost friend. Pushing my hips against hers, I silently asked for her to touch me, too. With a little hesitation, she granted me my wish. What I really wanted was to make love to her, but it wasn't advisable. Dr. Michaels had told us that she could already go into early labor, and I wouldn't risk that happening. Still, since it was Valentine's Day, I desired to show her I loved her.

An adorable hum filled the room when I caressed her intimate flesh. I joined her in vocalizing my pleasure at the attention she paid to my manhood. Each loving stroke tightened the coil in my groin. After not touching each other for so long, it didn't take long before we were moving in tandem toward the precipice. The sight of her emotions flashing across her face drove away the months of blank stares, her old self breaking through and shining like the sunshine outside.

When she finally fell over the heavenly peak, I was there to catch her. Clutching her close, I joined her in moaning out and releasing. The sigh she gushed washed over me. Leaning our foreheads together, we panted our love to each other.

After a few minutes, the time came to move, even though I didn't want to. "Come with me." I slid out of the bed, bringing her hands with me.

"Where are we going?" she huffed.

"To the bathroom to clean up." She giggled when I wiggled my eyebrows.

Turns out, she needed help getting up. I'd missed so many changes. Her baby belly, now round and heavy, hung lower than I'd ever seen. The guilt reinvaded my heart. I had chosen to sleep one room away from her. She hadn't pushed me away; I had done that all by myself. I'd used liquor to avoid my pain and my wife. I'd never get those moments back.

"Justin?" She looked at me, supporting the twins with her hands beneath them.

I scrunched my eyes shut. "We can't go back. I screwed it up so badly; how can you still want me for a husband?"

She cupped my cheeks. "I left you, too. I hid from you. How can you still want me?" She cocked her eyebrow in challenge.

"Because I love you." I shrugged.

"C'mon, we need a shower," she turned and gazed over her shoulder, "and, I love you, too."

Wrapping my arms around her, we waddled to the bathroom. I released her and started the water. When I turned back, she stood before me naked. Seeing the distended womb that held the twins captivated me.

"You're exquisite," I gushed.

My hands quickly removed my clothes, dropping them next to her night gown. With my guidance, she stepped in, letting the spray wash over her. I lathered up the lavender-scented shampoo she loved. Her head fell back against my chest while I washed her red tresses. Grabbing the shower gel, I soaped up a pouf and began cleansing every inch of her, even dropping to my knees to scrub her petite feet. Gazing up at her, I marveled at how she glowed. Everything looked different suddenly. Starting today, I'd lavish her with all the attention and love I'd denied her.

I shook my head when she wanted to return the favor, but shoving my shoulders back, she pushed me into the water spray and took over. Every touch sent shivers across my body. I let her have her way with me. If she wanted to do that, then I wouldn't deny her. Those days were over.

CHAPTER 24

ALEXIA MCNEAR'S LOST AND FOUND

After showering, dressing, and making coffee, the time to talk had arrived. "Justin, where did you go?" I whined, putting my mug down in front of me, unsure I couldn't keep it from shaking.

"A few of the guys at work took me to a bar they hang at." He looked away, arousing my suspicions further.

Heaving a heavy breath, I pushed, "So it was just the guys from work?"

"Yeah, well . . . okay, there were girls there, but nothing happened. It wasn't a big deal." When his gazed shifted to the floor, I knew.

"I know when you're hiding something, so fess up," I demanded.

"Alexia, please, can we just let this go?"

"No, I don't think so. Tell me what kept you from our bed!" It amazed me how strong my voice sounded, considering my insides were shaking.

"I slept on the couch," he mumbled.

"Justin?" I growled.

"A few girls propositioned me," he shook his head, "but nothing happened. I always came home to sleep on the couch. I didn't even feel it when they touched me . . ." Before he could say more, I staggered to my feet and teetered away.

He let them touch him! My mind swam with sights of faceless women pawing him just like before the wedding. The only difference being he'd now admitted to it, which made it worse.

I felt him following me, but it didn't matter. My heartbeat pounded in my ears, blocking all his pleas. He tried to grab me, only to be met by swats from my hand. My stomach seized when I snatched my pocketbook and keys that still sat on the table near the door where I'd left them months ago.

"Alexia, please, wait. It didn't mean anything." Those were empty words to an empty person.

Flinging the door open, I waddled away to my car. There was only one place I wanted to be at that moment, and it wasn't home. Justin banged on the window with his fists after I slammed the door in his face. With shaking hands, I started the car and threw it in reverse, nearly running him over in the process. Jumping backward, my front end just missed his legs. The look of sheer horror etched on his features would forever be branded in my mind. I watched in the rearview mirror to see him running behind the car, shouting. My eyes darted back to the road when he gave up and turned back toward the house with his head in his hands.

My quivering hands reached out to turn on the heat. Like an idiot, I had left without a coat. The raging anger kept me from feeling it at first. It was more than anger; I'd had my heart torn out again. By the time the heater started warming the car, I'd reached my destination. Rubbing my abdomen, I tried to calm the restless twin who kicked me from within. Sitting back, I closed my eyes and thought about my time after hearing of the death of one of my twins.

The minute the dreadful words had slipped from the doctor's lips, my mind had shattered. So many thoughts had run in swirling circles. My heartbeat had pounded in my ears, and crippling pain had seized my chest. I'd wanted to scream when they'd laid their hands on me to pray. God and my faith had turned their backs on me, mocking me with something they never intended to give me. They had taken my son from me.

With Donna's injection had come the promise of oblivion. My body became numb as my mind did. I'd welcomed it. The only time I'd felt anything came from the feel of Justin's skin against mine.

As the days had dragged on, his caresses became less frequent and eventually stopped. With him being absent, everything meant nothing to me. The will to survive left me with him. When I'd needed him the most, he hadn't been there. That was nothing new; he'd missed everything already; what was one more thing on the long list?

I'd stopped listening for the sound of him coming home. The weight of my pain had rippled through me every night when everyone would leave me to sleep. I had been a boat without an anchor, floating aimlessly through the sea of despair.

Even with my eyes sealed shut I had known the moment Justin came home. I'd heard the bitter squabble between him and our families, and I'd felt his pain when he screamed out. But it wasn't until I'd felt him touching our moving child that I had finally found my way out of the blackness that had enveloped my soul. He'd come home.

My body had hummed alive from his touch. After all that time and pain, I still needed and longed for him. For a few hours it had seemed as if things were back to the way they'd once been, until he'd told me about the women.

All my time in bed caught up to me when I started my trek across the snow-covered, uneven terrain. Fatigued, shivering, and gasping, I stopped in front of the small, white, carved lamb that marked Alicia's grave. I'd never told Justin about Alicia because it had never come up. You don't just throw out, "Oh, by the way, my twin sister died at birth."

I'd buried the guilt over killing her a long time ago. My parents had argued that it hadn't been my fault. They'd sworn that no one could have controlled the fact that my umbilical cord had wrapped around her neck. I'd once told them that a part of me felt missing. I felt incomplete. After a while we'd agreed not to discuss it, and eventually when I was old enough, I began to go to see her on my own.

Swiping the snow off the gravestone, I traced the etched name and date. "Hey, Alicia. I miss you. Everything is a mess right now, and I don't know what to do anymore. I need to ask you a favor." A stream of tears started to fall from my clenched eyes. "I know Kaiden is with you now. Take care of my son for me? He's just a baby and needs someone to look after him while he's waiting for me."

"You don't have to ask her to do that. She loved you, and you know in your heart she's already holding him for you," my mother's voice rang out.

"How would you know what she felt?" I chided.

"When Dr. Brackett did an ultrasound, we saw you two hugging. That's when we saw the cord wrapped around her neck. He tried to do an emergency C-section, but it was already too late. She died in your arms."

When I spun around, Justin and my dad stood by her side. Turning back, I refused to look at them. I had heard the footsteps when they arrived, but I'd assumed only my parents had come. The grave sat in the back of the cemetery adjacent to the church.

"Alexia, please hear Justin out. What happened to him . . . well, let's just say he wasn't the first to let his circumstances lead him down the wrong path."

"Dad, you don't know what I'm going through. You would never do that to Mom," I snarled.

"No, I didn't, but your mother did," he sighed.

"It was a long time ago, when my father contracted me to marry your father. I had a boyfriend I didn't want to give up, and well, your father caught us making out one night by the lake." Looking over my shoulder, I saw my dad moving to hold her.

"You chose someone else over Dad?" I asked, astonished.

"No, that night when I saw the pain in your father's eyes, I knew I couldn't hurt him again. I turned my back on Stephan and followed your father. It's where I belonged. I loved him, but I rebelled, much like Justin did."

"And you forgave her?"

"Yes, I loved her before the contract was reached. Though my opinion didn't matter, in the end my father chose her. She is my other half in every way."

"And you think I should forgive Justin?"

"Please, Alexia? I didn't even kiss them. You can ask anyone. If they tried to kiss me I turned away, avoiding them. I didn't want to feel anything, especially them," Justin begged.

Shaking my head, I tried to block out his pleas. In my heart, I knew he spoke the truth. I froze when he moved closer. I couldn't resist him if he touched me. It would be my undoing. A trill of warmth ran down my spine when he wrapped his arms around me.

"I'm sorry. You have no idea how much or how long I have been in love with you. It was wrong not to leave when they came on to me. I let the alcohol excuse it. I won't lose you over an arm touch, because that's all that ever happened."

"But . . ." I gasped.

"No buts. It will never happen again."

"Promise?" I huffed, shivering, my breath coming out in wafts of white mist.

He slipped my coat over my shoulders, placing his lips under my ear. "No one touched what you have always owned." I shivered again, and it had nothing to do with the chill in the air.

Spinning, I buried my face into his chest. Pulling me closer, he held me, tilting my head and crushing his lips to mine. If I hadn't heard my parents crunching through the snow, I might have been embarrassed when I moaned into his mouth before he pulled back, smiling.

"So . . ." He motioned to Alicia's grave.

Blushing, I introduced them. "Alicia, this is Justin, my husband. I've told you about him."

"I'm sorry we never met in person. And I am sure Alexia has told you of my utter failures, but I promise to get it right and make her happy." He kissed my head. "Please, I beg you, take care of Kaiden for us. My baby boy needs you," he choked.

Looking back at him, his tears flowed freely. Reaching up, I wiped the salty streaks from his cheeks. "She will. I know it in my heart."

Pulling his head to my neck, I held him while we both cried. With gentle touches, we healed each other's pain. When my knees buckled beneath me, the time to leave had come.

I yelped when he scooped me up. "Let's go home," he cooed.

CHAPTER 25

JUSTIN MCNEAR'S NORMALCY IS NICE

"Alexia, we're going to be late for Mass," I grumbled for the fourth time.

"I'm coming; it's not so easy nowadays." Seeing her teetering into the living room started me chuckling.

The poor thing looked absolutely huge. Her gray silk dress only succeeded in accentuating her baby belly even more, but I loved it that way. Seeing the way her body shifted to accommodate her swelling womb left me wanting to reach out and rub it.

"But you're so beautiful and round," I murmured with a smile plastered across my face, wrapping myself around her.

"Are you insinuating I'm fat?" she snipped, crossing her arms over her heaving chest and showing her hormonal changes were in full swing.

"Never. I love you. Now if we don't leave, we'll miss the dedication of the new church. And let's face it; you've had two months off," I teased, releasing her long enough to grab her hand to drag her out the door and ignoring her pouting lip that begged to be kissed.

Opening the door, I waited for her to plop in before I shut it for her. Running around, I joined her in my Mercedes. She slipped her small hand in mine, intertwining our fingers, no doubt, looking for a sense of security. Her shifting positions drew my attention. I knew why she fidgeted in her seat while we drove: it would be her first time being seen in public since she had melted down. I dragged our joined hands onto to my lap.

"Alexia, no one blames you for needing time to heal."

"But I missed so many Masses. They'll think I'm a heathen," she twittered, letting her nervousness show.

"Minister Jeff has already explained it to everyone, so we don't have to go through the ordeal of doing it ourselves."

"They're going to look at me funny. They'll want to blame someone for Kaiden . . ." His name caught in her throat.

I squeezed her hand tighter, placing light kisses on her knuckles. "No, they won't. I promise." I prayed I could keep that promise.

I had to admit, she was right about the stares we received pulling into the car park. Lowering her eyes to her lap, she refused to look up. I glared back in our defense. Everyone finally turned back to the white ribbon draped across the white and gold front doors. With smiles plastered across most of their faces, Madison, Ginger, Joey, and Johnny strolled up.

"There's the momma. It's so good to see you out again." Madison hugged her, grinning from ear to ear before passing her over to Ginger.

"I'm so happy to see you're doing better. Guess I'm out of a job," she laughed, faking a pout.

I chuckled. "Nope, we still need you if you're available." Pulling Alexia into my embrace, I continued, "She's to rest as much as possible until the time comes. I don't want her to do anything." The twin rolled under my touch.

"Cuz, you'd better be on your best behavior. If you pull another stunt like that, I'll sic my wife on you again." Crazy Eight cackled, hiding behind Madison, wiggling his eyebrows.

Johnny kept his distance but glared enough to tell me I wasn't forgiven in his eyes. Tugging on my collar, I tried to cool the heat from the intense stare down. It didn't work and I glanced away. He didn't need to remind me. I felt the shame that coursed through me every time I thought about my epic failure.

"Ladies, escort Alexia over while I have a chat with Justin." Johnny's stone stare sent shivers down my spine.

Alexia didn't seem too keen on the idea; as they led her away, she kept glancing over her shoulder. I could see her discomfort, but if what my gut screamed did happen, I didn't want her anywhere near me. Once the ladies reached the ribbon line he let loose. Grabbing my shoulders, he tossed me against my car. I didn't resist. From the sound of the metal giving way, I'd have a dent to remember his tirade. I deserved what he felt compelled to do.

Through clenched teeth, he growled, "I warned you! My promise was clear; if you hurt her, I'd hurt you!" He fisted his hand, and it shook from his immense anger.

Joey leapt at him, trying to get him to back off. "Dude, stop!" Johnny didn't listen, and his fist impacted my jaw with a snap.

"Johnny!" Joey tried again to get through Johnny's rage-induced haze, grabbing and wrestling with him before another fist could fly my way.

Finally Joey pulled him away by his arms, letting me slump to the ground with my back still against my front fender. Rubbing my jaw, I looked over to see Alexia waddling back our way with Madison and Ginger right behind her. They tried to grab at her, but Alexia swatted them away. She looked so horrified. I shook my head to tell her not to get in the middle, but she continued her trek, only stopping when she reached my side. Her horror morphed to fury right before my eyes, her pain evident.

"Johnny, what are you doing? How could you?" Slapping his chest over and over, she pushed him backward against the car next to mine.

"Alexia? He needs to learn! What he did to you . . ."

She snarled out in frustration when he latched onto her arms, stopping her from hitting him further.

"We lost a son! He needed to grieve!" she growled, pulling her arms free.

Alexia moved to my side, trying to soothe me and making light strokes across my tender cheek.

"Are you all right? Did he hurt you?" The love she felt shone in her emerald eyes.

"Come on, Justin, let me help you up." Joey extended his hand to me.

I slapped it away. "Nah, I'm good. Just leave me alone." I huffed, getting up on my own.

"Leave us alone. If that's how you treat your friends and family, we don't need you," Alexia snarled, pulling away from the girls when they tried to comfort her, leaving them looking bewildered.

Out of the corner of my eye, I saw my father and the minister approaching. Alexia sunk into my arms rubbing my cheek. "Justin, does it hurt a lot?"

I turned away from them for some privacy. "No, sweetheart, but you shouldn't have put yourself in the way. It's one thing if they hurt me," dropping my forehead to hers, "I couldn't bear it if they hurt you by accident."

"What's going on here, boys?" Minister Jeff looked to me for an explanation with his brow furrowed in confusion.

Shaking my head, I grumbled, "It doesn't matter. People are the same, no matter where you go." I led Alexia away in my arms.

She blanched. "I'm so sorry . . ." Spinning to face her, I cut her off.

"No! You did nothing wrong. Don't take the blame for me. If I'd been a better husband, none of this would have happened." I winced at the truth in my words.

Locking her eyes on mine, she cooed, "You did what you did because of how I reacted; so you see, it is my fault." She stroked my cheek again.

Closing my eyes, I wanted to release a frustrated scream, but I managed to hold it back. "You handled it the only way you could. So how about we both agree it wasn't either of our faults, and it was just what we needed to do to survive. Can we do that?" I pleaded, squeezing her tighter to me.

Glaring at the others coming up behind us, she whispered, "For you, I can." She shifted her gaze back to me. Her batting eyelashes sealed my fate. For her I, too, would do anything.

Minister Jeff, still shocked by our abrupt departure, took the center at the front of the church with Henry Atwood and the Council members. Waving his hands in the air, he called for everyone to settle down before he began. A hush fell over the group. "Welcome home. Our church is finally ready, and today we celebrate it. By cutting this white ribbon, we sever the pains of the past. Today we venture forward into our faith, with our Lord leading the way. Justin, if you would be so kind as to join us." He waved me forward.

Leaving a kiss on Alexia's cheek, I joined them at the front, unsure why they needed me. "Mr. Justin McNear is the man who designed the beautiful place of worship that stands before you today. He didn't ask for acknowledgement or praise; he just wanted to serve his faith with all that he had in him." My modesty won out, and a blush crept across my cheeks.

Henry smiled, handing me the mammoth scissors. I accepted the tool to cut the white silk ribbon with sweaty palms. I snipped it, releasing a sigh. Looking up, Alexia smiled at me with tears slipping from her eyes. She bobbled up beside me, grabbing my hand.

"No crying, love. Today's a whole new day. We're not going to relive the bad stuff. I'm sorry . . ."

She stopped my words with a simple shake of her head. Placing two fingertips on my lips, she sighed. "No more 'sorrys.' We can't change the past, but we can forgive and move forward."

I nodded, taking her by the elbow, and I led her inside behind Minister Jeff and the Council.

The chamber filled with the sounds of everyone's admiration; the sight inside left me feeling humble and full of hope. The new cream walls were adorned with hand-painted scriptures. The gray, tiled floor shimmered, multi-colored facets reflecting off it from the stained-glass windows. Each window depicted a different poignant scene from our Bible. New sculptures of all eight archangels stood proud beneath each window on white marble columns. The new cherry pews shone in their highly-polished state. Walking to the end, we gawked at the Italian black marble altar. Above the altar hung a golden metal cross depicting Jesus making his final sacrifice. As in the days before the fire, we took seats in the new pews that had replaced the charred ones.

With tears in his eyes, Minister Jeff began his sermon. Everything ran in the usual format until just before the end, when he suddenly looked angry.

His eyes hardened before he spoke. "I am appalled by the recent behavior of some of the members in this parish. When two of our own are enduring a tragedy beyond anything most of us has ever endured, some of you turned your backs on them, and others attacked them. These two souls need love, not hate; caresses, not punches; and words of kindness, not malicious slurs." Minister Jeff paced the new altar. "This church you're sitting in is the direct result of their love for us, our faith, and our community."

Alexia slid further into my arms, whispering, "I love you."

"And I love you," I murmured, kissing her hair.

While Jeff rambled on about the events leading up to his lecture, my eyes drifted around to see Johnny's head bowed, and from the way Ginger held him, he was battling his own demons. My parents seemed lost in their own thoughts, also. Krista showed us her support with a gentle smile. Leaning our heads together, we listened to the sounds of everyone shifting uncomfortably in their seats. The feel of Alexia's breath washing across my cheeks had my eyes fluttering shut.

When Minister Jeff finally finished, we all slipped from our seats and headed to the meeting room for lunch. Many of the once-gawking parishioners now walked past us offering pats of affection and slight smiles. It seemed that all they had needed was a reminder.

In the white cement-walled basement, tables of food were already being set up. After dropping Lexie off at a table with her parents, I headed to retrieve her some food. When Joey hopped in behind me, I knew he had something to say. Mrs. Michaels passed me two paper plates with plastic utensils when I moved past her.

"Justin, sorry I didn't see Johnny losing it sooner. We're twins, but we don't share one mind. I want you to know, I don't hold how you dealt with your pain against you. What you were and still are dealing with has to be the hardest thing in the world. Try to forgive him; he's running scared, too. They just found out Ginger's expecting in November. He's afraid." Joey looked over at his twin brother with concern in his icy blue eyes. "He's not strong like you are. It would kill him if they lost the baby. You and Lexie have been through something no one wants to think about." Not knowing what to say, I just nodded. "They aren't telling anyone outside the family." He huffed.

"Well, it's their choice. I don't know what you want me to say. There's nothing I can do to help them except to pray for them." I sighed.

Bouncing between his feet, he pleaded, "You can forgive him when he asks you to. I know he will, but if you go off on him, he'll crumble into a million pieces."

Grabbing two premade turkey sandwiches from the huge silver trays, I deposited them on my plates. "I always seem to be the one turning my cheek every time I get attacked. I'm tired of being abused. My family until now had never been the ones doing the attacking. I thought we were more than family, I thought we were friends, too. My assumptions were wrong." I turned my back on him, adding some potato salad to the plates.

Truth be told, it really hurt to have Johnny attack me, more emotionally than in the physical aspect. I had let them in where I'd kept others away. My trust had taken a beating along with my jaw.

Grabbing my arm, he halted my progress. "They weren't. You're more than my cousin, you're one of my best friends, and I'd like to keep it that way." He released my arm.

Scooping out some salad from the clear glass bowl, I decided to cut him some slack. "You're going to have to prove that to be true, but I'll give you the chance to do it."

"Thanks, dude. Do you think Lexie will forgive us?"

Shaking my head, I replied, "That's up to her; I won't force her. Not right now. The delivery can happen at any time, and I won't do anything to upset her." I pulled two drinks from the punch bowl, refusing to look at him.

"No, we don't want that either, although it would be good for her to be surrounded by friends." His expression looked hopeful. "One more thing. I overheard my parents talking about the retreat," he hissed before continuing, "I'm sorry he did that to you. No one has the right to hurt you like that. If we'd known . . ."

"It's in the past, but thanks."

With a final nod, he headed back to his table with his two plates.

Shuffling off, I hurried to feed my ravenous wife. She could be rather scary when left unfed for too long. Her parents chuckled when she almost ripped the food from my hands, growling like a bear that hadn't eaten all winter. Sitting down next to her, I helped her eat her food; not that she needed it, but I enjoyed doing little things to make her happy. Throwing her head back, she hummed in delight at the potato salad I fed her from my spoon. When her lips pursed, I knew something wasn't right. Alexia's head snapped forward, looking at her lap, and she wrapped her hands across her baby belly.

"Justin?" she whimpered.

"Alexia, is that . . .?" I gasped, looking at the puddle on her seat as it dripped to the floor.

"Oh, no, Justin, her water broke!" Katrina shrieked.

"It's okay, love. We can do this. Look at me!" I placed my hands over hers. "I love you."

CHAPTER 26

ALEXIA MCNEAR'S IT'S TIME!

"Justin, I'm scared." I looked up to see his own fear written across his features.

"The doctor will be right back. He's talking to the minister," he whispered in my ear.

After my water had broken at lunch, we were rushed to the clinic. Sharp breaths echoed in the small area. I'd never known anyone to go into labor during a church event. The room had turned into a chaotic mess when everyone scrambled to get us out. Justin had scooped me up into his arms with a grunt and carried me out, while Dr. Michaels ran ahead to get the clinic ready and to call Donna to come in. My parents, of course, had followed us, with Justin's family right behind them.

Even Madison, Joey, Johnny, and Ginger had come to wait outside the clinic. It hadn't curbed my anger toward them. The fact that they'd allowed Johnny to attack Justin had left my feelings battered. The fact it had come from family made it worse. They'd known how much Justin had suffered through my months of self-imposed imprisonment, yet not one of them had tried to help, with the exception of the intervention. I loved them, always would, but I had to protect my husband.

The contractions at first weren't so bad, just a tightening around my midsection every ten minutes or so, but an hour into labor they started to hurt beyond my expectations. The surviving twin wanted out in a major way. Justin flinched every time I screamed out; still he stayed by my side.

We knew today would be bittersweet. Our twins would be born, one surviving and one not. Kaiden's tiny body would finally join Alicia's. Together they would wait for us to join them when our time came. But first, we needed to be here for the one who had made it. The hardest part of all was that I couldn't hold that twin responsible for surviving; it wasn't the baby's fault. No one could be blamed for what had happened. That realization finally sank in, and with it, I finally forgave myself for Alicia.

"Oh . . . ow . . . no . . . no . . . no," I panted, my stomach seizing under my hands, my skin sweating, and my legs shaking.

"Breathe, Lexie. It will pass. I'm sure it won't be much longer." Justin wiped my brow with a cool, wet cloth. "I love you," he whimpered, looking like a little boy.

At that point, I needed a cool, wet blanket. My body was drenched in sweat, my hair clung to my face, and every muscle in my body ached. Panting and puffing, I tried to get through yet another round of pressure racking my belly. Nothing anyone had said to me could have prepared me for the excruciating pain – pain I would endure for the sake of the baby.

"That's right, love." He clutched my hands in his, locking his sincere eyes on mine. "Soon this will be over, and you can sleep," he cooed.

When the contraction finally passed, Justin lifted a spoon of crushed ice to my parched lips. I couldn't deny the love in his gem blue eyes for me. Licking the water from the spoon, I sighed at the relief it provided. Stroking my face, he pushed the sweat-coated mess I'd once called my hair away.

"Better now?"

"Yes," I moaned, shifting in a vain attempt to get comfortable.

His brow scrunched up as if he wanted to say something, and after a few tries, he succeeded. "Joey apologized."

"I see," I mumbled, not wanting him to see it still stung.

Shrugging, he said, "They love you." He turned away, looking out the window.

"Could have fooled me," I snipped. "Another one?" Whining, I felt the tightening burn starting again.

Justin glanced at the clock on the wall, lost in thought. "Two minutes apart now," he muttered.

"Well, how are we doing in here?" Dr. Michaels inquired, walking through the door.

"The last three contractions were two minutes apart." Justin winced when I tightened my grip on his hand.

"And they hurt!" I screeched. My body tightened to the point that my back arched off the bed. "I have to push!"

"Not yet. Let me check to see how dilated you are first."

Lifting the sheet, he positioned himself between my legs. He rubbed my tensed abdomen until it relaxed under his gentle strokes. Slipping one hand in, he smiled. "Very good. You're at nine centimeters. Just a few more minutes, I think, then you can push. We'll get everything ready. Justin, you should head out to wait with your family." From his snarl, I'd say he didn't agree with that idea.

"I'm not going anywhere. I don't care about the other fathers waiting outside crap. If you want me out of here, you're going to have to drag me out." His eyes blazed at the doctor.

"It's just customary for the fathers to wait outside; however, if you want to stay, there is no reason why you can't."

Justin smiled, seeming pleased with that idea.

Dr. Michaels nodded to Donna, who answered his with one of her own before she started moving everything into place. He also moved around, getting ready. A hiss slipped from my lips when a new contraction hit me hard.

By the time everything was in place, the contractions were one after the other. Justin did his best to keep me from screaming out. I think he would have been horrified by the things that begged to be said. Just thinking them had me blushing, not that he'd noticed with my whole body flushed from the pain. I could see he suffered every pain with me.

A ear-piercing shrill erupted from my chest when the hardest contraction yet slammed me. Shoving my heels into the mattress, I tried not to push. My entire body lifted from the sticky sheet while Justin struggled to keep me on the bed. The doctor again reached under the sheet to measure me.

"It's time. Justin, if you're going to stay, crawl in behind her and support her. You're going to grasp behind her knees and pull them as close to you as possible. It will help open her up."

Without waiting for further commands, he did what had been asked of him, wrapping his legs around my hips. Leaning into his chest, he pulled my knees to my chest, tilting them around my stomach and draped them over his thighs. He nuzzled my ear, sending shivers down my spine. His heated breath fanned across my exposed sweaty flesh, causing me to break out in goose bumps.

"Okay, Alexia, push on the count of three. One. Two. Three."

Taking several cleansing breaths, then one deep breath, I slowly exhaled while pushing as Justin counted backward from ten, ending with a full exhale. Slumping back, I groaned. The pain wouldn't stop. I cried for it to, but it refused to give me a break. So gasping in a new breath, I pressed off of Justin and pushed again. Dr. Michaels, who was now seated between my feet, encouraged me to keep going. I slumped against Justin, sighing once the pain relented.

"That's right, Alexia, you can do this. Justin, help her."

Justin nodded into my neck before leaning forward, helping me lean into the new contraction. "Push, Lexie. You're doing great! Together, okay?" With his hands laid over mine, he pushed downward. Honestly, neither of us knew what we were doing. At that moment, it would've been nice to have had some sort of instructions besides what my mother had said.

"I've got you, sweetheart," he gushed.

"Stop pushing. The head's out." Dead silence fell over the room.

No one even dared to breathe. I felt my heart breaking as the tiny body slid out and into the hands of the doctor. Without a word he snipped the cord and passed Kaiden to Donna to wrap. I couldn't stop the tears that fell, not that I tried. My son deserved those tears. Justin sobbed in my ear, holding me tighter. Turning, I buried my face in the crook of Justin's neck. Cheek to cheek, our tears merged, blending into one. Small unintelligible words rambled from our lips. Shifting, he pulled back, placing a chaste kiss on my tear-soaked lips.

"We'll love him forever. We'll never forget him."

"Never . . . forever . . ." I croaked.

Shifting in his arms, we both lost the ability to speak. The minutes slip by with us looking at the baby blue fleeced bundle. Everyone was lost in their own thoughts. The only sounds in the room were soft sniffles from everyone, even the doctor.

I hissed when the pain started again. "Okay, Alexia, one more time," Dr. Michaels coached, wiping away his tears with his sleeve.

Pushing the second time around was harder. Everything repeated as with the first time, but it was doubled. Double the pain, the stretching, the strain, the amount of pushes; it all wore me thin to the point where I didn't think I'd make it.

My flesh tore under the pressure. This time when the head was out, we paused so the airway could be cleared. With one last push, the baby slipped free, screaming along with me. Slumping back, we watched the remaining twin's cord being cut.

"Congratulations; it's a boy." That wasn't a surprise to us since we had known they were identical twins.

Lolled my head over, my voice cracked. "Is he okay?"

"He's perfect," Donna's calming voice rang out when she took him.

She moved closer, delivering him to our waiting arms. Placing him on my stomach, she backed away, giving us a minute to examine the newest member of our family. I had to unravel the swaddling; I needed to see he had made it through unscathed. Justin traced his tiny features.

"Welcome to the family, Jayden," Justin cooed.

Mocked By Faith

CHAPTER 27

JUSTIN MCNEAR'S IT'S NOT GOOD–BYE

Looking at the angelic face of my son cradled in our arms brought back all the emotions we'd struggled for months to keep at bay. Only this time, I had a better grip on how to deal with them. My heart broke for Kaiden but swelled for Jayden. Alexia examined every inch of him, looking for anything out of the ordinary. She finally smiled when she discovered he was perfect. Then again, it wouldn't have mattered if he wasn't. He'd survived, and that was all that mattered.

Alexia frowned when Donna needed to take him to clean, weigh, and measure him. I understood why. After losing one, she had to fear that something would go wrong; I knew I did.

Dr. Michaels settled back in and sewed the tear the baby had caused in his escape. Alexia flinched but kept quiet as the doctor repaired the damage. Times like these, I wished there wasn't such a tight restriction on medications. Prescriptions were only allowed for drastic cases. After listening to her screams for hours, I prayed she wouldn't suffer any longer than necessary.

Placing light kisses across her shoulder, I held her while Donna untangled and cleaned her of the residue from the last few hours. In the end, I did have to leave the bed so we could both go into another room for the night. I missed her touch the moment Donna moved her. It would seem my fear of loss extended to Alexia as well.

Scooping her up into my arms, I followed Donna to the room she had readied for us. Once Alexia rested in her new bed, I forced myself to leave her side. With one light chaste kiss, I slipped out the door, leaving her with Donna. I needed to make an introduction.

The doctor knew before I reentered the delivery room. "Ready to show him to your parents?"

Walking in, I noticed we weren't alone. "Yes, if he is."

"He is, Justin. Kaiden will be in his bassinette until tomorrow morning, if you and Alexia want a few moments alone with him." He bowed his head, his sadness showing.

Watching Minister Jeff praying over Kaiden, I answered the doctor. "I'll see if she's up to it, but I know I'd like to spend a while with him." I knew what I had to do, and I had stowed the necessary items in Alexia's overnight bag that I'd left in my trunk.

Dr. Michaels placed the blue fleece bundle in my arms and gave me a slight smile before turning to go and join Minister Jeff. Bowing their heads, they clasped their hands in prayer. I kissed Jayden once on the forehead, letting his new baby smell permeate my senses. Walking out into the waiting room, I'd admit, scared me. I wanted to be happy, and I was, but at the same time the sadness wouldn't leave my soul. It never would, but I needed to be happy, proud, and loving for Jayden.

"Hey, everyone, he's here," I announced, holding him so everyone could see him.

"Oh, he's beautiful," my mother gushed, rushing up.

"He looks like Alexia, but with your eyes!" Kat exclaimed, smiling.

"I can't believe you stayed in there. I wanted to when you and Krista were born; you're the first in our faith to do it. Well done, Justin." My father clapped my shoulder, seeming prouder of me somehow.

"Can we hold him?" Chris's hope shone in his eyes.

"Sure, you can. I actually need to step out into the car park." I nudged my head toward the group waiting there.

Chris laughed at my choice of words. After all my months here, I couldn't shake my accent or the word usages. Ten years in England had left them embedded.

"They've been checking in every half hour. They're worried about you both." Chris joined me looking out the window to see our four friends moving in the lot.

"How did you do it? Is it wrong to be happy Jayden survived?" I choked back a lump in my throat.

"It's not wrong. I won't lie, the pain never goes away; but you will learn to live with it. Jayden deserves all the love and affection you want to lavish on him. Don't hold back, thinking you shouldn't be happy, because you should be." Reaching out, he readied himself to take the baby from my arms.

"I'll be right back." I nodded, handing him Jayden.

Taking one last deep breath, I opened the door and walked outside. The chilly air nipping at my exposed skin didn't cause me to hesitate in my need to put them at ease. Madison. Joey, Johnny, and Ginger froze when they saw me walking toward them. Their panicked looks shifted back and forth between each other.

"Thank you for coming. Alexia's just fine. She delivered twin boys. Why don't you come in and meet Jayden?" A collective sigh of relief quieted my fears of facing them.

Everyone smiled except for Johnny. He seemed to still be torn, probably because of me. Those worries would have to wait. My attention belonged elsewhere. They started walking toward the door while I went to my car. I popped the trunk to my car and grabbed the bag for my wife. Trotting ahead, I reached and held the door while they filed in.

We all stopped and enjoyed the sight of the grandparents doting over their first grandchild. Jayden drew them in. The room filled with coos and gasps. Everyone's happiness seemed to permeate the air, making my next move easier.

I took the opportunity of their distraction to slip back into the delivery room. Kaiden lay waiting for me. Pulling my pad and pencils from the pouch, I breathed deeply before uncovering his precious features. There was one thing I could give our family that no one else could. In seconds, the outline sat complete. He resembled Jayden, only smaller. Lost in my drawing, I never heard the door behind me open or close.

"Justin?" Johnny startled me.

Clutching the pad to my chest, I spun to see him standing there. His eyes glistened with unshed tears. "I – I didn't hear you."

"Sorry about that. If you need to be alone . . ." The rest of his words lodged in his throat when his gaze fell upon Kaiden.

"Can we finish fighting tomorrow? I want Alexia to have something to remember him by."

"I don't want to fight anymore. Your father told me you never left Alexia's side. When most men would have run and hid in the waiting room, you didn't. You stayed for your wife and sons. She needed you, and you were there for her." His tears found their way down his reddened cheeks. Furrowing his brow, he continued, "It was wrong to judge you. Can you ever forgive me?"

"I forgave you already," I mumbled, returning to my sketchpad.

I expected him to turn and leave, but he surprised me by walking closer, his dress shoes tapping on the white linoleum. His next statement choked me up. "He was going to be my godson, wasn't he?"

"Yes," I croaked, wiping away my own tears.

"Can I hold him while you draw?"

I nodded, not knowing if I could actually say it.

Taking the tiny bundle from the bassinette, he moved to the rocking chair in the corner. Rocking, he hummed while I sketched. It wasn't until a knock on the door brought me out of my drawing haze did I realize it had been fifteen minutes. Putting the pad down, I walked over and retrieved my son. Johnny hugged us both before drifting to the door with his head hung low. I heard his muffled whispers, but I couldn't make out his words. Cradling Kaiden to my chest, I held my angel, my son.

I knew her touch the minute she placed her hand on my shoulder. Alexia. Sliding to the front, she joined me at marveling at the preciousness.

"Justin, he's in the arms of the angels. His soul flutters with the butterflies. He wouldn't want us to suffer while he's in the loving embrace of the Lord. We need to love Jayden and live for Kaiden. He's smiling down upon us; can't you feel it?"

I nodded, knowing she spoke the truth.

It ached less when I placed him back in the bassinette. I knew it wasn't goodbye; it was a 'see you in the hereafter.'

Wrapping my arms around my wife, I kissed her from the heart. My love flowed as our lips moved in tandem. I ended it when her knees went weak. Normally, I would've taken that as flattery about my kisses; in truth, the labor and delivery had left her spent.

Lifting her into my arms, I snuggled her close to my heart. "Come on, love, let's get Jayden and settle in for the night. You've had a long day." I paused long enough to grab my sketchbook and pouch.

"We all have," she breathed across my neck.

She fell asleep in my arms before we even reached her room. Donna sat watchful over Jayden's cradle on Alexia's bed. Seeing my approach, she moved to the bedside and pulled down the linens, only leaving once Alexia rested in bed. The room had two twin beds in it separated by two bassinettes. Dragging up one of the chairs that sat at the foot of the bed, I settled in for the long night ahead. There was no way I'd sleep with the emotions from the day still racing through my veins.

I spent the night watching them both sleeping and working on the drawing. Every precious breath of my son was a gift from God. Never again would I take life for granted. The hours slipped past while I added every detail I saw to the portrait. When a detail escaped me, I looked to Jayden to fill it in.

Just after midnight, he roused for his first meal. The sounds of his slight wailing filled the air, waking my wife in the process. Bringing him to her, I helped her sit up to feed him. Alexia, unabashed, released her left breast for his demanding mouth. I watched in awe while he suckled. It amazed me how she knew instinctively what to do. When the left breast ran dry, she shifted him to the right side. Together they drifted off to sleep with him still attached. Once satisfied, he released her. Cradling him to my chest, I patted his back until a tiny burp slipped from his mouth. For good measure, I kept it up until he'd released another one. I rubbed his back for a few minutes, soaking in his beauty.

I placed him back in his own bed and changed his nappy, leaving him sleeping. When I felt the drawing showed Kaiden's sweet reflection, I closed the book and placed it back in the bag on the floor. I slipped into Alexia's bed, pulling her flush to me. As usual, she spun in my embrace, resting her cheek against my chest. Fisting my hands in her long, curly red locks, I ensured she'd hear my heartbeat. Every beat belonged to her and the twins.

Jayden squawked again around four o'clock in the morning for another feeding. Poor Alexia could barely move, but with my help, all she had to do was lay there. Once he'd had his fill, I changed him again and resumed my position on the bed, this time allowing myself to drift off to sleep lost in her arms.

The next morning after Alexia had showered, eaten a proper meal, and nursed Jayden again, we spent an hour holding Kaiden before he needed to leave. Our parents joined us in saying a tearful good-bye. Dr. Michaels rode with Kaiden to the funeral home to be prepared.

A week after the delivery of the twins, we stood in the cemetery adjacent to the rebuilt church. Looking down at the plot next to my grandparents, we watched my son Kaiden's tiny white coffin being laid to rest, his spirit long in the arms of our Lord for safe keeping. A piece of my soul went with him. Jayden James McNear would be the one thing that held our family together.

Alexia wasn't aware that my family had once lived in The Gates until I told her when we were making the arrangements for Kaiden. My father had been the one to leave. He'd been the only one in his graduating class without a marriage contract. My grandfather had flown to England to secure him a wife. Within days of his arrival he'd found my mother, and like with Alexia and myself, the contract had been signed right away. For two years, my father had flown to England during summer holidays to get acquainted with his future wife. Not once did he miss an event in her life. My father had never looked back when he'd boarded the plane for England on his eighteenth birthday.

The summer I'd met Alexia on the beach, we'd flown in for my grandparents' funerals. They had died one rainy night while driving back from a shopping trip to Small River. A deer had dashed in front of their car, causing them to lose control on the wet roads. That was just one more reason I didn't like Alexia having to leave The Gates. I couldn't protect her out there.

Wiping away her tears, I kissed and held her and Jayden until we were all ready to leave the cemetery. I guess it shouldn't have surprised me that every member of our community attended, since the funeral was held during Sunday Mass. Minister Jeff had insisted that we had all lost a member, therefore it had to be done that way.

The meeting hall was packed to capacity when we finally made it there. I saw Minister Jeff surrounded by the council and Henry Atwood. For some reason, Henry didn't seem pleased. One by one, more people noticed the exchange. Soon we all knew what the issue was.

"What do you mean there's no money in the bank account? Where did all our donations go?" Henry yelled at the council.

CHAPTER 28

ALEXIA MCNEAR'S RUNNING ON EMPTY

My breathing all but stopped when Justin moved toward the angry voices at the front of the room. What did he think he was doing? From his stance, I knew he didn't like what he had heard.

"Henry, please, let us explain . . ."

Henry had no patience and cut Minister Jeff off. "Explain what? Why you can't pay me? Why I won't be able to pay my men? Who's gonna feed all those families?" he seethed, his face turning red.

"We didn't know he'd taken the money until it was already long gone," Mrs. Daigle pleaded.

"Who took the money?" James joined the crowd that had started to form around them.

"Minister Mark," Minister Jeff grumbled.

The room erupted in cackles and hisses, chairs flipped over with deafening crashes, and then the hollering started. Jayden cried out at the sudden change in noise levels. Shushing and rocking him, I did my best to keep up with everyone's yelling until Minister Jeff finally got some control.

"Stop! Everyone have a seat and be quiet! We'll tell you everything we know!"

The minister paced for a few moments while everyone quieted down and took their seats again. I'd never seen the council members look so uncomfortable in their own skins. Their aged features appeared even older and more worn than usual. Each one of them had a vacant glaze in their eyes. Justin resumed his spot next to me, wrapping his arm around my shoulders. Our parents and his sister shared our table. Each of us looked to the other for some sign of knowing what would come next.

Rubbing the back of his neck, Minister Jeff started, "Some of you may or may not know the situation with Minister Mark, so for those who don't know, I will disclose everything." He looked at Justin before continuing. "He was in full charge of our revirgining retreat; a place for those who had lost their way and needed intense counseling. Unfortunately, he took his authority too far and had physically harmed those in his charge." Justin shivered against me. "All the ministers from all our communities convened in a conference call and decided to remove him from his post. This all happened during his visit here to help in the rebuilding of our church." All heads snapped to stare at us with concern etched on their faces.

When Minister Jeff couldn't continue, Mrs. Arbella took over. "Minister Mark also controlled our master bank account. Each month, we always sent half our donations, and we sent all the money for the rebuild." A tear slipped from her eye. "Upon his leaving, an auditor was called in to balance the books. That's when we received the call that funds were missing. We had no idea how much at the time had been unaccounted for. Last night we got the call that the exact amount of money gone was eighty-five million dollars." Mrs. Arbella choked up, dropping her head into her hands.

The reactions in the room varied from faces flushed with anger to hands covering mouths and silent sobs. Justin, who had remained quiet, tensed around me. His body shook from the anger he was trying to hold back. The youngest members didn't seem to understand what had happened. Krista eyed us, hoping for some sort of explanation, but we had none to give her.

"The authorities are battling about who is in charge of this since the account was a foreign account. We have to rely on the other governments to figure out where the money went. Minister Mark and his family have disappeared somewhere in England. They haven't left England legally. Their passports haven't been logged out of the country. We have tried to hire private investigators to look for them, but so far they have come up empty." Mr. Boucher paused.

My head snapped to my dad. He had to have known about the

embezzlement and hadn't told us! From his bowed head and shame-filled expression, I had my answer. My mother looked between us and saw what I did. My father's eyes filled with tears. Grabbing his face, she forced him to look at her. All he could manage was a silently mouthed, "I'm sorry, I'm their lawyer. I had to keep it quiet until they announced it."

"Why aren't we going to look for him?" Justin surprised me by speaking up.

Minister Jeff looked shocked to hear from him as well. "We're giving the authorities a chance to find him. The most likely places he'd hide don't take well to strangers."

"All the more reason we should go. If he's hiding with others like us, we can get in before someone else could!" Justin slammed his hands on the table, causing Jayden to wail again.

Justin refused to look at me and the baby the whole time he seethed. His eyes trained on the group in the front of the room, his clenched fists grinding against the round white Formica table we sat at.

Holding his hands up, Minister Jeff offered a compromise. "We'll make you a deal; if they don't catch him in three months, we'll put together a group to head to England to try to find him." The room again erupted in noise when all the men demanded to be in the group.

Rocking my son, my heart raced when Justin yelled he wanted to be on the team. The thought of him leaving scared me to death. I wanted him home with us, not running around looking for the man who had made a mess of my husband once already. Releasing a shaky breath, I tried to calm myself down, but the news seemed to be getting worse.

Henry couldn't stay silent any longer. "Well, don't expect me to finish the shopping center or any more townhouses until I am paid for the church." My head snapped to see Madison growing paler by the second. Joey looked ghostly while he cradled her shaking figure in his arms.

"That construction will be on hold until we can get the money for it. We have gone into Small River to ask the bank for a loan. Unfortunately, we haven't heard back from them yet. All money transfers from our accounts here have been suspended until further notice. We're not the only ones. England, Mexico, and Argentina all lost their money." Minister Jeff's words brought very little comfort.

We all knew that our weekly donations would only sustain the church, not promote growth. For Madison and Joey, that meant they couldn't open their hair salon in two months after she graduated hairdressing school. Every penny they had from her dowry had been invested into it. They were counting on it to be their income. Now they would have to wait.

The war raged on inside me. I wanted to scream at Justin. I wanted to beg him not to go, but this was the wrong place and wrong time for a marital spat. However, when we got home that would change.

"Anyone who wants to go can enter a ballot in June if we haven't found Mark by then," Minister Jeff said as he, Patty, and their son Vincent left the meeting room.

"Let's go, Lexie. The baby must be tired." For the first time since the news broke, Justin looked at me.

"Yeah, whatever," I hissed, looking away.

I took his silence and grinding jaw while he grabbed the diaper bag as his realization that I wasn't happy with the turn of events. Following behind him, I dreaded what would come next. Justin held the doors for me, but he couldn't find it in himself to look my way. By the time I'd strapped Jayden in and had given him his pacifier, Justin had already started the car and was waiting for me to get in. He hit the gas pedal as soon as my door shut.

The deafening quiet on the ride home kept me glued to my seat, my hands under me to keep them from shaking. For the first time since meeting Justin, his driving scared me. He slammed on the brakes once he pulled into the driveway, sending me sliding forward into the dashboard.

"Justin!" I sneered, pushing myself back.

Snapping his face to look at me, he snipped, "What?"

"Stop now! I know you're mad about Minister Mark . . ." From the way he gaped at me, you'd think I sucker punched him.

"Don't call him that! Mark is not a minister anymore, and even when he held that title, he was a poor excuse for one."

I had no retort for that one, because he was right, and I knew it. Shaking my head, I got out and retrieved the baby from the back seat. He'd fallen asleep on the ride home. Justin handled retrieving the diaper bag and opening the door to the cottage. Moving past him, I headed straight to the nursery. When I heard the door shut, I thought Justin had stayed in the house, but when I heard the trunk to his car slamming, it became evident that my assumption hadn't been correct.

After moving Jayden into his crib, I looked out the window to see Justin leaning against the back of his car. He stayed out there for hours, only coming in after he thought I had gone to bed. Lying in bed, I pretended to be sleeping. Every sound he made while readying for bed reached my ears. Also the smell of alcohol on his breath found me, angering me further. He'd begun running from us already.

The next month passed without us speaking about the events again. We tried acting like it never happened, but it was an uncomfortable truce. My stomach churned every time I thought about him wanting to leave us so soon after the delivery of the twins. I couldn't help but wonder if he really did love us. If he willingly wanted to charge off after the maniac Mark, then maybe he didn't. Every day, I spent my time staring out at the water from the kitchen window, wondering what the summer would bring.

Justin went to work and returned as always, only each night I could smell the liquor on his breath. He tried to cover it by chewing peppermint gum, but it didn't work. On the weekends, he found excuses to run out to his car or errands that needed to be done.

Easter started our journey back to each other. Jayden was baptized with two other babies who had been born near the same time he was. Crazy Eight and Madison played the perfect godparents, even giving him his first cross. The ceremony remained festive until, of course, someone announced that Mark remained at large. Refusing to let that ruin our holiday, I let it pass without commenting on it.

The girls and I had had several conversations over the last few weeks about what would happen if the guys were to be chosen from the pool. Ginger also had announced that she and Johnny were expecting. They pleaded for me and Justin to be the godparents, which we accepted. Johnny even went as far as to come over and beg for me to forgive him. My anger had long dissipated, so I accepted his apology. More importantly, Justin had forgiven him.

After Mass, we ate dinner at the cottage with our families. My mom brought all the desserts, and Jane brought the ham, leaving me the side dishes, which I'd become much better at preparing thanks to Ginger's help.

Once everyone had left, I put Jayden to bed, grateful that he now slept six hours every night before needing another feeding. Getting more sleep helped with my overall attitude, making me less snippy.

I found Justin sitting in our bed with a baby blue wrapped package set on his lap. He looked up at me with an expression that reminded me of a lost boy looking for his mommy. Justin patted the bed near his crossed legs.

He made it hard to resist that offer, looking all cute at me.

Fiddling with the wrappings, he mumbled, "This is for you." He held it out to me when I walked toward him.

"Justin, I don't need gifts. I need my husband back." A gush of air escaped me when I dropped onto the bed next to him.

"I didn't buy it." His eyes cinched shut. "I made it."

His eyes popped open when I caressed his cheek. "Thank you."

"But you haven't seen it yet." He furrowed his brow in confusion.

Shaking my head, I replied "It doesn't matter. I love you. The fact that you're giving me something from the heart makes it perfect."

Smiling, he nodded, placing the pretty package on my lap. My hands shook when it was my turn to fiddle with the wrappings. Holding my breath, I ripped the wrappings away to find a picture frame holding three hand-drawn pictures, each in a heart-shaped matte within the eight-by-ten-inch silver frame. They were reminiscent of the one Crazy Eight and Johnny had given me for my last birthday with the picture of a young Justin in it. Stroking the pictures through the glass, a tear slipped down my cheek as I realized that it was a picture of Justin's heart. In the left heart was a drawing of Jayden, I sat in the center one, and Kaiden's tiny portrait sat in the right heart, all hand-drawn with love.

"Don't cry, sweetheart." He pulled me onto his lap. Wiping away my tear with the pad of his thumb, he whispered, "I love you."

My heart skipped a beat. It had been so long since he had uttered those words to me. Cupping his cheeks, I attacked his lips. "I love you, too," I murmured against his lips, not wanting to let them go.

My resistance melted away further. I missed his touch. Pressing myself against him, I found the needed proof that he wanted me. I licked his lips, begging for more. When he parted his lips, my tongue dove in, desperate to feel his caressing mine once more. My hands searched out his silky brown hair, pulling him further against me. My chest heaved against his.

He pulled away panting. "Not yet. The doctor said six weeks."

"It's been so long already." I huffed when he rolled us over so his chest rested against my back.

"One more week," he purred into the crook of my neck.

I fell asleep cradling the picture frame, taking comfort in the fact he still loved me and wanted me.

CHAPTER 29

JUSTIN MCNEAR'S MANY HAPPY RETURNS

The month of May brought with it more than just beautiful, aromatic springtime flowers; it brought Alexia's nineteenth birthday with it. I had missed it last year, so this year I wanted it to be special. Thankfully, I had cohorts in crime to help me with the planning. They were all too eager to help. I didn't want some elaborate, overcrowded party – just something memorable in case I did leave next month to search for Mark.

Just thinking his name had me reaching for a beer before driving home. I'd started leaving boxes of beer in my trunk after the announcement that the wanker had snuck off with our money. The prat needed to stop torturing us with his escapades. As much as I didn't want to leave my family, I wanted him found and stopped once and for all. That money belonged to our churches.

If Mark never left England, then I had an idea who could help us. Thanks to my time spent away from my previous community, I'd made several friends with questionable ties; the type of blokes who, when they owed you, you could get almost anything in return. They would prove very helpful.

To keep my wife in the dark about my drinking again, I also stocked up on mint-flavored gum. When she didn't mention it, I knew I had pulled it off. That only served to allow me to take more liberties with the mind-numbing elixir. By the beginning of May, I had Carlos buying me a box of

Foster's Lager every few days during his lunches at the dealership. They were needed to get me through the rough patch Lexie and I had hit after the embezzlement had been announced.

Unlike before, I didn't want to hide from my wife, so going to the pub after work was never a consideration. Even when the tension in the house became too thick to breathe, I wanted to be with my family above all else. I just needed the beer to get me through it.

Her mother had already agreed to take Jayden for the night of her birthday, so that we could celebrate it as a couple. After the delivery, we'd been told to wait six weeks to make love again; however, that had stretched into eight when her cycle arrived, then the baby came down sick with a cold. Lexie had barely slept that week with the baby being miserable. With her party tonight, I planned on making her very happy.

I'd spent my lunches in my car calling Ginger and Madison every few days for two weeks setting everything up. My cousins had agreed to take the ladies into Small River tonight, which for us usually didn't happen. They felt the same about their wives having too much exposure to the outsiders as the rest of the men in our community did. Tonight would be a special event. Leaving work at my usual time, I made it home by six.

"Lexie? Where are you, love?" I called out, entering the cottage.

"Feeding the baby in our room." I followed her sugar-dipped voice to the bedroom.

On the bed snuggling, she sat breastfeeding our son. A smile crept across my face as I soaked in the sight. Leaning against the door frame, I waited for her to finish. Stroking his cheek, she encouraged him to take as much as he wanted. When he detached, satisfied, she lay him on the black silk duvet. I might have whimpered when she put her breast back in her bra. Snogging them had always been one of my favorite pastimes.

"You're staring. Do you see something you like, Mr. McNear?" She cocked her eyebrow.

I probably should have been embarrassed for gawking, but I wasn't. "Yeah, without a doubt," I licked my lower lip, "but that will have to wait. Let's go." Before I could take her up on her offer, I went to leave my jacket and tie in the bathroom with the rest of my clothes for the cleaners.

"Where are we going?" She huffed, following me down the hall.

"I have a surprise for you." Her adorable lips puckered in a little O.

Looking down, her brow furrowed. "Should I change?"

"Nope, you look perfect. Now, come on," I twittered, my excitement surging through my veins.

Her white, spaghetti-strapped cotton sundress hugged her just right. I loved it on her. Two months after the delivery, and she'd already regained most of her womanly favors. Not that I minded seeing her with her baby weight, but now she looked more like the woman I'd married almost a year ago. After not making love to her for so long, just the thought of what lay hidden under that dress had me wanting to tear it off of her.

"Are you going to tell me anything?" She eyed me with caution, snatching the baby's bag from the floor near the door.

"Lexie, meet me in the car." Pouring on my charm, I grinned and pranced out the door, leaving her gaping at me.

Once at my car, I slipped the extra items Ginger had picked up at the shop for me into the bag. Alexia rushed out the door, looking a little frazzled with the baby in her arms. Her red curls bounced free and uninhibited around her shoulders. I didn't ever remember seeing her looking so flustered when she strapped Jayden into his car seat. A gush of air escaped as she threw herself into the seat beside me.

I chuckled at the precious pout she gave me. "Relax, love. I wouldn't leave without you."

I grinned, tapping her lower lip to free her upper lip from her teeth. The short ride to her parents had her spinning her head in every direction. A deep chuckle erupted from my chest. Pulling up in front of her parents' home colored her face in confusion, her eyes darting back and forth, then over her shoulder at the baby.

"He's staying here?" she gasped in horror.

"You stay in the car. Your mother had you for lunch. I have you for the night." Grabbing her by the nape of neck, I pulled her to me for a passionate kiss.

"But . . ." she tried to protest. I wagged my finger at her.

"Shush. You're mine." Before she could wage a rebuttal, I jumped out, moving to the back door.

Jayden had fallen asleep on the ride; he didn't notice when I lifted him out of his seat. Grabbing his bag, I hip-checked the door to shut it behind me. I knew Alexia watched my every move; the hairs standing up on the back of my neck proved that. Her parents' front door flew open, and Katrina emerged, looking a little too eager. Shaking her head, she giggled through her broad grin.

"Everything set up?"

"Oh yeah, Chris has it all under control." She wiggled her fingers to demand possession of the baby.

"I wrote everything on a note in the bag." I laughed, passing Jayden into her arms.

"Justin, I'm fairly certain not much has changed since Alexia was a baby." She waved to the birthday girl.

"Well, okay then." Turning to leave, I paused, looking back. "I'll have my mobile if you need us." It was harder to walk away than I'd thought it would be, but for Alexia I did manage to walk back with only two glances over my shoulder.

"Have fun!" she called out, turning to go back inside.

Lexie lifted her hand, placing it against the window, her heated breath fogging up the window. The heartbreaking expression on her face almost had me running back for my son so her pouty lower lip would stop quivering. The woman could kill me just with her eyes; add in "the lip," and I was history.

Hopping into the car, I grabbed her and pulled her to me again. Crashing my mouth to hers, I devoured her lips. The feeling of them moving against mine had my eyes drifting shut. Desperate for more, my tongue plunged into her hot, wet mouth. Our tongues swirled, caressed, and teased each other's and elicited a moan from deep in her bountiful chest. Just hearing that magical sound escaping from her had me hardening in my trousers. Leaning back, I forced myself to release her, leaving us both breathless.

I saw the fear in her emerald eyes return before she'd even had a chance to verbalize it.

"He'll be fine, love. Now, this evening is about you. I've made plans to celebrate your birthday. Sit back and enjoy it just this once." Holding up my index finger, I emphasized the 'once.'

I meant it; the thought of her going out and doing what I had planned, alone or with her friends, would have killed me. Tonight we would be doing something our community had not done in decades. Rebelling, indeed.

Slipping the car in gear, I headed toward the front gate. Once we passed the guard's glass booth, waving to Luc, we turned toward Small

River. The familiar winding road flew by as we drove. Alexia kept her eyes trained out the window, looking all too ready to jump out at a moment's notice. Her nervousness reminded me of the day we'd married. Back then, she'd never been seen naked by a man.

I pulled into the car park of the best restaurant in town. Stelladora's was rumored to have the best seafood for miles around. Decked out with twinkle lights, the front of the building resembled an Italianate villa complete with red carpet and two potted trees on each side, highlighting the door frame. Nothing but the best for my wife, I thought. Moving around to the passenger's side, I took her hand in mine, helping her out of the car. Lexie suddenly frowned and smoothed out her dress. When would she learn?

"Stop, Alexia. You look fantastic tonight," I cooed in her ear.

Pointing at the building, she fidgeted again. "Justin, this place is the fanciest restaurant in town. I'm a mess."

Guiding her chin up, I tried to put her at ease. "You and mess don't belong in the same sentence." Wiggling my eyebrows, I earned myself an adorable giggle.

Dragging her by the hand, we left the car park and headed to the entrance. She tried to resist by leaning back, shaking her head and biting her lip, but that wouldn't work. Like it or not, she was walking in there. After a few grumbles, she relented when I held the door open for her, nudging my head toward the hostess's station. The hostess knew we were coming since I'd stopped by at lunch to make the reservations.

Looking up from her seating charts, Suzie smiled. "Welcome. Dinner for two?"

I wrapped my arms around Alexia's waist from behind, kissing her below her ear. "Reservation's under McNear," I hummed.

"Right this way." Picking up two menus, she turned for us to follow.

I guided my wife through the tables, weaving a path to the back of the restaurant. Suzie waited until we were behind her before she threw open the curtain-covered glass french doors, revealing the private room I'd reserved. I had chosen this one for its rich-colored red and gold decor. It matched Alexia's hair in the sunlight.

Alexia squealed in surprise when Johnny, Joey, Madison, and Ginger yelled, "Happy birthday!" Wrapping myself around her from behind again foiled her escape.

"How? When?" she stammered, taking in the sights of the room.

Her eyes shot to the Black Forest cake – complete with her name on it – then the gold, heart-shaped balloons. Finally setting her eyes back on our friends' beaming faces, I breathed into her hair, "Happy birthday, love."

Whipping around, she buried her pink cheeks into my chest. Everyone, including me, chuckled at her embarrassment. "Pink's your color, Lexie Ann," Crazy Eight chortled.

"Oh, come here, Lexie!" Madison gushed, rushing up with Ginger hot on her heels.

Letting go, I nudged her toward her friends. Bringing her into the room, they each took turns hugging her. I hung back, letting them have a few minutes to ease my wife's jitters. When they were finally done, I pulled out Lexie's chair for her to have a seat. She slipped into it, glowing from the excitement of her shock. Her looking up at me put me at ease as well. You could feel the waves of happiness rolling off her exquisite form.

Her cheek turned deeper rouge when I stroked it with the back of my fingers. "Pink is definitely your color."

With the guest of honor seated, we joined her at the table. Passing out the menus that were stacked there, everyone chatted while they decided what they wanted. Crazy Eight winked at me, letting me know none of the wives knew what would happen after dinner. If they had known, they'd be too excited to eat. The waitress arrived, wishing my wife "happy birthday" as well. Once our orders were all taken, she slipped back out, leaving us to celebrate. The wait passed quickly with us talking about Alexia's past birthdays. By the time our food arrived, my sides hurt from laughing so much. I loved seeing her eyes lighting up from the tales of her childhood.

Once the drinks and entrees were served, we all quieted down and enjoyed the meal in relative silence. The fish and chips were delicious, maybe even the best I'd ever had. After the dishes were removed from the table, the waitress began lighting the candles. Waving my hand, I signaled for the her to deliver the cake to Lexie. She looked so beautiful with the candlelight shimmering off her porcelain skin. Blushing again, she blew out the candles when we were done singing to her.

I leaned my elbows against my knees and tucked my hands under the table to keep her from seeing them shaking. My fingers fiddled with the hem of the golden linen tablecloth. A beer would fix that; it always did. However, it would have to wait until we left. She would notice if I slipped out.

Laughing, Alexia cut the cake, dropping the pieces onto the small plates that had been left on the table. I was pleased with how the night had been going thus far. I draped my arm around her shoulders and we snuggled, feeding each other mouthfuls of cake until every last bite had passed our lips.

She radiated contentment when, one by one, we presented her with her gifts. Madison and Crazy Eight had given her a new pastel pink sundress. Johnny and Ginger finished off the outfit with a new white wristlet purse and matching sandals. I saved mine for last. Her jaw dropped at the diamond-crusted hair clips I lavished her with. She was worth every penny I had spent on them; more even. When she jumped into my lap, smothering me with kisses, I knew she liked them.

"Thank you!" she gushed, latching her mouth to mine, still tasting like chocolate frosting.

"You're very welcome," I muttered against her soft, ruby lips.

From the desire simmering in her emerald irises when she gazed into my eyes, she knew I enjoyed her exuberant acceptance. My trousers couldn't hide the fact that having her heated core so close made me hungry for something only she could provide. A whimper slipped from my lips when she left my lap.

Just after eight, I paid the bill with my credit card, and we headed for the car. Once she was safely inside, I went to the trunk to deposit her gifts and chug down a beer, tossing the empty can back in the box. I popped in a piece of gum from my pocket before heading back. Feeling the stress leaving my body, I joined her in the car. I grabbed her hand and pulled it into my lap. I smiled, squeezing it once.

"Everything was perfect. Thank you," her soft voice purred in my ear.

"We're not done yet," I laughed, knowing our next stop would leave her in complete bliss.

"We're not going home? Jayden will be hungry soon."

"I bought him a formula that Dr. Michaels recommended. He said it would be fine." I shrugged, hoping it wouldn't make her upset and ruin the evening.

"Oh . . . I . . . they hurt. That usually means it's time for Jayden to eat." She glanced down at her swollen breasts.

I cupped one in my hand, teasing the clothed nipple with my thumb.

"I'm sorry they hurt. Is it wrong to want them to myself for just one night?" I pleaded.

"No!" Her guttural moan tickled my ears.

I released it and turned on the car, throwing it into reverse and backing out of the spot. My cousins and their wives followed us out of the lot. Careful not to lose them, I drove to our next destination. It was only two blocks away and we could have walked but then we'd have had to walk back, not to mention I wouldn't be able to frequent the trunk if I needed to.

A sharp gasp reverberated from her chest when I pulled up to the front of the Lion's Den. Snapping her head to face me, she looked adorable all bewildered.

"That's a club." She pointed to the ominous red door.

"So I've heard," I chuckled, "and it's for people under twenty-one." I nodded, grinning at her gaping mouth.

Looking behind us, she saw Johnny's 2005 Audi A4 pulling in and parking. "They're coming, too?" She broke out in hysterics, throwing her head back and laughing so hard she cried. "Which one did you have to bribe?" she gasped short of breath, clutching her sides.

"Johnny. Joey was easy," I chuckled, hopping out.

I really didn't want to tell her what it had cost me. Let's just say that tomorrow, Johnny would be picking out a new car at a drastic discount, though I had failed to tell him my father would have insisted on the same discount for family anyways. That was my little secret.

Alexia was still wiping away her happy tears when I opened her door for her. Helping her out, we waited for everyone else to approach before moving to the door. The music from inside already pounded through the air, a dance rhythm beating in time with my racing heart. All three ladies looked ready to vibrate out of the own skins, their excitement palpable in the air. The blokes didn't look all that happy; they looked more ready to be heading off to battle. I guess in a way we were. If one prat looked at our wives the wrong way, there would be trouble.

Joey held the door for us to walk in, and the noise rose to deafening levels. In the center of the room, there had to be one hundred people bouncing and swaying to a dance beat I'd never heard before; however, the words being screamed had my ears flushing red. Did he really just say 'booty?' Most of the lyrics didn't make sense to me, but I would tolerate anything for my wife.

Lexie grabbed my hand, holding it securely against her hip. She wasn't scared; by the way she grinned, I had to say she was even more excited. Dodging and bobbing between the other patrons, we made our way farther into the mass of jumping, sweaty bodies toward the dance floor. Together we started to sway and follow the rhythmic music until we, too, were jumping and dancing to the fast-paced beat. Madison and Ginger also dragged my cousins onto the floor. The six of us let go and allowed our bodies to do whatever the music demanded.

The next few hours flew by with us dancing and kissing with our wives. Alexia was a vision with her hands waving in the air, her red curls swirling under her fingers when she buried them in her hair and pulled them on top of her head, the breasts I loved heaving in heavy pants, and her hips gyrating to the music. Every time her bottom wiggled against my straining trousers, I shuddered in anticipation.

I made sure to take a few trips to my car while the ladies used the loo and the blokes grabbed us bottles of water. Before we knew it, it was time to leave. Stepping out into the cool air, we laughed our way to our cars. A stream of hugs and kisses followed. Settling into the car, I sighed looking at my wife's hungry eyes as she openly ogled me.

"Like what you see, Mrs. McNear?" Biting her lip, she nodded. "You can have anything you want once we get home."

She didn't reply, settling back in her seat instead and waiting for me to drive us home. Maybe it was my impatience to get home or the fact that I couldn't take my eyes off of my wife's bare legs for more than a few seconds at a time, but we were home and rushing into the cottage by the time my brain caught up with my body.

Alexia spun the moment she heard the door shutting behind me. The desire reflected in her eyes mirrored my own. We'd both waited so long to ravage each other. Rubbing the lapels of my shirt, she shoved me back against the door, trying to undo the buttons in a rush. As promised, I let her have her way with me. I had it easy; two tugs on her straps and her breasts were mine. Careful not to make them hurt, I thumbed the peaks until they pebbled. She mewled at my ministrations as I caressed them. I then understood why they hurt; they were rock hard under my hands, ripe and ready for my son to nurse.

When she finally had my shirt unbuttoned, she pushed it from my body, which allowed her to take the same liberties I had. Her hands left a blazing trail when she glided them across my shoulders, pecs, and abs. I shivered at the intensity of her touches.

Smashing my lips to hers, I claimed them as mine. From the force I used, I knew they would be swollen, but I couldn't stop myself. The need outweighed any rational thought. Her lips moved against mine in the same demanding fashion. Desperate for more, I lapped at her lower lip looking for entrance, which she granted me with no hesitation. I hummed when I tasted her on my tongue, so sweet.

Her roaming hands settled on the button to my trousers, her tiny fingers undoing it fast and furious before moving the zip down and releasing me to her wanting hands. I gasped when her heated palm wrapped around me. Hearing her soft giggle when she felt my hardened member pulsing just for her sent shivers up my spine.

Rolling, I moved her back against the wall. I grasped both her hands with one of my much larger ones and yanked them over her head. With open-mouthed kisses, I made my way from her ear, down her neck, across her chest, and landed on her bountiful bosom. Arching her back, she pushed her hardened bud between my lips. A groan vibrated around her breast when I swirled my tongue around it.

"I've missed this," she whimpered, licking her lips.

Pulling away, I purred, "You smell good enough to eat."

Thrusting into her hand, the point of no return evaporated. I needed her! Grabbing her hip, I drew her to me, grinding against her already moist curls. Releasing her hands, I withdrew from her hand, dropped to my knees, and kissed and licked her stomach. When I gazed up, I couldn't get over the sight of her glowing with a light sweat. Her red hair was strewn everywhere, her emerald eyes hid behind the thick lashes, and her fingers caressed their way down to where I sat on the floor between her knees.

My tongue darted out and lapped at her folds. Her eyes snapped open to see what I was doing. Wrapping my arms around her thighs, I stopped her swaying hips. We'd never done that before, but I'd been told it was quite satisfying for a woman, and I wanted her satisfied.

"Justin," she moaned, dropping her hands into my hair and tugging on it.

I draped her leg over my shoulder to gain better access. Her sweet taste tingled on my taste buds when I delved in further. Trapping her lower lip between her teeth, she mewled, letting me know she did indeed like it. That was the only prodding I needed to keep going. Using my fingers, I spread her folds to expose her perfect pink womanhood to me. Since it was the first time for both of us, I licked around the tender flesh until I found her clitoris, which seemed to give her the most pleasure. Using it as a guide, I continued lapping, sucking, and nibbling until she convulsed above me.

"Justin!" she screeched, pushing further against me as her release rocked her body.

I didn't give her a chance to think about what I'd just done; instead I dragged her to the floor. Crawling over her, I kissed my way back to her lips. In her frenzy, she locked her lips to mine, devouring them. Once I settled between her legs again, I slipped straight into her moist heat in one thrust.

"Oh, Alexia, you feel so good," I mumbled into her mouth.

Latching onto my bottom with her hands, Alexia pushed me in further, lifting her legs around my hips. I became lost in the euphoria of being inside her. Her slick walls allowed me to slip in and out at a fast and desperate pace. Our lovemaking had never been so aggressive. The desire would be quenched. Each thrust I made had her pushing up to meet mine. Grabbing both of her hips, my strokes became uneven and more erratic. I was ready to lose control, and from her pants, so was she. Lolling her head on the floor, she let me ravish her form until I couldn't hold back.

"I can't stop!" I growled in her ear.

She gasped her agreement. "Yes! Please?"

Her begging sent us both over the edge of oblivion. I wouldn't deny her tonight. Together we thrashed our sweat-coated bodies against each other as our climaxes shook us to the core. Left breathless, we held each other until I could pray for us. Too tired from the night's activities, we never left the floor; instead we snuggled and fell asleep where we lay.

CHAPTER 30

ALEXIA MCNEAR'S TIME IS UP

"Justin! Alexia! Wake up! There's an urgent meeting at the church in a half hour!" Joey's bellowing and banging on the door jarred me awake.

Stretching, I discovered we'd fallen asleep on the floor in front of the door where we had made love the night before. Justin stirred in my arms as the yelling continued.

"Twit!" he grumbled, hugging me closer. "I like it right here." He gyrated his hips to show me how much he preferred staying naked on the floor with me.

But his affections came to a crashing halt. "They pulled the lottery for the group going after Mark!" Johnny growled.

That woke him right up. "Get dressed." He huffed, extricating himself from our entangled mess.

My chest constricted when he pushed away from me. Scrambling to my feet, I ran for our bedroom, still stark naked. With shaking hands, I grabbed the first dress from the closet and shimmied it on without caring about how I looked or what color it was. We were expecting another two weeks before the decision came in. If they were calling an emergency meeting, then something had gone drastically wrong. Breathing deeply several times, I tried to stop my body from quivering.

Justin stormed in and went straight to his drawers, rummaging through and grabbing his favorite black Armani jeans and his white polo shirt. A sigh slipped out when he threw them on in a hurry. What if I didn't get to see that sight for a while? His eyes darted to mine when he heard it. He froze for a moment, then dropped his tensed shoulders. With slumped shoulders, he strolled up, taking me into his arms. Leaning my cheek to his chest, I heaved a heavy breath from the relief his touch brought.

"I promise, if I get selected, I'll hurry home as soon as he's found." His strong hands stroked my hair and down my back until they rested on my bottom. "We can't worry about it just yet. I might not get picked." Peeking up, I could see the thought disappointed him.

I grasped onto him, not wanting to let go. "I don't want you to go. We have things here that need to be settled."

"Like what, love?" he gasped.

Pulling away from him, I squared my shoulders ready to confront him once and for all. "Like the fact that you're drinking again, and have been for a while."

That left him gaping at me as he tried to find a retort. "I . . . but . . . when?" he stammered.

Turning my back to him, I looked out the window. "Since the delivery," I croaked, my emotions getting the better of me.

"I had hoped you hadn't noticed," his mumble grew closer.

Looking back over my shoulder, I hissed, "How could I not notice, and you really didn't think the gum hid the smell, did you?"

A shiver rocked my body when he traced from the nape of my neck, across my shoulders, and down my spine. "It relieves the stress, that's all," his honey-coated voice purred.

"You can't stop, can you?" I sighed.

I tensed when he growled, "Of course I can!"

Closing my eyes, I provoked him, "Prove it. Stop today. Stop drinking, and show us we're more important than the alcohol."

"You're the most important thing in my life. The beer just makes me forget the other stuff." Did he really believe that would pacify me?

"If that's true, then agree to quit today, no stalling." I crossed my arms over my chest, refusing to budge.

Sliding up and wrapping his arms around my waist, he calmed my rattled nerves. "If it will make you happy, then I will. I'll quit today, but can we talk about this later? The meeting's going to be starting soon," he whined.

"Fine." It would have been hard for him to have missed the sarcastic tone I used. "What about Jayden?"

Kissing my neck, he chirped, "I'm sure your parents will be there. They'll bring him, and we'll take him home once it's over." Apparently he did miss my bitter remark.

His arms dropped away, leaving me feeling empty and hurt. Dragging my heels, I trudged behind him when he headed for the car. He was so excited about the meeting that he didn't even open my door. Justin always held my door. Dropping into the seat, he hit the gas before I'd had the chance to shut my door.

I yelped when the sudden jerk sent me further into the seat. "Justin!"

"Calm down, Lexie. I don't want to be late." Shaking my head, I tried to let the fight die down, though it wasn't easy.

When he hit the gas pedal again, I let him have it. "Well, I want to make it in one piece!"

His fingers wrapped tighter around the steering wheel, he glared out the windshield, refusing to look at me. I then realized the problem when his head cocked to the left then right as he stretched his shoulders. The lack of alcohol in his system was making him edgy and jumpy. Reaching out, I placed my hand on his forearm, squeezing in. When he nodded, I knew he understood I still supported him. We found the parking lot bustling with a flurry of activity when we arrived. Those who were running late, like us, dashed through the door, hoping not to miss the announcement.

For the first time since we had woken to the news, Justin looked at me with apprehension in his deep blue eyes. "You believe me when I tell you I love you, right?"

Chewing my lip, I knew what he needed. "I do."

He smiled and got out to go around and open my door. Entwining our fingers, we walked into the meeting room together. My parents jumped up when we approached them. They wore the same expressions as everyone else in the room. Confusion, panic, and frustration colored everyone's faces. We rushed up and hugged them; a family hug seemed in order.

Krista delivered the one thing I needed to focus: Jayden. Taking his carrier into my arms squelched some of my fears. I looked at the angel in my arms, stroking his delicate cheek. He had no idea what was happening. Justin and I greeted his parents when they joined us at the table. Justin's smile looked genuine; however, I knew mine wasn't. I placed Jayden's seat down on the table. After a new round of hugging, we settled down and waited with bated breaths, each one of us clutching our neighbors' hands in our own for support.

A sudden silence fell over the room when Minister Jeff and the council entered through the front door. From their determined march, they weren't in the mood to take any back-talking today. Their hard, cold stares left their features looking stony and impenetrable. Taking center stage, they whispered amongst themselves before addressing us.

After hissing out a long breath the minister began, "Thank you for coming. We're sorry for the rush, but we were left with no other option." With his chin resting in his hand, he paced back and forth. "Our three other churches had a revolt of sorts." The room filled with gasps and hisses, but he ignored them and continued, "The rectories were stormed by parishioners refusing to wait any longer. They demanded an immediate response. Last night, there were four lotteries drawn, one for each of the four communities. It was the only way to appease the crowds. Even though we didn't partake, we had to do ours as well."

My hands started shaking when he held up three folded pieces of paper. "These are the names that were drawn. We haven't read them yet." Minister Jeff looked back at the Council, and they each nodded. "I wanted everyone together when we did. The three chosen here will fly to England tonight to join with the nine from the other churches. The search is being funded by Mr. James McNear, Mrs. Catherine Chesterfield from England, Mr. Jose Martinez from Mexico, and Mr. Pablo Dali from Argentina." The room shifted their gazes to my father-in-law.

"It's the least I can do since I couldn't be part of the lottery." Justin was the first to start clapping, followed by the rest of congregation.

With tears staining her cheeks, Jane rubbed his back. James had asked for his name to go in, but because of his age and financial responsibility, he'd been declined. Personally, I thought it had something to do with the fact that he would kill Mark on sight for the torment he'd inflicted on Justin.

"Now for the names. Each one of you will have one last chance to back out, then you'll go home and pack to leave." When his hands shook too much to unfold the first paper, Mrs. Arbella relieved him of the notes.

She sighed after seeing the first name. "Johnny McNear." Ginger whimpered hearing her husband's name being announced.

"I'm in!" he exclaimed, running up to the stage.

I held my breath saying a silent prayer. "Joey McNear." Mrs. Arbella grimaced.

"Going!" Crazy Eight kissed Madison on the cheek before he, too, went to the stage.

With one name left, I closed my eyes, intertwined my fingers, resting my forehead against them, and prayed harder it wouldn't be Justin. Time stood still as she unfolded the last paper. "Justin McNear." My heart skipped a beat before leaping into my throat.

My eyes snapped open to see his reaction. "Yes!" Justin pumped his fist in the air while he made his way forward, never looking back at my heartbroken tears streaming down my cheeks.

The room erupted in a celebration like none other, leaving me, Madison, and Ginger to wallow in our pain. Passing Jayden off to Krista, I went to meet them in the middle of the room. No one noticed the three of us latching onto each other, the noise of the celebration covering the painful sobs wrenched from our chests.

"We'll get through this together. Right?" Madison groaned.

Nodding my head, I confirmed her need to be as one on this. "Yes, we will. Friends forever, from birth to eternity, never judging, always as one. Together we will fear no one, because together we are stronger," I recited our childhood vow.

"Friends forever!" Ginger cried out, clutching us closer.

"Friends forever." Madison nodded with new tears filling her eyes.

"Ginger?" Johnny's voice startled us, forcing us to pull away from each other.

Shaking her head at him, Ginger bolted away and out the door, leaving Johnny watching her dumbfounded. He took off running behind her.

Joey and Justin arrived, laughing and grinning until their smiles fell. They each looked as if someone had smacked them when they saw our reactions to the news. When Justin reached for me, I pulled away and stomped back to the table.

"Alexia, wait!" his muffled voice begged, but I didn't care. "Don't do this!"

"I'm not, you are." I sobbed, dropping my face into my hands, my chest heaving.

"Please?" He grabbed me, pulling me into his arms. "Don't be mad."

"I don't want you to go! Stay here, stay with us," I pleaded, my tears running down my cheeks.

"Let's talk about this at home." He huffed, releasing me and grabbing the baby and his diaper bag.

Looking to my parents, I could see they were worried for me. My father tried to hide the tear that refused to stay in his eye. My mother didn't bother with pretense and sobbed, wrapping herself around me. "We're right behind you. We want to say good-bye, too." Sniffling, I nodded.

There was no doubt in my mind that they would all come to see him off. Whether I liked it or not, last night would be the last night I had Justin to hold me in my sleep for a while. Now that he had permission to go, he wouldn't stop until they found Mark.

Feeling drained and emotionally abused, I followed Justin to the car. I didn't want his leaving to be an ugly fight, but I was willing to fight for my family. He refused to talk on the ride to the cottage. I could see his set jaw, cold stare, and twitching fingers. The car slid into the driveway without Justin even looking at me once. Slamming it into park, he jumped out and retrieved the baby.

It took all my energy to trudge into the house. Justin placed Jayden at my feet and went about packing to leave. I pulled the baby from his seat and sat on the couch with him in my arms. When his nose wrinkled and a gentle whimper slipped from his lips, I knew he smelled me, ripe and ready for his taking. Sighing, I released the one thing he wanted, my engorged breast. His little lips wrapped around the nipple, suckling in earnest. Looking up at me with the same bright blue eyes of his father, he nursed from my bosom. I stroked his tiny, soft red curls he had inherited from me.

Jayden had just finished feeding from the second breast when Justin dropped his suitcase and carry-on by the door. "Where are you going?" I muttered.

"I have to grab a few things from my car and park it out of the way," he grumbled, but kept walking.

The sound of two cars arriving had me rising to my feet. Cradling the baby to my chest, I rocked him until his soft, even breaths found my ears. I moved to the yard to see who had arrived. Justin stood in the yard chatting with his sister and our parents. Justin was so lost in his conversation he never saw me approaching. Krista saw me and met me halfway to take the baby.

Walking up behind him, my heart lodged in my throat.

"Yeah, you don't have to worry, Dad. I've got this. He's going down. I don't care if it takes a year, I will find him."

Justin's head snapped around when his father pointed to me. He stared at me with his jaw slack. He hadn't expected me to hear him.

"Lexie, I . . ." he choked, but the rest of his words fell away.

Taking two steps closer, I smelled it, proof that nothing had changed. "You're still drinking?"

"It was just a beer!" he snarled in his own defense.

"Just go! We don't mean anything to you!" I screeched, running into the house and leaving him flabbergasted in the yard.

I threw myself onto the bed and let all the tears I'd been holding fall. He couldn't even stop for one day. The sobs raked my body. He had betrayed my trust. He'd lied. I lay on the bed long after the last tear fell. With my red and swollen eyes closed, I waited for him to come in and say goodbye.

When a hand gripped my arm, I knew it was the wrong hand. "They're gone."

MOCKED BY FAITH

HEALING THE FAITH

CHAPTER 1

JUSTIN MCNEAR'S LOST

I knew what I did was wrong before the car ever left The Gates, yet I did it anyway. I had left my wife of less than a year in tears, feeling unloved. She'd needed me to remind her of my love, and I had denied her. The consideration that leaving to search out the man who had single-handedly tried to ruin my life would cause her such distress had never crossed my mind, when it should have been the first thing I'd thought of.

I had spoken with my cousins in the weeks leading up to the lottery, and we had agreed that, in the event one of us had been picked to go, the others would care for our wives. We'd never thought we'd all be selected. By the time we boarded our flight to England, I was an utter mess. My chest ached for absolution from Alexia; my hands shook, craving to touch her as I had the night before when we'd desperately made love on the living room floor; and my thoughts swirled with ways to make up for all my mistakes I'd made since June.

Once the plane had taken off, I used the onboard phone, hoping to reach her and to plead for forgiveness, for understanding. My heart sank into my stomach when no one answered. The pained expressions on my twin cousin's faces mirrored my own. Their wives had taken our departure just as bad as Alexia. Madison, Alexia, and Ginger only had each other now that we were gone.

Grabbing my sketchpad, I flipped it open to the last drawing I'd done of her emerald eyes, the same eyes I had seen in my dreams for ten years before my father had found her and arranged our marriage. Stroking the sketch with my fingertips, visions of seeing those eyes filled with tears when she had run from me in the yard of our cottage filled my mind. Releasing a shaky breath, I pulled a pencil from the pouch and began writing her a letter to send when the plane landed. My tears started falling before the pencil touched the paper.

Dear Alexia,

I did this to us. Never think this mess was your fault. The need to face Mark once and for all overrode my ability to think correctly when it shouldn't have. I know nothing I say will heal the wounds I left behind, but I will find the right words to tell you I love you. You're everywhere I look. My heart breaks when you're not there. When this is over I will return to you and Jayden. I'll beg you both to forgive me. If I have to kneel at your feet in front of the whole community, I will. When I told my friends you owned me, I meant every word. My soul, heart, and body are always yours. You and my son light my world; without you, everything is lost in the darkness. Maybe you would be better off without me, but I can't let you go even if we were allowed to divorce. I love you too much to be without you. Right now you think I am gone, but I am right there beside you. I left my heart with you; take care of it until I come home. I will be the man you deserve. Please still be waiting for me.

I love you forever,

Justin

www.ingramcontent.com/pod-product-compliance
Lightning Source LLC
Chambersburg PA
CBHW051148030726
47504CB00004B/1104